In the

SHADOW

of

LAKECREST

OTHER BOOKS BY
ELIZABETH BLACKWELL

While Beauty Slept
The Letter

In the

SHADOW

of

LAKECREST

ELIZABETH BLACKWELL

LAKE UNION
PUBLISHING

Published by Lake Union Publishing, Seattle

www.apub.com

Amazon, the Amazon logo, and Lake Union Publishing are trademarks of Amazon.com, Inc., or its affiliates.

ISBN-13: 9781503941847
ISBN-10: 1503941841

Cover design by Christian Fuenfhausen and Cyanotype Book Architects

Printed in the United States of America

To the other Elizabeth Blackwell

PROLOGUE

1937

Last night, I dreamed Lakecrest was on fire. I watched, indifferent, as flames devoured the brocade curtains and wood paneling, ashes coating my tongue and face. The windows shattered in a violent blast of heat, and turrets and walls and paintings crumbled around me. Lakecrest was dying, and I was content to see it burn.

I woke into that eerie uncertainty when a dream feels as real as a memory. I could make out the usual shapes from my bed: the bureau against the wall, the arched entrance to the bathroom. There was no smell of smoke, no sound other than my husband Matthew's rumbling snores. Still, I knew I'd never get back to sleep if I didn't make sure the house was safe.

I slipped out from under the sheets, walked to the hallway, and peered down the stairs. I heard only the usual creaks and moans. Years ago, those sounds scared me. Before I learned what it really means to live with ghosts.

Had the dream expressed an unconscious wish? I thought Lakecrest and I had come to a truce, that my feelings had dulled with time. Maybe I still hated it—more than I'd ever admit.

I made my way slowly down the hall, avoiding the squeakiest floorboards. I peeked into Stella's room, which was dimly illuminated by a night-light in the shape of a twirling ballerina. My daughter looked like an angel in the amber glow, with her rosy cheeks and swirls of golden hair splayed across the pillow. I crept closer, unable to resist kissing her velvety skin. It wasn't until I was almost at her side that I realized one of her arms was wrapped protectively around a figure huddled against her. Robbie.

I'd laid down the rules many times: boys don't share rooms with their sisters. But he was afraid of the dark, and Stella was always the one he turned to for comfort. His defender. That very afternoon, at the beach, I'd heard them giggling and whispering. When I asked what they were talking about, they refused to tell me.

Keeping secrets already.

If I picked up Robbie and moved him back to his room, he'd only wake up and start shrieking. The whole house would be in an uproar. *What's the harm?* I could imagine my friend Eva saying. *They're so sweet!*

I watched my sleeping children and remembered Jasper and Cecily, Matthew and Marjorie. A weakness passed from one generation of Lemonts to the next, a pattern I was determined to break. I'd sacrificed everything for my children. Done terrible things to protect them. If Lakecrest was invading my dreams, maybe it was because I still hadn't made peace with what I'd done here.

I don't believe in ghosts—not anymore. But I've seen how a house can be haunted by its past. I looked at Robbie and Stella, at their perfect, beautiful faces, and wondered how I'd ever keep them safe. How I'd ever escape Lakecrest's shadow.

Is it possible to be haunted by the future?

CHAPTER ONE

I never should have met Matthew Lemont.

I'd seen him on the ship, of course, stretched out on a deck chair, his impossibly handsome face staring intently at his book. I'd noticed his irritation when one of the pushy, overdressed flappers hovering around tried to strike up a conversation. I'd thought those few days at sea were my last, best chance to meet the kind of man my mother had always urged me to marry: someone well-off and well-bred, the gateway to a stable future. But Matthew seemed beyond my reach. A man like him—obviously rich, with a preference for solitude—would never cross paths with a girl like me. Until July 18, 1928, a date branded in my memory as clearly as my own birthday.

As I stood alone at the rail of the RMS *Franconia*, I saw him approaching from the corner of my eye. I could have ignored him, let him pass. I knew nothing then about the Lemonts or Lakecrest. I knew nothing of the infamous Labyrinth and the secrets it held. Even if I had, I doubt I would have been able to resist. I leaned out a touch too far, looking intently at the horizon, and gave Matthew an opening to approach me.

He took it. And everything changed.

"Stop!"

Strange, to think that was the first word my future husband ever spoke to me, as if he were warning me away from what was to come. But on that bright summer day on the upper deck of a grand luxury liner, my body simply responded to the command. My hands tightened against the glossy wood railing, and I froze in place, one foot propped against the lower rung. I turned my head and saw him take a few running steps toward me, then jerk to a halt so abruptly that his body wobbled with the effort of stopping. The wind ruffled the dark-blond waves of hair along his forehead, and I clutched at my hat as a gust threatened to waft it off into the water.

"Forgive me," he said in a crisp, formal manner that suggested a lifetime of the finest schools and debutante parties. "I thought . . ."

"Thought what?"

"I thought you were about to jump."

I stepped away from the railing, casting my eyes down and then shyly up, unsure whether to laugh or appear contrite.

"I saw something in the water," I said. "I know we're too far north for dolphins, but I could have sworn that's what it was."

A pause, as he considered whether to believe me.

"You must think I'm very silly," I said.

"No, no. I'm the one who should apologize. I shouldn't have bothered you."

How odd, I thought fleetingly, that he saw a young woman admiring the view and immediately feared for her life. The Atlantic stretched around us, seemingly endless and utterly calm. Who sees death in the middle of a clear blue sea?

"I probably was leaning out too far," I said. "So maybe you saved my life after all."

He laughed, an outburst of genuine pleasure that seemed to take him by surprise. His shoulders softened, and his legs relaxed, settling into a standing position rather than gearing up for a brisk exit.

"Who's to say you didn't see a dolphin?" he said. "I rather hope you did."

"I rather hope so, too, Mr. . . . ?"

I watched his face register confusion, then amusement. Pretending not to know his name had been the right tactic; he was delighted by my ignorance.

"All right, then," I said firmly. "I'll call you Mr. X. My mysterious would-be rescuer."

"And you are?"

"Hmm. I suppose I'll be Miss Z."

"A pleasure to make your acquaintance." He nodded and propped one elbow against the rail. "Are you enjoying the voyage?"

"Oh, yes," I said. "On the way to England, I was too nervous to take it all in. It was my first ocean crossing, you see, and I was worried about seasickness and icebergs and getting lost among the decks."

He smiled wryly as I babbled on, doing my best to sound amusing and carefree. A girl with no worries.

"Go ahead and laugh, but I'd never left the state of Ohio before, let alone the United States, so you mustn't poke fun. I'm proud to say I have put those fears behind me and given myself over to the romance of shipboard life. It's rather dreamy, don't you think?"

"I envy your youthful enthusiasm." Matthew sighed as his gaze drifted away and over the water.

To say he was handsome would hardly convey the overall effect of his looks. He had all the features you'd expect in a good-looking man: narrow, straight nose; high cheekbones and strong chin; shoulders and arms that suggested a streamlined strength. But there was none of the heartiness or brash self-confidence that usually goes along with physical perfection. His lips curved slightly downward, and his dark-blue eyes appeared to be caught in a restless search for a reassurance that would never come. His reserve didn't deter me. Matthew offered a challenge, and every smile I wrangled from him felt like a victory.

"Are you on your way home?" I asked, trying to pull him back into the conversation.

"Yes."

"Let me guess. New York?"

"No, Chicago."

"Really? My cousin moved there about a year ago, and I've been dying to visit. You hear so many stories."

"It's worth seeing, so you'll know which stories to believe," he responded with a certain defensive pride. "Besides, a trip to Chicago will be old hat now that you've been to Europe. What brought you so far from home?"

"My job. I've spent the last three weeks touring literary sites of the British Isles and teaching two young ladies poetry so they can impress their father's friends at parties."

He looked appraisingly at my white cotton dress and T-strap shoes. "You look much too young and cheerful to be a governess. Mine were always dowdy old dragons with permanent scowls."

"Oh, I've only been hired as a summer companion. But even real governesses bob their hair now."

"How shocking! The next thing I know, you'll be dancing the Charleston."

I laughed. "The Charleston! I can barely manage the foxtrot."

"I'll bet you know your way around a dance floor better than I do. They're having one of those tea dances in the Garden Lounge—shall we give it a whirl?"

Of course I wanted to say yes. But if he was the sort of man who'd always been handed what he wanted, maybe he'd be intrigued by a girl who didn't come easy.

"That's very kind, but I've got to get back," I said, looking down in embarrassment. "The girls will be finishing their badminton lesson in a few minutes."

"What about dinner?" he asked. "I'd be delighted if your party joined my table."

Was he daring me to break the rules? Or did he truly not understand the social gulf between us?

"I'm allowed up here on the first-class deck as long as I'm with my charges, but I have to stick to the second-class restaurant for meals," I said. "Thanks for the offer, but I can't accept."

I turned away before I could regret my decision. Maybe I'd gone about this all wrong. There was no reason for him to seek me out, no reason for me to expect anything to come of one conversation. But I'd enjoyed pretending I was someone else. Someone untroubled by doubt and regrets.

Behind me, I heard him exclaim, "Your name! I don't know your name!"

It took Matthew less than a day to find out.

I was standing with Lillian and Maisie by the shuffleboard court the following afternoon, waiting for an opening, when I saw him again. He was leaning against a lounge chair, his elbows and arms resting along the back. Our eyes met, and he tipped his hat in acknowledgment, his lips curving into the subtlest beginning of a smile. It was all I could do not to grin back at him.

Lillian, following my gaze, threw her hand upward in an enthusiastic wave. At fourteen, her behavior swung unpredictably between that of an expensively educated young woman and that of a temperamental child.

"Mr. Lemont!" she exclaimed.

"Miss Headly," he called back in greeting as he straightened up and began walking toward us. I glanced at Maisie, who looked as thrilled as I felt.

"That's Matthew Lemont," Lillian whispered to me hurriedly. "Of *the* Lemonts. Father says they're rolling in money." Louder, so Matthew could hear, Lillian called out, "What a pleasure to see you again. It was so refreshing to dine with someone younger than Methuselah at breakfast this morning."

"Lillian," I admonished, instantly regretting the schoolmarmish tone.

"I was delighted your father invited me," Matthew chuckled. "And grateful to you girls for the entertaining conversation."

Lillian and Maisie hadn't told me Matthew had joined their table that morning, and I felt a dark stab of jealousy that I'd missed it. My morning meal, as usual, had been delivered on a tray to my cabin.

"You haven't introduced me to your companion," Matthew said. His gaze met mine and held it.

"Oh," Lillian replied dismissively, as if I wasn't worth his notice. "This is Kate."

"Kate Moore," I said, holding out my hand.

"Matthew Lemont."

There was no jolt of electricity as our palms pressed together, but what I felt was something deeper, a bond being formed, as we silently agreed to say nothing of our previous meeting.

Lillian abruptly turned and motioned toward the shuffleboard courts, where a raucous family was about to vacate a space.

"Now's our chance!" she exclaimed. Maisie scurried off after her sister, leaving Matthew and me alone.

"Matthew Lemont," I said, sounding out each syllable with dramatic emphasis. "How mortifying. I had no idea, yesterday . . ." I looked away, as if I were too embarrassed to face him.

"Don't apologize," he pleaded. "I enjoyed my secret life as Mr. X."

"I'm quite sure I never told you I work for Mr. Headly. What a coincidence that you should have breakfast with him the very day after our meeting!"

To my delight, Matthew laughed at being caught. "I'll confess," he said, "I was so curious about you that I stalked the smoking room last night in search of a father with literary tastes. I met Mr. Headly, and we spoke about his love of British poetry and his two daughters, and before I knew it, he was insisting I join them this morning."

"I hope you're not too disappointed," I said. "Kate Moore is awfully boring compared to Miss Z."

"On the contrary," Matthew said. "I find the mystery more compelling than ever."

He took a step forward, and I pretended to be flustered while I tried to work out what to do next. Matthew wasn't the type to have his head turned by fluttering lashes and girlish giggles. I heard Lillian shout out in triumph, and I nodded at Maisie, urging her on. If she gave up in frustration, as she so often did, I might never get another private conversation with Matthew.

"I'm quite ordinary," I said. "A governess traveling with a widowed father, his ancient spinster aunt, and two daughters who will use any excuse to escape their lessons."

"But who is she, this governess?" he teased. "I know nothing about her."

Why would he want to? I was passably attractive (my mother's words, forever imprinted on my memory), but had none of the glamour I'd assumed a man like Matthew would be drawn to. My dress was simple white cotton, and my dark-brown hair was cut in a practical chin-length bob. My figure was all wrong for the fashions of the times: bosomy on top and rounded at the hips, so dresses clung stubbornly to my curves rather than cascading elegantly downward.

I had to pretend none of that mattered. I'd risen above the miseries of my childhood because I was determined not to let my past define my future. Self-confidence was the only advantage I had.

"If you were a detective—Sherlock Holmes, say—you could deduce everything you need to know," I said in a breezy tone. "I'm practically penniless, as you can tell from the scuffs on my shoes and the fact that I'm wearing the same clothes as yesterday. I'm well educated; otherwise, Mr. Headly would never have hired me, yet I also told you I'm not part of the family's regular staff. When the girls go back to boarding school in the fall, I'll be out of a job. And I haven't the faintest idea what I'll do next.

"Now for the most damning evidence of all: I am confessing all this to a man I hardly know, which must mean I am either terribly forward or terribly lonely. There you have it! A complete portrait of Miss Kate Moore. I warned you. It makes for a very dull story."

"Then why is it I'd rather talk to you than any other person on this ship?" Matthew's voice had dropped to a whisper, and he was so close, his breath tickled my cheek.

Before I could respond, we were interrupted by an irate Maisie, who ran over from the court and threw her stick at my feet, the clatter echoing along the deck.

"Lillian cheated!"

"Don't blame me for your clumsiness," Lillian snapped as she walked over to join us.

The spell was broken, and Matthew's playfulness vanished. With formal politeness, he leaned forward in a bow and said, "Ladies, forgive me. I promised to join a game of cards this afternoon, and I'll be forced to walk the plank if I'm not there to make a fourth at bridge."

Thrown off balance by his sudden change in tone, I barely had time to nod before Matthew walked away. Moments later, I heard a familiar tap-tap-tap and guessed the reason for his quick departure. The girls' great-aunt, Constance, came tottering toward us, her slouched upper body jolting with each movement of her cane. One of Cincinnati's haughtiest social doyennes, she had been taken aback to discover that her reputation didn't carry beyond the Ohio state limits. The humiliation had made her more high-handed with the few of us still subject to her commands.

"Miss Moore, we mustn't allow the girls to tire themselves with recreational pursuits. Surely these hours should be set aside for their studies?"

"Yes, of course," I said, mentally pushing aside the irritation that swelled up whenever Aunt Constance shared one of her self-important pronouncements. I told Lillian and Maisie to get their books from the cabin and meet me in the ship's library.

"I can't say I approve of Preston buttering up the young Lemont fellow," Aunt Constance said. "It won't do for the girls to be seen with him at every meal."

"Why not?" I asked. "He seems very polite."

"Don't you know anything about the Lemonts?" Aunt Constance glared at me, irritated, as if my stupidity was beyond her comprehension.

"They're rich," I said, trying to keep my voice calm. "That's all that matters, isn't it?"

"We are unfortunate enough to live in a time when hedonism is celebrated rather than condemned," said Aunt Constance mournfully. "The Lemonts' money keeps them from being ostracized. But they'll never be respectable, no matter how much they spend."

I couldn't understand it. Matthew looked and acted like a perfect gentleman. It's what had drawn me to him, from the very first time I spotted him on board.

"There's always been something strange about that family," Aunt Constance continued. "They'll stop at nothing to get what they want—that's what everyone says about the Lemonts." She shook her head in haughty disapproval. "That young man's father and grandfather were the subjects of unsavory rumors for years."

I was taken aback by the vehemence of her tone.

"A girl disappeared at their estate, you know. Simply vanished!"

"What happened?" I asked.

"Honestly, I can't remember. It happened years ago. But I will not have Lillian and Maisie tarnished by association. We must distance ourselves from Mr. Lemont for the rest of our journey."

We? Aunt Constance wasn't concerned about my welfare; it was Lillian and Maisie she wanted to shield from whatever bad influence the Lemonts represented. Not that I took her suspicions seriously. At the time, I dismissed her as a bitter old woman, jealous of another family's good fortune. I never considered that her accusations might be true, that something dangerous might be lurking beneath Matthew's refined exterior. I looked at her pinched, judgmental face and nodded obediently, hiding my disappointment and frustration. I'd hoped our flirtation might last beyond the voyage. Now, thanks to Aunt Constance's meddling, I'd never speak to Matthew again.

But I was wrong. That night, when I returned to my oppressively tiny cabin and the rattling snores of the elderly woman who had been assigned as my bunkmate, I found a cream-colored envelope sitting on top of my mattress. I ripped the seam open with one finger and pulled out a thick note card with *Matthew Lemont* embossed in gold letters at the top.

My dear Miss Z, he wrote in a narrow, angular hand.

> *With our voyage approaching its conclusion, I find myself much concerned with your plight. As we will both be traveling westward, I cordially invite you to join me in my family's private railcar, which will be departing from Pennsylvania Station two days after the* Franconia *docks. I would be happy to escort you to the station of your choice in Ohio, but I hope you will consider continuing on for a visit to Chicago. The thought of giving up our lively conversations is enough to send me jumping off the deck at the earliest opportunity, so your answer must be yes.*

It was all there, had I chosen to read between the lines: Matthew's impetuousness, his disregard for proper etiquette, the entitled expectation that I would do whatever he asked—even a joking reference to the inner despair that would take me so long to truly understand.

Yet all I saw was an invitation into a world I thought forever denied me, a world of luxury travel and hovering servants and notes dashed off on extravagantly expensive stationery. What had begun as a lark—a challenge to see if I could catch Matthew's attention—had taken a more serious turn. I'd been dreading our arrival in New York, when I'd be out of a job and forced to start fresh. I'd thought about staying on in the city, but a future as a shopgirl or secretary already felt like defeat. I remembered Matthew's face as he stepped closer to me by the shuffleboard court, the mix of apprehension and hope in his eyes. Why not go to Chicago? I had nothing to lose.

I brought the card up to my face and brushed it against my lips, breathing in the scent of the paper and ink and imagining Matthew's fingers skimming against the page. I already knew what my answer would be.

Yes.

CHAPTER TWO

I'd known, from as far back as I can remember, that I had to make my own luck. I may have come from nothing, but that wasn't how I intended to end up. My mother always told me that getting in good with a rich family was the easiest, best way to pull myself up from poverty. She'd done the opposite and paid a heavy price.

Ma was seventeen, pregnant, and penniless when she married my father, Brian "Binny" O'Meara. Not a promising start, and things went downhill from there. Binny was a drunk, a gambler, and a fool; if he'd been any two of those things, we might have scraped by, my mother liked to say, but all three? Our family was doomed. The little money he earned went straight to whiskey and cards, and his few, rare winnings never made it back home. When she asked him for money to buy milk, he hit her. Until the day he went too far and the anger she'd held in came hurtling out in one burst of rage—one strong enough for her to plunge a knife into his stomach.

I don't remember it happening, though I was there. I was later told I'd crawled right through the puddle of blood that seeped across the floor. I was sent to Aunt Nellie's while Ma was in the asylum. Those two years left me with only faint impressions of floury aprons and murmured voices, of warm hands tucking me and my cousins into bed. A real home. But Ma got better and took me back, vowing to make a fresh start. She was still young. She might have done all right, if she'd gone about things differently. But Ma never did think beyond her next meal, or mine. Her moods made it impossible to hold down a regular job, and she was too proud to fall back on her older sister's charity. Ma's stubborn that way.

Eventually, Ma turned to the kind of work any girl can do if she's pretty and not worried about eternal damnation. When her "callers" came to visit, she'd scoot me under the kitchen table and tell me to stay hidden behind the oilcloth. I'd hug my ragged stuffed bunny and wonder about the grunts and howls I heard from the bedroom, thinking it was some kind of game. When I was older and knew better, I would go out to the back porch when her visitors came so I wouldn't have to hear them. It was rough in the winter, swaddled up in her winter coat and mine, but it was better than being inside. Even when it was just Ma, spiraling down into one of her moods, I'd escape to that porch, put my hands over my ears, and swear I'd get out.

Ma wanted me to get an education, but only as a means to an end. At college, she told me, I'd meet the right kind of man, the steady, dependable sort who wouldn't desert his wife in favor of a bottle or slap her around for speaking her mind. By the time I was twelve, Ma had saved enough to send me to St. Anne's, a snooty Catholic boarding school where eagle-eyed nuns kept a close watch on the students' virtue. I'd never amount to anything as an Irish cook or laundress named Kathleen O'Meara, Ma said, but if I started copying the St. Anne girls, I'd improve my prospects. I was enrolled as Katherine Moore, and Ma told me to put the word out that my mother was an invalid who wouldn't be making any visits. When no one questioned my story, I discovered I was good at lying.

A talent that served me well in the years to come.

My roommate at St. Anne's was an orphaned girl named May, who was being supported by the church. She'd lost her parents but not her faith, and she liked to say that God would provide. I couldn't help thinking that God didn't seem all that concerned with my day-to-day life on earth, and he'd certainly never provided anything for my mother. *No,* I thought, *I will provide.*

Now, my perseverance had paid off. I'd impressed Matthew Lemont, a man so rich I'd never have to worry about money again.

I had doubts, of course, before stepping on the train. I had sent a note back to Matthew accepting his offer and telling him I'd be staying at the Knickerbocker with the Headlys, but I hadn't seen him during the following three days of fretting and second-guessing. Our only communication was a brief message sent to my room informing me where and when I should meet Matthew at Pennsylvania Station.

I made no mention of Matthew when I told the Headlys I was going to visit family in Chicago, and I was equally cautious in the telegrams I sent Ma and my cousin Blanche. Mr. Headly looked surprised when I told him I'd already booked my ticket, but he wished me luck and gave me an extra fifty dollars, most of which I spent at a Fifth Avenue boutique recommended by the hotel's head porter.

Staring at myself in the mirror in my new dress, shoes, and hat, I faced up to the enormity of what I had agreed to: traveling halfway across the country with a man I barely knew. Aunt Constance's warning echoed in my mind, and I wondered if I was making a terrible mistake.

Too late to turn back now, I told myself. *Don't look; just leap.*

By the time I got to the station the next day, I was afraid Matthew might have changed his mind. What if the attraction he'd felt toward me was nothing more than a shipboard flirtation? I saw him, waiting on the platform. Though he had favored loose linen jackets on board the ship, he wore a precisely cut dark-blue suit and had liberally applied pomade in a vain attempt to tame the natural wave of his golden hair.

He raised his hand in greeting. I hurried forward and was suddenly aware that I had never stood face-to-face, almost eye-to-eye, with such a striking man. He looked charmingly relieved to see me.

"Kate."

"Mr. Lemont."

There it was, in a simple greeting: the unalterable gulf between our stations in life. He smiled, amused, and said, "Matthew. Please."

With a discreet nod of his head, he caught the attention of a man in a blue uniform, who took my suitcase and hatbox with an efficient flourish. Matthew gently took hold of my elbow to usher me up the steps, then introduced me to the staff of three. There were no other passengers; I'd be alone with Matthew for most of the journey. The thought was both unnerving and exciting.

"We'll be off before long," Matthew said. "Care for a drink?"

"Yes, thanks. It's so beastly hot."

"Isn't it? I was just making sure we had enough ice on board. Charles, two gin fizzes!" He opened the first door off the narrow hallway and ushered me inside. "I hope you'll be comfortable here."

The compartment was clearly meant for female passengers, with floral wallpaper and a serene cream color scheme.

"It's lovely," I said. I wondered whom the room had been designed for, and if other women who weren't part of the Lemont family had stayed here before me. "How many people can you sleep on board?"

"Twelve, if we're all packed in. There are four sleeping compartments. Mine's at the other end."

Matthew shot me a quick, meaningful look. I wasn't sure if he was trying to reassure me that he'd stay as far away as possible or signaling that I was welcome to visit him there. I wasn't sure which of those underlying messages I wanted to hear. I leaned against the doorjamb and gave him a shy smile. Matthew reached a hand toward my face, and my stomach twisted with anticipation. I hadn't expected him to be so forward, so soon.

"May I?" he asked, and I realized he was offering to take my hat. I pulled it off and ran my fingers through the damp hair around my ears while he hung it on a hook.

"Good," he announced. "Here's Charles with the drinks."

Matthew led me on a tour, and any apprehension I'd felt in my sleeping compartment was quickly soothed by the easy flow of conversation. A dining room and parlor filled the center of the car, and it was there that we settled onto settees upholstered in red velvet. By the time the train pulled out of the station, it felt like we were friendly acquaintances exchanging gossip from the *Franconia*, and the discussion became even livelier when Charles brought us each a second cocktail. I'd been worried Matthew and I wouldn't have enough in common to fill the hours ahead, but he seemed interested in my travels around England, just as I prodded him to tell me all about Chicago and which sights I mustn't miss. By the time Charles announced dinner, I felt pleasantly tipsy. I wasn't used to drinking alcohol, but Prohibition didn't seem to apply to families like the Lemonts.

After pulling out a chair for me in the dining room and then taking his own place, Matthew looked me straight on and spoke with a forthrightness that caught me off guard.

"I can't tell you how much I'm enjoying this. I've had my mind on nothing but business for weeks. Talking to you is a very welcome change."

I tried not to show how much the compliment thrilled me. "You must have some time for fun."

"What some consider fun isn't always worth the effort. Not for me."

Before I could ask Matthew what he meant, Charles arrived with a silver tureen and served a chilled vegetable soup; he was followed by another steward carrying a bottle of white wine and two goblets. The food distracted us for a few minutes, but when we leaned back in our seats, glasses in hand, an expectant hush settled over the table, as each of us waited for the other to determine the way forward.

"So, what do you consider fun?" I asked at last.

"Honestly, I don't know," he said.

"How sad!" I took a sip of wine, telling myself to keep the conversation light. I'd ruin the mood by revealing too much too soon. "I'm having a great deal of fun right now."

"Yet I suspect you know exactly what I mean," said Matthew. "You've got spirit, but you're no flapper."

"Not like the other girls you know?" I teased.

"My sister, her friends . . . they're always off to some party or another, looking for the next good time. You strike me as more serious than that."

"I was a very serious little girl," I said. "Always had my nose in a book."

"Let me guess. You imagined you were Alice, disappearing down the rabbit hole. Then, when you were older, you devoured *The Sheik* and dreamed of being carried off by a dark, mysterious stranger."

"Close enough. I did use books as an escape."

"Escape from what?"

Best to stick close to the truth. Tell Matthew the facts, but not the terrible stories behind them. "My father died when I was very young," I said. "My mother didn't have an easy time of it after that. She worked very hard so I could afford to go to good schools. It was a rather lonely childhood."

"What sort of work did your mother do?"

I looked at him directly, my gaze posing a challenge. "She's a housekeeper, in Cleveland."

He didn't flinch. If anything, my revelation seemed to impress him. "She must be very proud of you."

"Yes, she is."

"We're not that different, you know."

I had to laugh. "You must be joking."

"Do you want the world to judge you based on what your mother does?"

I shook my head. If Matthew knew half of what my mother had done, I wouldn't have been sitting at the table.

"Then don't I deserve the same chance?" he asked. "How about this. Tell me everything you think you know about me, and then I'll tell you the truth."

I looked into his eyes and saw his hunger for an honest conversation, for someone who wouldn't choose flattery over honesty. I took a gulp of wine and felt the tart warmth expand through my chest, surprised to find myself feeling sorry for this man who had everything but happiness.

"Lillian told me you're very rich," I began. "I don't know where the money comes from, but I assume you were raised with maids and butlers and therefore must be spoiled rotten. You have some role in the family business, though I have no idea what, because you don't like talking about work. I've seen your name in the society pages, along with the words, 'Chicago's most eligible bachelor,' and I've seen your sister's picture in the papers, too. She's beautiful and has a reputation for outrageousness. Not you, though. You're reserved, even shy. And yet you strike up conversations with strange girls on ships."

I could picture Aunt Constance's disapproving face, egging me on.

"There is one more thing. I was warned the Lemonts are strange and have a very unsavory reputation. So I guess that includes you as well."

Matthew, to his credit, looked amused rather than shocked. "All that may be true," he said. "But it's hardly a complete portrait."

"All right," I said. "Tell me what I missed."

"My father died, too, when I was thirteen." There was an ache to his voice, as if the pain of the loss was still fresh. "He was a remarkable man. Smart as a whip, bursting with confidence—the kind of person who fills up a room. Then, suddenly, he was gone, and I grew up knowing I could never fill his shoes. My mother was the one who kept Lemont Industries going while I decided to rebel and study medicine. Thought

I'd be noble and save lives. When the war came along, I was so anxious to prove myself that I signed up with the Medical Service Corps. I was eighteen years old and an innocent fool. A few months in France were enough to turn me against doctoring forever. Turns out I'm not so noble after all."

"You must be proud of serving your country," I began.

But Matthew brushed me off. "I am rich," he said, "and I'm probably spoiled. But I'm not lazy. I've spent the last few years learning everything I could about the business and planning for the future. I spend every minute of every day weighed down by my family's expectations, wondering if I would have made my father proud."

"It can't be that terrible," I said. "You must be invited to all sorts of parties and weekends at glamorous country houses."

"A man in my position has responsibilities, as my mother likes to say. Just because I go to charity balls doesn't mean I enjoy them. I usually spend the night fending off pushy mothers who keep telling me I simply *must* meet their daughters."

"Why fend them off?" I asked. "Why not meet their lovely daughters?" I looked straight at him, daring him to answer me honestly. I was wondering why such a good catch hadn't been snatched up years ago.

"Because I won't marry a woman who wants to marry Matthew Lemont." He said the name with contempt. "I'm waiting for a woman who will marry me despite my name, not because of it."

The declaration hovered between us, fraught with weight. He'd practically handed me the key to his heart. All I had to do was use it.

"You're the one who brought up marriage, not me," I said lightly. "Now, tell me more about this sister of yours. What's the wildest thing she's done?"

But Matthew seemed reluctant to talk about his family, as if he regretted telling me as much as he had. We sat in silence as Charles cleared the soup bowls and brought in plates of poached salmon and grilled vegetables. Everything had been perfectly cooked, but I couldn't enjoy it. Not until I found a way to lighten Matthew's mood. Finally, I asked him if he liked going to the pictures.

"Sure. I hardly ever do, though."

I asked if he'd seen *Wings*, and when he admitted he hadn't, I told him he simply had to and began describing the aerial dogfights until he got lost in the story and his tense posture loosened. By the time I moved on to Buster Keaton's exploits in *The General*, Matthew was smiling. I thought about refusing the after-dinner port Charles offered along with our dessert of orange sorbet, but before I could say anything, my glass was full, and Matthew was holding his up for a toast.

"To a delightful dinner, with a delightful companion."

"Same to you," I said. Our glasses clinked, and I tried not to grimace as the bitterness trickled down my throat. Hours of being charming had tired me out, and my cheeks were uncomfortably flushed.

"What do you say to some cards?" Matthew asked.

"Sure," I said, standing up, but the floor seemed to shift under my feet. I lurched forward, grabbing at Matthew's arm to steady myself.

"I'm sorry," I muttered. "Forgot I was on a moving train."

I tried to concentrate as Matthew laid out double solitaire in the parlor, but cards kept slipping from my fingers when I played them, and I couldn't keep track of my moves. My hands felt like they'd been numbed, forcing me to make slow, deliberate movements, and an unsettling dizziness was making me nauseous. *So this is what it's like to be drunk,* I thought distractedly.

When I stifled a yawn, Matthew looked at me sympathetically and said, "You look done in. I'll see you to your room."

I kept one hand pressed against the wall as I tottered along, my body swaying with each tilt of the train. When we came to my compartment, I saw the bed had been made up, and the sheets were turned down in a neat triangle. I stepped inside and turned around. Matthew was standing in the doorway. I moved back until my legs pressed against the edge of the berth. Suddenly, the gravity of the moment cut through my foggy, unfocused thoughts. I was alone in a bedroom with a man I barely knew, unchaperoned. The staff quarters were at the other end of the car. No one could see or hear us.

I looked at Matthew and realized whatever happened from this point on would be my choice. If I took a step toward him and leaned against his chest, he would kiss me. If I threw my arms around his shoulders and pulled him toward the bed, he would follow.

For a fleeting, thrilling moment, I thought I'd do it. Then a clear, commanding voice told me to stop. Matthew was my lucky break, my best shot at a better life. He might even be a man I could one day fall in love with. All of that would be at risk if I moved too fast.

"Thanks," I said, tipping my head in dismissal.

"Are you feeling all right?" he asked.

"One too many drinks, that's all," I said. "I'll be fine."

"Good night, then," Matthew said. "Sleep as late as you like. We won't be getting to Chicago until the afternoon."

And with that, he was gone. Though I was relieved to have the uncomfortable moment over with, I couldn't help feeling a twinge of regret. I'd wanted him to kiss me, very much.

After being closed up all day, the compartment was stifling. I pulled the window open, but the air was too humid to offer any relief. After waiting in vain for a cross breeze from the windows in the hall, I closed the compartment door and stripped down to my slip. No point changing into a nightgown and getting it sticky, too. Splashing cold water on my face and chest helped, but I felt sick every time I leaned over the sink. I decided to skip my usual nighttime reading and go right to bed. I didn't want to face Matthew the next day looking like a wreck.

I turned off the light and lay down, pushing the top sheet and thin blanket aside. The click-clack of the wheels seemed to pound into my brain, and I felt the first throb of an impending headache. I tried to settle my body and thoughts, but I couldn't get comfortable. The walls seemed to shift unnervingly whenever I changed position, and the pillowcase soon felt as warm as my face.

I considered getting a glass of water, but standing felt like an impossibly grueling task. My arms and legs were weighed down with exhaustion, and I knew sitting up would send hideous darts of pain shooting through my head. I lay in overheated, uncomfortable misery for what could have been minutes or hours, my mind drifting between fragments of memories and dreams. The steady chug of the train punctuated visions of my mother, urging me on. I saw Constance Headly, shaking her head, telling me to stay away from the Lemonts. I remembered the steward Charles handing me a cocktail with a deferential smile and treating me as an honored guest. As if I deserved to be here, as if I belonged at Matthew's side . . .

The train took a sudden turn and jolted me to the edge of the mattress. The whistle shrieked, and I opened my eyes. A bright flash illuminated the bed, and I realized we were passing through a town, the streetlamps forming an alternating pattern of darkness and light as we zipped by. Groggy and disoriented, I lifted my head and was confused by a strange, bulky mass that seemed to be looming over me. Then another burst lit up the room, and I saw it was Matthew, wearing blue-and-white striped pajamas. He was standing perfectly still, staring at me.

My body tensed with something that went beyond terror, a fear not just of him but also for myself and my own sanity. The man in front of me looked like Matthew, but it wasn't the same man I'd seen across the table at dinner. His arms and legs were rigid, the muscles tightly clenched, as if he was using all his force of will to hold himself back. His agitated eyes swept across the bed, and I realized to my horror that I was nearly naked, with my slip halfway off my shoulders and the skirt hiked up my thighs.

I wanted to scream, to burrow under the sheets so I wouldn't have to look at his disturbingly blank expression. But I couldn't move. The scene had the peculiar unreality of a nightmare, and I felt the same helplessness I'd experienced in my dreams: legs that wouldn't obey when I tried to run, a voice that couldn't be summoned when I called out for help.

"Matthew . . . ," I whispered. I felt my lips form the name, but I couldn't tell if I made a sound. The room went black as the train left the town and raced through the countryside. I stared into the darkness. A narrow beam of illumination crept through an opening in the doorway, enough for me to see that the compartment was empty. Matthew was gone.

The door slammed against the wall as the train sped up, and I leapt up, throwing my body against it and shutting the bolt. I couldn't remember if I'd locked it before. I curled into the farthest corner of the bed, shaky with motion sickness, my head prickly with pain. I tried to think logically, to find a reasonable explanation for what I'd seen. Matthew could have been sleepwalking. He might have come by to check on me and been too embarrassed by my disheveled state to say anything.

But I knew Matthew hadn't stopped in for a friendly chat. His wild eyes and tense body had frightened me. Or had I frightened myself? The whole incident was so odd, so out of character. I was half-delirious with the heat, and an impending hangover made it hard to concentrate. It must have been a dream.

But I couldn't help remembering Aunt Constance's warning. I'd brushed her off because I didn't believe Matthew could be dangerous. Now I did.

CHAPTER THREE

Matthew was already eating when I walked into the dining room the next morning. I smiled warily as he stood up and pulled out a chair.

"Good morning," he said. "Did you sleep well?"

There was no hesitation, no trace of embarrassment. No acknowledgment of what had happened in my compartment the previous night. I sat down and stared at the serving platter piled with eggs and bacon and toast in the middle of the table. If Matthew was putting on an act, it was perfectly played.

"I did have a rather strange dream," I said at last.

"Oh?"

Matthew's face revealed nothing other than polite interest. *Had* I been dreaming? Looking at Matthew in the bright morning sunshine, content and well rested, I began to doubt my own memory. It already seemed ridiculous that I'd thought of him as frightening, and I didn't see how I could bring up the incident without offending him.

"It's not important," I said nonchalantly. "I've already forgotten it." And maybe it was better I did.

"Well, I'm glad you were able to sleep in," he said, "because we've got a big day ahead. We'll be arriving in Chicago earlier than expected, and I thought I'd show you around."

"Are you sure you have time?"

"Don't you worry about that. I've telegrammed the office and told them I'll be taking a few days off. You accused me of never having fun—well, I'm going to prove you wrong."

Matthew was so charming, so obviously pleased about our upcoming adventure, that it was easy to dismiss any lingering doubts. When we arrived, his car and driver were waiting at Union Station, ready to take us on a tour of the chaotic city. I craned my neck at the soaring office buildings that reached toward the clouds and marveled at the crowds along State Street, a horde of strangers propelled by a common ambition. The whole experience had an air of unreality, as if I couldn't possibly be here with Matthew in this sprawling, unfamiliar place. These hours might be only a brief interlude in my otherwise humdrum life, but those downtown blocks hummed with a restless energy that resonated with my own hopes.

Like me, Chicago was striving for more.

I begged off dinner, saying my cousin was expecting me, and Blanche was amusingly flabbergasted when I told her who'd dropped me off at her boardinghouse. Though we hadn't seen each other in years, I'd made a point of staying in touch with Aunt Nellie's family, remembering their kindness when they were my guardians. Blanche had moved to Chicago the year before and was working as a nightclub coat-check girl while she tried to make it as a singer. She had the kind of bubbly personality that puts people instantly at ease, and I guessed she wouldn't be stuck behind a counter for long.

Blanche told me she'd seen Marjorie Lemont at the club, but never her brother.

"He's quite a man of mystery," she gushed. "The very last person I'd expect to sweep a girl off her feet!"

For the first time, I saw the puzzlement that would be directed my way in the weeks and months to come: *Why would someone like him be interested in someone like you?* I had no answer. There was nothing to set me apart from the hundreds of prettier, more sophisticated girls Matthew must have met in his lifetime. I still couldn't quite believe it myself.

When Matthew picked me up for lunch the next day, I resolved not to drop any coy hints about my expectations or how long I planned to be in town. I'd be a happy-go-lucky traveler, seeing the sights with my new friend.

"Are we friends?" he asked.

"I certainly hope so," I said. "Otherwise I've made a complete fool of myself, and I'll have to scurry home in shame."

"Well, we can't have that. I'm determined to make you fall in love with Chicago."

"Why's that?" I asked, eyebrows raised.

"So you'll stay."

I grinned, delighted that he was already talking about the future.

Over the following week, Matthew insisted on acting as my companion, rediscovering the city he claimed as his hometown but didn't really know. The product of a New England boarding school and college, he'd spent most of the past few years in Europe on business, so in many ways he was as much a sightseer as I was. When I heard about the roller coaster at Riverview Park, I begged Matthew to take me, even though he jokingly rolled his eyes and said it wasn't his usual crowd. I screamed and clutched his hand as we careened down the stomach-churning drops, and as our car slowed to a stop, he wrapped one arm around my shoulders. It was the first time Matthew offered an opening, and I took it. I leaned my head up, and he leaned his down, and we kissed in full view of the factory workers and their families, the bored ticket takers and the disapproving nannies. It wasn't more than a quick peck, but it felt like I was back at the top of the steepest drop, my skin tingling with nervous anticipation.

Then Matthew was standing, offering me his hand, and the ride was over. He let go of my fingers as we wound our way to the exit, and there were no more displays of affection, though I tried to signal they'd be welcome by brushing against him when I could. We reverted to our friendly but cautious selves, as if the kiss had never happened. I was beginning to wonder if he regretted it, and then he suggested dinner at the Drake Hotel.

"It's time I took you somewhere nice."

I told him I'd have to change before going to such a swanky place, but Matthew laughed and said I looked just fine. His look of pleased satisfaction was enough to reassure me until we arrived at the hotel, where I had to pretend to ignore the glances and whispers exchanged all around us. Matthew nodded curtly to a few fellow diners, but he didn't greet anyone by name, and he grew steadily more silent as the meal progressed. Confused and disappointed, I tried to revive the romantic sparks between us, but Matthew answered my flirtatious questions in a monotone voice. When the waiter asked about dessert, Matthew abruptly demanded the check and said we had to leave for another engagement.

We emerged onto Michigan Avenue, which was hazy in the dim light of sunset.

"Where are we going?" I asked.

"It's a surprise." He hailed a taxi, and we were soon settled inside. "Won't take long. It's not far."

Only a few days earlier, I would have been thrilled to be whisked away on a mysterious outing. Now, I was hurt by Matthew's secretiveness and by his eagerness to avoid anything below the surface of our conversations. Throughout dinner, I'd waited for him to mention our kiss, to acknowledge that it had meant something. Because if it hadn't, I'd judged Matthew—and myself—all wrong.

"I need to tell you something." I lowered my voice so the driver wouldn't overhear. "I got a letter from my mother yesterday. Asking when I was coming home."

She'd had plenty more to say, too. Questions about whether I'd landed my big catch and exactly how much money the Lemonts had. But Matthew didn't need to know about that. I'd burned the letter right after reading it.

"There's no rush to get back, is there?" Matthew asked. "We're having such fun."

"Yes, but I can't live off Blanche's charity forever. I need a job and a place to live. I have to start being practical."

"So, you want to stay?"

"Why wouldn't I, with this kind of welcome?"

Matthew took hold of my hands. "I'm so glad, but I don't want you worrying about money. Let me help."

"No! Can't you see how that would look? Like I was some sort of . . . kept woman."

The mortification on Matthew's face made it clear he'd had no such intention, thank God. I wouldn't be tempted to follow my mother's example.

"Don't worry," I said. "I'll figure something out." I decided not to tell him Blanche had offered to get me a job at the Pharaoh's Club as a cigarette girl, vamping around in a gold slave-girl costume. I already knew he wouldn't approve.

The taxi pulled to a halt, and the driver announced, "Chicago Theatre." I stepped out and gawked at the enormous illuminated sign across the street.

"You said you'd never seen a talkie," Matthew said from behind me. "Now's your chance."

The lobby and the sprawling movie palace inside were so ornate that I wondered how anyone could concentrate on the pictures, but Matthew barely responded to my eager comments. I followed him up to the balcony, where only a scattering of seats were filled, and settled in next to him. When the newsreel started, he reached his arm around me.

"I'm sorry I've been so dense," he said.

"It's all right." Already distracted by the images on the giant screen, I was ready to escape into a fantasy world. To let go of the questions that churned through my mind whenever I was with Matthew: *What are we doing? What comes next?*

"I don't want you worrying about money," he said. "I don't want you worrying about anything. From now on, I'm going to take care of you."

"I already said—"

"I want to marry you, Kate. I'm head over heels in love with you, so why wait?"

My heart surged with a relief so intense and overwhelming I could hardly breathe. I'd done it. I'd convinced Matthew Lemont to marry me.

Or had I? Matthew was in love with Kate Moore, a role I'd crafted to please him. He didn't know the truth about my family; he didn't even know my real name. I'd pursued Matthew the way my gambler father chased a royal flush, never really believing it would pay off. Now I had the proposal I'd dreamed of, but I couldn't think of a thing to say.

"Dear God, I'm such a dolt," Matthew said. He looked nervous and fretful, a little boy craving reassurance. "I've gone about this all wrong. I should have bought you flowers and chocolates and asked your father for permission . . ."

He stopped, flustered, remembering my father was dead. I imagined Matthew telling my mother, how she'd shriek with joy. Matthew's polite reserve giving way to shock when she told a dirty joke or let slip a compromising detail from her past.

"Are you sure?" I asked.

Matthew's anxious expression softened. "I want to marry you. More than anything."

Unlike Matthew, I wasn't deliriously in love; I'd spent a lifetime keeping my emotions locked tight. But I genuinely liked him, and I knew he'd be kind. *Don't think,* I told myself. *Leap.*

"All right."

In retrospect, it seems impossible that such ordinary words could have ushered me into an entirely new life. It never occurred to me that Matthew had secrets of his own, that we'd both been modeling our best selves for the other's admiration. I had no idea what it meant to link my future with his. No idea what I'd be driven to do for his sake.

Matthew spoke quickly, abuzz with nervous energy. "We can have any kind of wedding you want. Here, Ohio—I don't care. I'd be happy with a judge at the courthouse."

He might have been joking, but it struck me as the perfect solution to the problem of Ma's big mouth and unpredictable moods. We'd avoid her until after it was done. When it was too late for Matthew to change his mind.

"I'd like that," I said. "Just us, no fuss."

"Tell you what," Matthew suggested. "Mum's hosting a party next weekend. What if I surprised her by arriving with my new wife?"

Matthew liked to think of himself as open-minded, but at heart, he believed in rules and order. I didn't think he was serious. "She'd disown you," I said.

Matthew laughed, as if such a thing weren't possible. "She's been pestering me to get married for years. I can't wait to see the look on her face when she finds out I've finally gone and done it."

Despite his lighthearted tone, I felt uneasy. Matthew was talking about marriage as if it were a practical joke—or a kind of revenge.

"Wouldn't it be better to tell her first?" I asked.

Matthew looked unconcerned. "She'd take charge and insist on a formal wedding with hundreds of guests. No."

"If you're sure that's what you want."

Matthew leaned halfway out of his seat so he could wrap me in his arms.

"The only thing I want is right here."

I pressed against Matthew in dazed wonder as he kissed me, a kiss that in my memory lasted through the entire first feature and into the second. Knowing we were engaged loosened the hold we'd kept on our physical urges, and the reticence that seemed as much a part of Matthew as his immaculate suits and neatly combed hair disappeared. He reached up my skirt, and I shifted my legs, encouraging him further, moaning softly when his fingers tickled the skin at the top of my stockings. I ran my hands through his hair, tugging gently to pull his kisses deeper, then reached inside his jacket, clutching at the solidness of his back. My quick, heavy breathing matched his as we explored the shape of each other's bodies, staking our claim by touch. It was the first time I'd been with Matthew and simply did what I wanted rather than second-guessing every move and decision. For once, I felt like the real me.

By the time we emerged into the sticky night air, giggling like guilty children, I believed it would really happen. I would become Mrs. Matthew Lemont.

"This party your mother's throwing," I said. "Will it be awfully stuffy?"

"Not at all. It's a garden fête at Lakecrest. Where I grew up."

I remembered Aunt Constance telling me that a woman had disappeared at the Lemont estate. Was it just gossip? It didn't seem like the right time to bring up the story with Matthew, especially when I didn't trust Aunt Constance's motive for telling me. There'd be time enough to figure it out later.

"All right," I said, "I am curious to see your childhood home. But I'm terrified of meeting your mother."

"Silly girl. She'll love you."

He said the words a touch too forcefully, willing them to be true.

Matthew and I got married at city hall and spent our first night as man and wife at his apartment on Goethe Street, walking distance from downtown and the Lemont Industries offices. He apologized for the masculine décor while I protested it was perfect; both of us were on edge, nervous about what we'd done and what was to come.

Matthew pulled a bottle of champagne from the icebox—"To celebrate," he said, with self-conscious jollity—and a few glasses helped calm our nerves. After kisses on the sofa, Matthew led me to his bedroom, telling me not to be nervous, that he'd be gentle. Before I knew it, I was on my back in nothing but my chemise, Matthew lying on top of me, his head buried in my hair. Everything I'd dreamed of was there in my arms: My rich, handsome husband. My happily ever after. But all I could think of was a different bed, a different man looking down at me, a seduction gone terribly wrong. Would Matthew be able to tell?

I tried to make my mind go blank to erase the past. A few minutes later, Matthew rolled off, flashing me a bashful smile and asking if I was all right. If I was disappointed by my own lack of emotion—by the feeling that we were still little more than strangers, making small talk on the *Franconia*—that worry was soon eclipsed by relief. Matthew didn't know. He thought he was my first. And when I whispered that I loved him, he believed me.

The next day, we drove to Lakecrest.

CHAPTER FOUR

Memories can be shifty and unreliable, but I'm convinced the feelings I recall from that first visit haven't been overshadowed by the knowledge of what came later.

When Matthew's driver pulled through the front gates, I thought Lakecrest was the ugliest house I'd ever seen. Unruly and disorienting, it was a mishmash of competing elements all fighting for attention. The roofline was so staggered I couldn't tell if the building had three or four stories, and offshoots sprang out from the central structure with no clear pattern or purpose, one constructed in a half-timbered Tudor style, another with the stone facing and tall, narrow windows of a medieval cathedral. My eyes skimmed from a stone turret to a stained-glass bay window to a pair of gargoyles that seemed to be staring directly at me.

I wanted to tell the driver to turn around. To take me back to the city, where I'd be safe. I told myself I was just nervous about meeting Matthew's family, that the house itself had nothing to do with my ominous sense of dread. But that didn't make it any easier to face what was coming.

The driver stopped halfway up the curved front drive, where a half dozen cars were unloading passengers, and got out to open my door. I twisted the gold ring on my left hand as I cautiously stepped onto the gravel and stared up. The arched stone entrance was carved with an inscription that I guessed was Latin.

Matthew smiled at my bewildered expression. "My grandfather Obadiah bought up mansions in Europe and shipped the pieces over here. Monstrous, isn't it?" He threw out the insult with affection, as if describing a decrepit but beloved family pet. "Ready?"

"I don't know if I'll ever be ready."

Matthew took my arm and ushered me toward the door. His eyes darted to the other guests around us, then back to me. He was nervous, too.

"You'll be fine," he said.

I knew as soon as I stepped inside the house that I wouldn't be. The two-story entryway was enough to intimidate anyone, given that every square inch was covered in marble. Statues of two women in flowing togas flanked a staircase that rose up from the center of the room, splitting in the middle to soar in opposite directions. But it wasn't the grandeur of the space that upset me; it was the lack of grandeur in my fellow guests. The people exchanging greetings and sipping glasses of lemonade wore simple white dresses and cream linen suits. My midnight-blue New York dress, with its silver trim and rows of shimmering glass beads, looked flashily out of place. I wished I could slip under the stairs and hide until the party was over.

"I've got it all wrong," I murmured to Matthew. "I'm completely overdressed."

"You look swell," he said. "I can't wait to show you off."

He veered off to the right, and I followed. We passed a huge dining room that looked like a fairy-tale castle's banquet hall, then walked into an equally enormous sitting room. A stuffed moose head loomed menacingly over haphazard groupings of armchairs and card tables.

The floor was covered with at least five Oriental carpets in mismatched shades of green, red, and yellow. I'd known the Lemonts were rich, but I couldn't imagine how much money it had taken to build such rooms, then fill them with that much furniture and art.

Matthew said dryly, "My grandfather was a great collector. Of everything."

We emerged onto the terrace, a stretch of flagstones that ran along the back of the house, where at least a hundred guests mingled among white wicker furniture, potted bushes, and flower boxes bursting with blooms. A vibrant green lawn seemed to extend into the sparkling waters of Lake Michigan. It looked like a magazine photo of a summer resort. Not quite real.

The crowd enveloped us as soon as we walked outside. There was an atmosphere of anticipation as everyone jostled to get closer to Matthew to shake his hand or greet him. He moved determinedly through the well-wishers, introducing me simply as "Kate," his eyes focused elsewhere. I did my best to be gracious, but it was impossible to remember anyone's name, let alone how they knew Matthew.

"Matts!"

A woman lunged into Matthew, tossing one arm around his waist while I dodged the cigarette held in her other hand. "Where have you been? I'm so bored I could *die*."

He leaned into her, his back blocking my view of their faces. She had the sort of long, lean body that every woman wishes for and so few achieve, and her cream silk dress emphasized her slender shape. She whispered something in Matthew's ear, pressing her chest into his arm, her lips so close to his face I could have sworn she'd kissed him. Her hand ruffled his hair, and I felt a twist of unexpected jealousy. She looked like just the sort of rich, spoiled debutante Matthew claimed to dislike, yet here he was, completely under her spell. He whispered something back, and the woman swirled around to face me. Her dark-blonde hair cascaded in neat waves along either side of her face, framing round blue eyes. Her narrow lips and sharp chin gave her looks a certain severity, but she was undeniably gorgeous.

"Kate, this is my sister, Marjorie," Matthew said.

"A pleasure to meet you," I said.

I reached out my hand, and Marjorie waved her cigarette in the air between us. Her smile came uncomfortably close to a smirk. Though I disliked the way she fawned over Matthew, I didn't feel the same visceral hate for Marjorie that I felt for Lakecrest. There was something fascinating about her elegant self-assurance, and I naïvely believed she'd be welcoming when she found out about the marriage. For Matthew's sake, at least.

"Aren't you precious!" she exclaimed. "Remind me where you're from? Kansas?"

"Ohio."

"I knew it was somewhere like that. A place where people are *nice*." She made it sound like a disease. "Tell me. How does a sweet young thing from Ohio land a husband as hard to please as my dear brother? You must reveal all your secrets."

Taken aback, I turned to Matthew. He looked down, embarrassed, and muttered, "I called Marjorie this morning while you were asleep."

"A secret wedding!" Marjorie gushed with exaggerated delight. "So romantic. I must tell you, Matts, I almost begged off this boring party, but I *had* to see Mum's reaction. I never thought you capable of such intrigue."

"Kate and I didn't want a fuss."

Marjorie looked at me with mock concern. "Oh, I see. There's a special delivery on the way?"

"No!" I protested, mortified. "I'm not expecting."

Marjorie drawled, "We'll find out soon enough, won't we?"

"Stop," Matthew admonished. Weary rather than angry.

"Heavens," Marjorie said. "I didn't mean to impugn the honor of your new bride. I'm tainted goods myself." She smiled at me, with no apparent shame. "Two broken engagements, and Mum's terrified I'll end up an old maid." She squeezed Matthew's upper arm. "You haven't told her yet, have you?"

"No," Matthew said.

Marjorie looked me over, inhaling deeply from her cigarette. She pursed her lips into a perfectly round *O* and leisurely blew the smoke out.

"I wouldn't miss this for anything," she said. "Let's go."

Anyone who didn't know them would think Marjorie was Matthew's wife from the way she took his hand and led him forward. I tried not to mind, not to dwell on the way Marjorie was looking at Matthew and pulling him close, acting like a protective lover rather than his sister. With their fair hair and striking features, they looked like they belonged together, a perfectly matched set. Yet Marjorie was blunt and brittle, her brother unassuming and polite, and I didn't understand how they'd turned out so differently. It wasn't until much later that I realized those differences were only superficial, that deep down they were both Lemonts. Raised to believe they should get what they want.

A taller-than-average woman in a high-necked white lace gown was standing at the edge of the crowd, surveying the party with an air of authority. Here, at last, was the person the party revolved around, the woman who so intrigued and frightened me: Matthew's mother, Hannah Lemont. She must have been in her late fifties or early sixties, given Matthew's age, but time hadn't harshened her face as it had my mother's; Hannah had the kind of classic, even features that aged well. She watched me with the same guarded expression I'd seen on Matthew when we first met, warning me off rather than inviting me in.

"Mum, this is Kate."

To my relief, Matthew pulled away from Marjorie and placed one hand protectively against my back. His support shored me up as I nervously stepped forward.

"So nice to meet you," I said. "You have a lovely home."

Hannah tipped her head. "Lakecrest has many impressive qualities, but loveliness is not one of them."

"Then I can honestly say I've never seen anything like it."

Matthew laughed, and Hannah's eyes flickered back and forth. Her face remained resolutely blank, but I could tell she had been momentarily thrown off balance. I wasn't sure if I'd offended her.

"I'll take you on a tour later," Matthew said. "Once Mum releases me from my hosting duties."

"From what I hear, you've released yourself from all sorts of duties since Kate came to town," Hannah said tartly. She offered me a tight smile. "How long are you visiting Chicago?"

My mind swirled with all the things I could say—*I'm not visiting; Matthew and I are married*—and I glanced at Matthew, expecting him to come to my rescue. Instead, he looked oddly unsure of himself as the silence lengthened. It had been Matthew's idea to surprise his mother, yet here he was, avoiding the very situation he'd brought about. Standing next to Hannah, my once-confident husband looked somehow diminished. Afraid.

Finally, Marjorie interjected herself into the uncomfortable family tableau. "Matts, tell Mum your big news!"

Hannah looked at Matthew, and Matthew looked at me, and I glanced down at my ring, which had rubbed my finger red with all my fiddling. Hannah followed my gaze and instantly understood. With a few twitches of her lips, her expression shifted from calm to furious. But her body remained motionless, and her voice, when she spoke, was measured.

"Congratulations to you both."

If Matthew had intended to declare his independence by marrying me, the plan had failed. He looked like a miserable schoolboy, awaiting his punishment.

"Clearly, we have much to discuss, but now is not the time, nor is this the place," Hannah declared. "Matthew, why don't you show Kate to the buffet?" She gave me what would have looked like a friendly smile to anyone who couldn't see the coldness in her eyes. "You look as if you enjoy a good meal. Marjorie and her friends are so keen on staying slender, it's a novelty to see a girl with meat on her bones. If you'll excuse me . . ."

She gave us a dismissive nod and turned away. I flushed at the insult, feeling more out of place than ever in the expensive dress I'd once adored. Hannah was right. No matter what I wore, I couldn't help but look dumpy and ugly next to someone like Marjorie.

Matthew grabbed my hand and squeezed. "She'll come round."

I wasn't at all sure, but I forced a grateful smile.

"I'd say we deserve a drink. Mum keeps Lakecrest dry, but Margie's friends usually sneak in some booze. Ah—Jack might know."

Jack turned out to be Jack Turnbull, who'd gone to Yale with Matthew. It wasn't long before Matthew and I were surrounded by a huddle of Jacks and Jocks and Jims, all of whom were identified by whether they went to Harvard or Princeton or Yale but seemed otherwise interchangeable. Almost immediately, Matthew slipped into the kind of man-about-town behavior I'd never seen from him before, slapping his friends on the back and laughing raucously at jokes I didn't understand.

The women who had accompanied these men formed their own separate cluster nearby, one I felt excluded from even after Matthew had introduced me and they'd squealed at the news of our marriage. Though I tried to fake an interest in their talk about housekeeping and babies, I couldn't think of a thing to say, and I felt cut off from their easy camaraderie. I was still an outsider, as I'd been all my life. I glanced around the terrace and saw Marjorie brandishing a cigarette with dramatic self-assurance, surrounded by a rapt group of men. I caught Hannah glaring at me before I turned pointedly away. I felt detached and light-headed, like I'd faint if I didn't get away from all these strangers and their shrill chatter. I slipped in next to Matthew and told him I wanted to take a walk around the grounds.

"I know I promised a tour, but could it wait?" he asked. "I haven't seen these fellows in a while."

"I'll go on my own. I don't mind."

"I'll find you soon." Matthew brushed his fingers along my cheek, an unexpectedly intimate gesture. I hoped Hannah had seen it.

I stepped off the terrace, and my heels sank into the thick grass. Ahead, I could see a path running along the bluff that overlooked the lake; to my right was another trail that led into a cluster of pine trees. I set off to the left, toward a white structure in the distance. A stone walkway curved past a fountain surrounded by rose bushes, each at its fragrant peak. I walked on, under trellises and through rows of columns that looked like the remnants of an ancient palace. The terrain became less orderly the farther I went, with dandelions running unchecked through the grass and crowding against a gazebo set atop a hill.

I walked up and stood inside. The building was small—no more than ten feet across—but lavishly constructed, with an intricate frieze carved into the lower portion of the dome that formed the ceiling. It seemed to have been inspired by Greek mythology: figures in flowing dresses and tunics were carrying sheaves of wheat and bunches of grapes. I looked back toward Lakecrest, a ramshackle dollhouse in the distance. The steep bluff dropped down to a private beach, where I could see tiny figures moving around on the sand. A yacht was tied up at the end of a long wooden dock—Matthew had made offhand references to sailing—and the water twinkled with reflected sunlight.

My eyes wandered along the shore, and as I turned my head northward, the bucolic landscape was interrupted by a hulking wall of deep-red brick. The remnants of a path leading toward it were barely visible under a carpet of weeds. Strangled by ivy and crumbling from the pounding of countless harsh winters, the building loomed menacingly over the untended terrain. Except for the drone of cicadas and an occasional birdcall, this part of the estate seemed to be deserted. That is why I was so startled to see a woman appear around one corner of the brick wall and walk toward me. She was somewhere between middle-aged and old, with a plump stomach and wobbly chin, and I could tell by the immaculate white of her shoes and gloves that she had money. Her smile was cautiously friendly.

"I didn't know anyone else was out here." She held out her hand. "How do you do. I'm Mabel Kostrick."

"Kate Moore. That is—Kate Lemont."

It was the first time I'd said the words aloud, and they suddenly sounded preposterous. How could that possibly be my name?

"Matthew's wife," I explained.

"Ah, Jasper's boy," Mabel didn't look taken aback or even particularly interested. Here was one person, at least, who hadn't been gossiping about me.

"That building over there," I said, pointing to the near ruin behind her. "What is it?"

It was as if I'd admitted to being unfamiliar with the *Mona Lisa*. Mabel's eyes widened, and she stared at me, considering her words. Finally, she simply said, "The Labyrinth."

I'm no believer in omens, but I felt a shiver of distaste. I knew, just from the way Mabel said the word, it was a place I should avoid.

"This is my first visit to Lakecrest," I explained.

"Oh," she said, confused, as if my unfamiliarity with the property was no excuse. Then, deftly changing the subject, she asked, "Shall we rejoin the party?"

I was in no hurry to get back to all those curious, judgmental stares. Or to Hannah. Befriending Mabel was a chance to find out more about the family I'd married into. I dawdled on the path, making no move to leave.

"Have you known the Lemonts a long time?" I asked.

"Oh, yes," she said. "I grew up nearby."

"Lucky you," I said, smiling. "It's beautiful out here."

Mabel glanced out at the lake. "We lived closer to town. I always envied this view." She sighed, and the exhale of breath seemed to drag her features downward, making her look older. Then, in a voice so quiet she might have been talking to herself, "It's not the same, though."

I could have let it pass, pretended not to have heard. Instead, I waited expectantly.

"You know about Cecily?" she asked cautiously. "Matthew's aunt?"

Embarrassed by my ignorance, I nodded and pretended to recognize the name.

"Matthew's told me a bit," I said. In fact, Matthew had never even mentioned her name. "I'm still sorting out who all the Lemonts are."

"Cecily was an extraordinary woman," Mabel said. "She's the one who started these summer fêtes, you know. I was quite in awe the first time I came! She was so beautiful, and I was completely tongue-tied in the receiving line, but she couldn't have been more gracious. 'Lakecrest's at its best come summer,' she used to say, and do you know, they always had the most glorious weather for those parties. Cecily would say the gods were smiling on her."

The gods? I glanced at the stone gazebo; Cecily clearly had had a taste for ancient Greek art.

"She called that the Temple," Mabel said. "This whole section of the estate was her idea, her design. She wanted to create a refuge for female artists, where they could be inspired by nature."

There was nothing inspirational about the place now. Cecily's monuments were gloomy, forgotten ruins. I looked back at the Labyrinth. Its stark, unwelcoming façade was a jarring contrast to the open airiness of the Temple and the decorative columns scattered around the landscape. I noticed cracks in the mortar and gaps where bricks had crumbled away. How long before the whole thing collapsed into a pile of rubble?

Mabel followed my gaze. "I'm surprised it's still here," she murmured. "I thought they'd have torn it down years ago."

"Why?"

Mabel turned to me, startled. "Hasn't Matthew told you?"

I shook my head.

Mabel looked away. Adjusting her hat to avoid looking at me, she said, "I'm sorry. I thought you knew."

"Knew what?"

Mabel began walking back toward the house, and I hurried to catch up with her.

"Mrs. Kostrick! What happened?"

She kept her eyes fixed ahead. "It hardly matters, after all this time."

Mabel seemed determined to ignore me until we arrived within earshot of the terrace and I uttered a final "Please!" I couldn't see Matthew, but I glimpsed Hannah sitting in a high-backed armchair. The queen surveying her court.

"Cecily walked into the Labyrinth," Mabel said brusquely, "and she never came out."

Before I could ask any more questions, Mabel scurried ahead, through the French doors that led into a glass-walled conservatory. The party had begun to fragment; a few young men were attempting a boisterous game of croquet on the lawn, while ancient dowagers and their equally decrepit spouses took refuge from the sun under the awning that extended out from the back of the house. Only a sprinkling of people remained on the terrace, with Hannah at their center.

To my dismay, she beckoned me over. "Kate. I've been looking for you."

Her hangers-on drifted away, and Hannah waved a hand toward the chair at her side. I sat, perched on the edge, hoping my upright posture gave me an air of confidence. I couldn't let her see how much I was dreading this conversation.

"I must admit, your sudden marriage to my son came as quite a surprise."

I met Hannah's stare with a similarly impassive expression. I knew enough about bullies to let her attack first. It would give me time to study her tactics.

"You can understand my concern," Hannah said, unruffled by my lack of response. "Matthew is quite a catch."

I smiled as if we were sharing a joke. "*Matthew* caught *me*, not the other way round," I said. "I didn't even know who he was when we first met."

"He can be quite charming, when he wants to be, and you seem like a delightful girl. But you must see you have no future together."

I told myself to keep calm. Hannah was baiting me, hoping I'd lash out.

"Matthew loves me," I said firmly.

"That is inconsequential," Hannah said. "Matthew is the head of this family, and you are not equipped to shoulder that burden. One day you will see my honesty as a kindness."

Her smug self-satisfaction was all the more awful for being delivered with such feigned concern. I could defend myself against straightforward insults, but how do you win against someone who pretends to take your side?

"I cannot let this marriage stand," Hannah went on. "I will arrange a quiet annulment, and we'll put it all down to youthful hijinks. If you leave quietly, you'll receive a handsome settlement. I can be quite generous with those who see things my way."

For the briefest instant, I considered it. But not long enough for Hannah to confirm her suspicions about me. Standing abruptly, I said, "Thank you so much for your hospitality. I'm going to find my husband."

I walked away briskly, trying not to show how the encounter had shaken me. I knew Hannah wouldn't welcome me with open arms; no mother in her position would want her son settling down with a penniless nobody. But I'd never expected such a blunt, face-to-face confrontation at our very first meeting. Had I played it all wrong? Maybe I should have been meek and groveling, telling her how pathetically grateful I was to be part of her *remarkable* family and married to her *wonderful* son.

I quickly headed into the conservatory and then through the first door I saw, which led into a room so dim I had to pause for my eyes to adjust. The walls were covered with books, thousands of them, and from the musty smell, most had been sitting there for years. A desk sat in a corner, dusty with disuse. The library, I guessed, but it did nothing to help me get my bearings, because I'd never seen it before.

I kept going, hoping to find a quiet room where I could shrug off my disappointment and decide my next move. I found a hallway that seemed to run the length of the house, and I veered down it, glancing through each doorway I passed, but nothing looked familiar. Lakecrest, daunting enough from the outside, seemed even larger from the inside. Every room was decorated in a different theme, from French Rococo to Arabian Nights, and I wondered how anyone could feel at home in a place constructed from other buildings' ruins.

The hall narrowed and ended In a door that sat slightly ajar. Hearing voices coming from the other side, I knocked cautiously. The door was pulled open abruptly, and a maid peeked out.

"Yes?"

Behind her, I could see a counter and sink, both filled with glasses in various stages of being washed.

"Sorry to disturb you," I said. "I'm afraid I'm lost."

"Where did you want to go?"

Overwhelmed by all the bric-a-brac and mismatched wallpaper and staring animal heads, I felt close to tears. I told the maid I needed to get outside, and she led me through a warren of tiny rooms where servants were cleaning up the party's aftermath. I stepped out of a narrow side door and into the kitchen garden, where gravel paths bordered neatly tended beds of vegetables. A footpath led to the bluff that overlooked the lake, and I headed toward it, drawn to the stairs that led down to the water.

A few children were running along the sand, trying to fly a kite, but otherwise the beach was deserted. I walked down the wooden steps, pulled off my shoes and stockings, and stood at the water's edge. I'm not sure how long I was there, my feet rooted in the wet sand. I wondered if Matthew would fight for me, what I'd do if he obeyed his mother instead. I heard the stairs creak behind me, but I didn't turn until I heard Matthew's voice.

"Kate."

He was looking at me from the bottom step. Contrite. "I heard what happened."

"That your mother tried to buy me off?"

A look midway between anguish and frustration crossed his face. "She hasn't gotten to know you yet. Give her time."

"They all think I'm a gold digger," I snapped. "Your family, your friends. At least your mother was honest enough to tell me to my face."

I pulled my feet out from the sand and awkwardly tried to brush them clean. The horrible truth was that Hannah was right, that I was lying when I said I had no ulterior motives. How long would Matthew believe me over his mother?

"It's all been sorted out," Matthew said briskly, as if he'd cleared up a minor domestic spat. "Come back to the house."

"No!" I snapped. "I'm leaving!"

The children stopped to stare at us. Clutching my shoes and stockings in one hand, I scampered around Matthew and up the steps. I didn't stop until I'd reached the top, where a movement from the house caught my eye. Hannah was looking down at us from a second-floor balcony, like a hawk tracking her prey.

Defiantly, so she could hear me, I raised my voice. "I don't want any of this!" I shouted, struggling to keep my wind-whipped hair out of my eyes. "I never did!"

Suddenly, I realized I wasn't protesting solely for Hannah's benefit. I didn't want Lakecrest and all the responsibilities that came with it; I didn't want to spend the rest of my life facing Hannah's and Marjorie's disapproving glares. Hannah had offered me a way out. I could take her money and never see this place again.

Matthew stared at me, bewildered by my loss of control. The distance between us had never felt so vast.

"Kate." His voice was almost a whisper. "Please."

I looked at Matthew's stricken face and didn't see the glittering prize I'd worked so hard to claim. I saw a man in pain—a man I'd promised to stand by, for better or for worse. Did I really want to give up on him so soon? I reached out, and he practically fell into my arms. I kissed him on the cheek, then the lips, pressing my chest against his, hoping Hannah was still watching.

"Let's sneak out," I said softly. "Go home."

Matthew tapped a finger on my nose, looking tempted. "Naughty girl."

"Come on, then."

Matthew sighed and extracted himself from our embrace. "I can't. Got to stand by Mum till the bitter end. But you can go if you want. I'll call the driver."

"You don't mind?"

"Not at all. You can get started on the packing."

"Packing?"

"I told you. We've got it all sorted out."

I looked up at him, bewildered.

"We're moving to Lakecrest. Mum insists."

CHAPTER FIVE

There must have been some kind of mistake. Matthew hadn't even asked me.

"We agreed to move, didn't we?" Matthew asked briskly. "The apartment's much too small for a married couple, and there's no space for entertaining. We have to maintain certain standards."

"But, your work," I stammered, queasy with dread. "You'd be so far from the office."

"I'll keep the apartment, of course," Matthew said, as if the arrangements he'd worked out without me should be perfectly obvious. "It will be useful for the nights I work late. But you'll be much better off up here."

I wanted to scream, *"I hate Lakecrest!"* I pushed the frustration down and tried to keep my voice level. "I don't want to live so far out in the country. What will I do all day?"

"Mum will show you the ropes," Matthew said. "You'll have Marjorie for company, too."

That was hardly a comfort. "Why don't we find a larger apartment?" I offered. "We can come out on weekends."

"I can't see why you're being so difficult—"

"Because I have no interest in living in that miserable house!"

Matthew's face hardened into an obstinate expression that was a mirror image of his mother's. "It's already been decided."

It was our first fight. I could feel the hurt and anger radiating off Matthew as he tried to keep his voice calm. Saw his determination to prove he wasn't the kind of husband who gave in to his wife's complaints. What would I gain by dragging it out? If I gave in gracefully, I could gradually change his mind over time. I thought I'd be at Lakecrest a few months at most, not knowing how much I'd be changed in even that short time and never guessing how hard it would be to leave.

"All right," I said, summoning an apologetic smile. "You can't blame me for being nervous, though, after what your mother said."

"Don't you worry about that," Matthew said. "She and I had a very frank talk. I told her you're my wife, and we're madly in love, and I won't hear a bad word against you. This invitation is her way of making amends."

I looked up at the house. Hannah was no longer on the balcony, but her watchfulness seemed to linger, casting a shadow over our conversation. *It's good news,* I told myself. *It means Matthew stood up for you, and Hannah's accepted the marriage. Who knows? She might even insist we go shopping and buy me the trousseau and jewelry I'd told Matthew I didn't really need.*

In the distance, I saw Marjorie approaching, moving with the graceful ease of a dancer. Her dress and hair swirled in the breeze.

"Lovers' spat?" she called out cheerily.

I dropped the arms that had been folded across my chest and squeezed Matthew's hand. "Wonderful news," I gushed with fake enthusiasm. "We're moving to Lakecrest."

"Yes, Mum told me."

I tried not to show my irritation. Why did everyone else seem to know about my new living arrangements before I did?

"The party's breaking up, and some of us are going downtown to hear a new band," Marjorie said. "Want to come?"

I looked hopefully at Matthew. At that moment, I wanted nothing more than to escape into the lights and noises of the city. To put Lakecrest behind me.

"Oh, let's," I pleaded.

Matthew shrugged. "You know I hate nightclubs."

Marjorie's smile to me was unexpectedly warm. "Forget my fuddy-duddy brother," she said. "We'll have a lot more fun if he's not along."

"Go on, Kate," Matthew urged. "Time you girls got to know each other better."

Despite my apprehension about spending time with Marjorie on my own, I knew I'd be a fool to say no. Showing her I was game for a good time might win her over, and I'd need all the friends at Lakecrest I could get. I kissed Matthew good night and said I wouldn't stay out too late.

Marjorie laughed and linked her arm with mine. "Don't wait up!" she called out to Matthew as we headed to the front drive. She leaned into me and whispered, "Feels like breaking out of jail, doesn't it?"

"Poor Matthew. He promised your mother he'd stay till everyone's gone."

"Dependable old Matts," Marjorie said. "Always doing his duty."

"The burden of being the oldest child, I guess."

"Oldest?"

"Oh, I'm sorry. Is it Matthew who's younger?"

Marjorie gave me a strange look. "We're twins," she said. "Didn't you know?"

I mumbled something about being forgetful as I blundered through the same disorientation I'd felt when Mabel Kostrick told me about Cecily. Content inside our private cocoon, Matthew and I had barely spoken about our families and our pasts. It was jarring to realize the man I'd married was still a stranger, and I wondered what else I didn't know about my new husband.

Marjorie seemed on the verge of quizzing me when we were waved over by a group of people huddled by a gleaming Rolls-Royce. Marjorie made rushed introductions—I forgot most of the names immediately—and we crammed inside.

Throughout the drive to Chicago, everyone competed to be the most outrageous, while I giggled shyly and pretended to look shocked. When we pulled up at the Pharaoh's Club, my heart sank. Blanche would be there. The coat check wouldn't be busy in the middle of summer, and she'd be eager to talk about the wedding and my meeting with Matthew's family. I imagined the reaction of my new companions, these privileged men and women who talked about their family yachts and who did what in Newport, when I introduced her as my cousin. They'd roll their eyes, exchange snobbish smirks.

In a split-second decision I'm ashamed of to this day, I slipped behind Marjorie, hoping Blanche wouldn't see me. But she did. I caught a quick glimpse of her surprised expression and instantly hated myself for snubbing her. But I didn't go back.

To block out my guilt, I drank more than I should have. It was easy to lose track of exactly how much I'd had, with glasses of spiked lemonade appearing in front of me seemingly by magic and being refilled without my asking. A hazy sense of well-being flooded through me, and Marjorie flashed me a radiant smile from across the table. She was enjoying herself—I was enjoying myself!—and whatever frostiness there'd been between us had melted in a blaze of alcohol and jazz. She leaned over to say something, and the man on the other side of me reached out for her hand, begging for a kiss with a slurred tongue, and I laughed as his elbow tipped a drink into my lap. It was all so funny, and I couldn't understand what Marjorie was talking about, except it was something to do with Matthew, and that made me laugh even harder. What would he think if he could see me now?

I dabbed the drink from my dress with a napkin, and when I looked up, one of Marjorie's friends was standing above me.

"Would you like to dance?" Dark-haired and ruddy-cheeked, he was nicknamed Boots, for reasons no one had explained.

"All right," I laughed, feeling emboldened by the liquor coursing through me but unsteady on my feet as soon as I stood up.

Boots was too polite to comment on my stumble as he led me to the dance floor. If he wasn't the most graceful dancer I'd ever partnered with, at least he didn't step on my toes.

"Matthew's a lucky man," he shouted, but the music was too loud to have a real conversation. We wove through the crowd, backward and forward, until I began to feel dizzy. I looked toward our table. Marjorie was sitting in a man's lap, one of his hands wrapped around her waist. George? Joe? All I could remember was that he owned his own plane and bragged about having met Charles Lindbergh.

Marjorie was an image of glamorous perfection, leaning forward as he lit her cigarette. But her beauty had a reckless edge, a trigger for dangerous emotions. The man's lips hovered by her neck, and her eyes caught mine, issuing a silent challenge. Was she ordering me not to tell her brother? Or daring me to?

Boots spun me to the left, and I ended by flopping awkwardly into his chest. He pressed his hand harder against my shoulder blades, where my dress stuck uncomfortably to my back, and pulled me close. His jacket brushed against my stomach.

"I'm tired," I said loudly over the music, wanting him to hear me. I felt flushed and uneasy, but he didn't loosen his grip. His breath blew hot and bitter against my cheek.

"You're a real doll," he whispered, and then his tongue flicked against my earlobe.

I recoiled, twisting my head away as Boots forced me into another turn. My heart was racing with panic as we passed by Marjorie's table. The faces were a blur, but I could tell they were looking at me and laughing, Marjorie loudest of all. Her voice had developed a harsh rasp, and her vivaciousness had toughened into something darker.

It was hard to think straight with my head buzzing and my steps clumsy from the alcohol, but I suspected I was the reason they were all roaring. Marjorie had never intended to befriend me; she wanted to see me humiliated. I pushed Boots away with an abrupt shove to his chest, and there was nowhere to go but toward the door, stumbling as tears blurred my vision.

A hand grabbed my arm, and a gentle voice asked what was wrong. I wiped the back of my hand across my eyes and saw Blanche. My dear, loyal cousin, whose kindness I didn't deserve. The thought made me start crying again, and Blanche pulled me into the coat check, telling me to hush.

Through choked-back sobs, I apologized for ignoring her earlier.

"I get it," she said. "No hard feelings."

How easy it was to talk to her, how easy to confess my feelings of shame and self-doubt. With her, I could be the best version of myself, a fun-loving girl who went to the pictures and rode the streetcar. An independent girl with no worries.

"I want to go home," I said impulsively.

"All right," Blanche said hesitantly. "Want me to hail you a cab?"

"No," I explained. "Home with you."

I'd been happy in that boardinghouse, surrounded by other young women who didn't think further ahead than what they'd eat for dinner that night. I could get a job, earn my own way, and never see Marjorie again. Or Matthew. I remembered the rush of feeling I'd had on our wedding day, my belief that we could be happy. But that fleeting regret wasn't enough to overpower my longing for escape.

What if I'd done it? Rejected my marriage and the Lemonts and marched off with Blanche that night? I like to think Matthew would have come after me, but Hannah might have convinced him I wasn't worth a second chance. He might have listened when she urged him to file for divorce. Our lives would have continued on divergent paths, and if that meant I would have been spared the horrors that followed, it also meant I would have missed out on the kind of love I didn't know I was capable of. That night at the Pharaoh's Club was a crossroads, one of those rare moments when one decision determines the course of a life. In the end, it wasn't really a choice at all, because Blanche refused to take me in.

"You're drunk and hysterical," she said bluntly. "Otherwise, you'd never be talking like this. Tell you what—you sleep it off, then call me in the morning. I'll bet ten bucks you thank me for talking some sense into you."

"Matthew wants to move to Lakecrest," I told her. "It's miles away and absolutely hideous. I'm going to be miserable."

"Oh, boohoo," Blanche laughed. Then, imitating my sullen voice, "I have to live in a mansion and be waited on hand and foot. Poor me!"

I smiled in spite of myself. "Try living there with my new mother-in-law. Not to mention Marjorie."

"You'll probably hardly ever see her. Seems like she's out every night."

"I don't know how she keeps it up. I'm worn out."

"Maybe she has some help."

Blanche said the words quietly, looking down, hinting at something I didn't understand.

"What do you mean?"

Blanche beckoned me to the doorway of the coat check. She tipped her head toward the dance floor, where Marjorie was being swung around by her aviator friend, her head flung back in rapturous release.

"She's soused," I said. "Like the rest of them."

"It's more than that," Blanche said. "I've been here long enough. I know the signs. She's on some kind of dope."

Dope? I thought that was for the lowest of the low, the failures who'd do anything to escape their miserable lives. Marjorie Lemont had everything: money, good looks, and a crowd of adoring friends. Why would she want to escape into a drugged fog?

I didn't want to believe it, not at first. But the more I thought about it, the more I realized there'd been something jittery about Marjorie, just beneath the surface. As I took a taxi back to the apartment that night, I decided not to tell Matthew. Marjorie's secret would be tucked away like a secret treasure, held in reserve for a time I might need it.

~

Twenty-four hours later, Matthew was giving me a full tour of Lakecrest, my home for the foreseeable future.

He explained that a series of architects had been given the impossible task of unifying all the odds and ends Obadiah had shipped from Europe, and eventually they'd given up any attempts at balance or harmony. Rooms and staircases and hallways were added on as needed, with no grand plan or consistent design. Thus, the Arabian Room, with its painted blue tiles and colorful peacock mosaics, led directly into the Gallery, a somber medieval-style showcase for Obadiah's collection of marble statues and oversized landscapes. The ballroom was done up in a gaudy approximation of Versailles, complete with mirrored walls, while the library was a masterpiece of Victorian gloom, with dark wood paneling and heavy crimson drapes.

"Grandfather wasn't very discriminating, as you can see," Matthew said. It was the thrill of the hunt that excited Obadiah, the act of claiming something beautiful and rare as his own.

The grand front staircase led directly to the main wing of bedrooms on the second floor, but there were other staircases that snaked through the rest of the house like mouse tunnels, some going directly up to the servants' quarters on the top floor, others stopping unexpectedly after only a few steps and ending in a storage cupboard or washroom. And everywhere, from the main reception rooms to the lowliest back cupboard, there were *things*: objects and artworks that seemed to cover every flat surface. Paintings of Italian noblemen in elaborate gold frames and marble busts of grumpy-looking Roman emperors. Chinese fans and jade vases. Rainbows of South American butterflies pinned onto black velvet backdrops. It was a celebration of excess, and were Lakecrest a museum, I would have admired its brash extravagance. But I didn't see how it would ever feel like home.

To my great relief, Matthew's bedroom was Spartan compared to the rest of the house. Here, at last, was a place I felt at ease. Larger than the apartment I'd grown up in, it was bright and uncluttered, with a four-poster bed, a wide bay window overlooking the lake, and a scattering of worn armchairs and settees. The walls were for the most part bare, which made the one painting tucked in a nook near the bathroom all the more striking.

It showed a young woman walking through the grass, barefoot, a crown of flowers on her head. The artist had given the composition an appealing sense of motion: the woman's legs were caught midstride, and her hands were tangled in the billows of her white dress. Her hair, a shade between blonde and brown, cascaded over her shoulders, tendrils of it lifted by the wind. Her face was in profile, captured as she turned to look over her shoulder. There was an impression of beauty, but I couldn't tell exactly what she looked like, as if paint were too solid a medium to capture her essence.

Matthew came over and stood beside me, looking pleased by my interest. "Do you like it?" he asked.

"Very much. Who is she?"

"My aunt Cecily."

So this was the mysterious woman who'd disappeared into the Labyrinth. I had a dozen questions, but I didn't want to upset Matthew by looking too eager for family gossip. Safer to hold back what I'd heard from Mabel and get his side of the story first.

"She painted this herself," Matthew said. "It's the way I like to remember her."

I thought it was odd that Cecily would obscure her own face in a self-portrait. Mabel had said she was beautiful, so what did she have to hide?

"You loved her," I said quietly. I could see it in his eyes, the way he looked wistfully at this woman who would always be turning away, out of his reach. For a moment, Matthew looked as if he were sorting through memories. Deciding which to share.

"Aunt Cecily was the most inspiring person I've ever known," he said. "She lived her life like it was a grand adventure—painting and writing and studying great art. Grandfather loved to boast about her being the first American woman to sit for the ancient languages exam at Oxford, but she wasn't stuck up. She was always so kind to me and Marjorie."

It didn't seem possible that one human being could encompass all those virtues, and I wondered what flaws she might have kept hidden from her adoring young nephew. It's easy to idealize those who die young.

Gently, I asked, "What happened to her?"

Matthew didn't answer. He took a few steps back and sat in an armchair, motioning for me to join him. I curled up at his feet and put my head in his lap.

"I don't know," he said at last. "It's eaten at me for years, not knowing. It's been . . . my God, more than fifteen years since I last saw her. The summer of 1912."

Matthew stroked my hair in a soothing, steady rhythm. Calming himself more than me.

"Aunt Cecily was like a second mother," he said. "She lived with us here at Lakecrest. Mum was always so busy; Aunt Cecily was the one who told stories and took me and Marjorie to play at the beach. She was the kind of person who made you feel like anything was possible—for years I thought she was actually magic! In time, of course, I got older, and Aunt Cecily went through some bouts of bad health, so we weren't quite the chums we'd once been. But I still adored her."

He paused, bracing himself for what came next. "I was twelve when it happened. Aunt Cecily hadn't been well, so she kept to her room for a few days. I stopped in after dinner to say good night, but she didn't want to talk. She barely even looked at me. So I acted like a spoiled brat and stormed out. And that was the last time I ever saw her."

Matthew sounded so sad that my heart ached for the boy who'd lost his beloved aunt and for the man who still grieved for her.

"I've gone over those minutes so many times," he murmured, "wishing I'd been kinder."

"You couldn't have known," I reassured him. "It's not your fault."

Matthew nodded slowly, trying to convince himself. "Later that night," he continued, "one of the maids was drawing the upstairs drapes when she saw Aunt Cecily walk across the lawn, to the other side of the estate. There's a building there."

"The Labyrinth," I blurted out.

Matthew gave me a puzzled look, and I told him I'd seen it, the day of the fête. For now, I decided not to mention Mabel Kostrick; I didn't want him to think I'd been gossiping.

After a brief pause, Matthew continued. "The maid didn't think anything was amiss, because Aunt Cecily often had trouble sleeping and was known to wander around at all hours. The next day, when the maid brought up Aunt Cecily's breakfast tray, she saw the bed hadn't been slept in. Mum told Marjorie and me to stay upstairs, so we'd be shielded from what was going on, but I saw the police arrive. They searched the Labyrinth and sent boats out on the lake, but it was no use. Aunt Cecily had vanished."

"Do you think she's dead?" I asked.

"She must be. If she left, for whatever reason, I can't believe she'd never have written."

"What does your mother think?"

Matthew let out a short, dismissive laugh. "We never talk about it. Not openly, anyway. Mum's dropped hints about Aunt Cecily taking her own life, but it's ridiculous. They'd have found her. That is—found her body."

There was another possibility. That Cecily had been lured away from Lakecrest. Kidnapped, possibly murdered. But this wasn't the right time to raise such suspicions. Better to nuzzle my head against Matthew in silent sympathy.

"I've got something to show you," he said.

He gently pushed me up so he could stand. Then he walked toward the window and opened the top drawer of a bureau. He pulled out a slim book bound in dark-green leather and handed it to me. I read the words embossed in gold on the front cover: *Twelve Ancient Tales. Cecily Lemont.*

"My grandfather had them printed for her birthday, years ago," Matthew said.

I flipped the book open and read the inscription on the title page.

My steadfast, mighty Matthew,
*   Be the hero of your own life. Dare to live as you*
dream.
*   With love from your devoted Aunt Cecily*

I could almost see her pen forming the angled letters, and I was overcome with a sudden regret that I'd never known this strange, spirited woman. The pages of text were interspersed with colored illustrations of cavorting nymphs and columned buildings; a bearded god scowled as lightning bolts shot out from his fingers. A word jumped out from the text—Labyrinth—and I glanced at the title of the story. "The Princess and the Bull." Curious, I began scanning the page.

"Time enough for that later," Matthew said, pulling the book from my hands and jarring me back to our conversation. "The room," he repeated. "Do you like it?"

I looked around again. "It's fine. But your mother told me a woman in my position should have her own bedroom."

"I like sleeping together," Matthew said. "Don't you?"

"Sure." I blushed when I said it.

"Then you'll stay here, with me."

I grinned at this further proof that Matthew could stand up to his mother. Who knew what other things I might convince him to change? I glanced at the table in front of the window—just the spot for morning coffee—and the armoire against the wall and the shabby but comfortable furniture. Then I realized what was nagging at me: there was nothing of Matthew here. No childhood toys or mementos from his college years. No clues to his character.

When I asked why, Matthew explained it used to be his grandfather's room. "Mum thought it would be more appropriate, now that I'm married. You can do it up however you like."

I told him I didn't care about decorating, but I wondered how long it would be before I turned into one of those wives whose greatest accomplishment was buying new drapes. Now that I was living at Lakecrest, someone else would buy my food, cook it, and serve it. I'd have my clothes sewn by the family's dressmaker, and maids would wash and mend whatever I wore. I was cut off from the life of the city, stranded on an estate without anything to do but stare at the lake. I'd been so caught up in the idea of marrying Matthew that I hadn't stopped to think what I'd do once I got him.

For a fleeting, chilling instant, I felt like a mythical princess, locked in a tower. Buried alive.

Then Matthew was reminding me that it was time to change for supper; his mother was expecting us downstairs. He showed me a dressing room where my clothes had already been hung, my shoes arranged in a neat row below, and I shook off my gloomy mood. Time to be the perfect daughter-in-law and perfect wife, biding my time until Matthew was firmly on my side. Then I'd convince him we should move out.

I was still naïve enough to think I could do it.

What Hannah called her nightly "social hour" was cocktail hour for Marjorie, who'd stashed a silver flask behind a potted plant and discreetly offered me a splash for my iced tea. I declined. We said nothing about my sudden exit from the Pharaoh's Club the night before, and I wondered how much she even remembered, given Blanche's suspicions. Maybe her boisterous laughter had nothing to do with me at all. Hannah welcomed me with a seemingly genuine smile, showing no trace of her earlier haughtiness. If anything, she paid too much attention to me, insisting I join her at one of the card tables and examine an elaborate family tree she'd laid out on top. Apparently, my first duty as Matthew's wife was to suffer through a lecture on the grand and glorious history of the Lemont family.

The trunk of the tree was Henri de Le Mont, a Frenchman who'd immigrated to Canada and followed the rivers westward as a fur trader. The next branch up was his son George, who had Anglicized the family's name and founded the shipping line that made them rich. George's son Obadiah, Lakecrest's builder, was memorialized in a portrait that hung over the fireplace. With his broad shoulders, muttonchop whiskers, and semi-scowl, he was the epitome of a gruff Victorian patriarch.

"Don't forget the Indian princess," Marjorie said offhandedly. She looked at me and whispered melodramatically, "The black sheep."

"Marjorie," Hannah snapped. Then, for my benefit, "There's no proof the story's true."

"They say old Henri fell in love with the daughter of an Indian chief," Marjorie went on. "Married her and took part in some sort of blood-brother ceremony to show his loyalty. Of course, Mum's horrified that the Lemont family tree may be tainted with Indian blood. But you don't care, do you, Kate?"

"It's nonsense," Hannah said to me. "A legend. We have no idea who Henri's wife was."

"Because only the men's stories survive," Marjorie said. "Isn't that what Aunt Cecily used to say?"

There was a moment of stillness, sharp and clear. Hannah stared at her daughter, aghast, and I privately savored the image of her looking so flustered. Recovering herself, she deftly changed the subject to Obadiah's collection of Greek vases, and Matthew chimed in, anxious to smooth away the awkwardness. Cecily, it seemed, was off limits.

When Edna, the cook, announced supper was ready, Hannah led us into the cavernous dining room, a space built for banquets that felt intimidatingly vast with only four of us at the table. Gone were the days when Lakecrest had a live-in staff of twelve. Only Edna lived at the house now, in quarters off the kitchen; the two maids, Alice and Gerta, would go to their homes in the nearby town of East Ridge after the evening meal was served. The servants' quarters had been closed for years, a forgotten remnant of more opulent times.

I looked at Matthew and Hannah and Marjorie taking their first bites of vegetable terrine and was overcome by what felt like a vision from the future. I saw all of us at this same table decades from now, making the same polite conversation, eating off the same gold-rimmed china. This was where we'd celebrate holidays and milestones, and in time I'd no longer feel like a nervous, self-conscious interloper.

These people were now my family.

"Cheers to Kate for making it through her first day at Lakecrest," Matthew said heartily, raising his water glass for a toast.

Hannah nodded and waved her glass in my direction. "I hope you'll be very happy here." Her rigid expression softened, and I wondered if she had genuinely made peace with my marriage or was simply putting on a show for Matthew.

I heard a snort from Marjorie, but when I turned to look at her, she was staring down at her plate, the picture of innocence.

"Thank you," I said. "I'll admit that I feel a little overwhelmed. It's going to take a while to learn my way around."

"Goodness, yes," Hannah said, giving me a surprisingly warm smile. "I still remember my first days here. Jasper—Matthew and Marjorie's father—expected me to swoop in and take charge when I could barely find my way to the kitchen! I was quite beside myself."

For the first time, I was able to think of Hannah as a real person, someone with weaknesses and fears.

"Well, I'll be depending on you to show me everything," I said. "I'm sure your mother-in-law was a great help to you, too?"

"Oh no, Jasper's mother had been dead for years when we married. There was a housekeeper, Mrs. Briscoe, but she was elderly and quite hopeless. Lakecrest was a disaster when I moved in."

"Mum was raised very differently," Matthew explained. "German family, very Lutheran and orderly. Her father was a doctor—"

"A professor of medicine," Hannah interrupted.

"Yes, Herr Doctor Professor," Matthew acknowledged, with exaggerated solemnity. "If he wanted something done, you did it. With no complaints. We used to joke about it—remember, Marjorie?"

"Clean your room! Doctor's orders!" Marjorie barked.

Hannah allowed herself a wry smile. "The home where I grew up could not have been more different than Lakecrest."

"Good thing you arrived to whip everyone into shape."

Marjorie had a talent for delivering insults as if they were compliments, but Hannah continued as if her daughter hadn't spoken.

"You can't imagine how difficult it was to plan a simple dinner, with Obadiah keeping such irregular hours. He might sleep till noon, then demand a roast at midnight."

"Not to mention Cecily and her acolytes," Marjorie said.

I caught Matthew's quick shake of his head and saw Hannah's face stiffen.

"Acolytes?" I asked, all innocence.

"Her devotees." Marjorie looked at me. "She'd have girls come to stay. They'd study art and Greek tragedies and run around in the moonlight. Among other things."

"Now, now—" Hannah tried to wrest back control of the conversation, but I took advantage of her hesitation. I was curious why Marjorie didn't share Matthew's worshipful attitude toward Cecily.

"She sounds like quite an interesting woman," I said.

"She was," Marjorie said. "Nearly ruined the family, though. Isn't that right, Mum?"

Hannah glared at her daughter, willing her to be silent. Matthew was looking back and forth between them, strangely lifeless, his self-possession chipped away once again by his mother and sister. I'd have been irritated if I wasn't so set on hearing more about Cecily.

Marjorie turned her attention back to me, her voice bubbly with mischief. "There were all sorts of lurid rumors. How Aunt Cecily was a *bad influence* on her poor innocent students. What they got up to, frolicking around the grounds. Do you know, I even heard a rumor about a human sacrifice, right here at Lakecrest."

"Stop!" Hannah's voice crashed down with an almost physical force. Marjorie jerked back in surprise, and my body tingled, all my senses warning me of danger. Matthew stared at the table, shoulders sagging, looking as if he wished he were anywhere else.

"I will not have such talk in this house." Hannah took a deep breath. Then, shifting with disconcerting ease into her usual formal tone, she asked me, "Shall I ring for the next course?"

Just like that, Cecily was banished. But I will always wonder if that conversation was the spark for what happened later that night, the night I will always think of as the true beginning of my marriage.

I'd begged off spending more time with Hannah and Marjorie in the drawing room after dinner, and Matthew followed me to our room soon after. Drained from a day of forced cheeriness, I read a book while Matthew wrote letters, a comfortably domestic arrangement that I hoped might become our regular routine. Afterward, we went through our usual bedtime intimacies: under the covers, in the dark, in polite silence. He ended as he always did, with a contented sigh and a kiss, and I wondered if our marital relations would ever develop into something more. But I couldn't find a way to ask without hurting Matthew. I didn't want him to think I was unhappy, not with our relationship still on such new, untested ground.

Matthew had an endearing way of slipping one arm over my chest and pressing his leg against my side, anchoring us together as we fell asleep. I eased my body into his, soothed by the thought of him watching over me. I closed my eyes, forcing myself to think only of that security, not what I'd been through that day or what would come tomorrow. It couldn't have been a few minutes before I drifted off.

I was wrenched awake by a harsh wail that sent my heart pounding with terror. Struggling to orient myself in the dark, staring at dim shapes in the unfamiliar room, I saw the outline of the bedside table and fumbled for the lamp. When I pressed the switch, the sudden burst of light made me wince, and it was a moment before I could make out the source of that awful, tortured noise. Matthew was huddled against the headboard, his eyes clenched shut, his pajama shirt damp with sweat. He was crying out in pain and despair, a sound that seemed to pour from the depths of his soul. I touched his shoulder, and when he didn't respond, I squeezed his arm and called out his name. I had no idea what was wrong or what I could do to help. All I wanted was for the screaming to stop.

I will never forget Matthew's face as he slowly opened his eyes and looked at me. Panic had twisted his perfect features into something terrifying. He lunged forward, forcing me back onto the bed, pressing his arms against my chest so hard I gasped for breath. Then he locked his fingers around my neck and squeezed.

CHAPTER SIX

Panicked, heart pounding, I tried to breathe. My mouth gaped open in a desperate search for air, and my feet writhed in revolt, but the weight of Matthew's body kept my chest and hips crushed against the bed.

Time stopped. I thought I was going to die.

"Oh, God! Kate!"

Matthew's hands flew away from my throat, and he jerked backward. I gulped in the precious air, my muscles tense, legs poised to leap from the bed and run. Matthew's shoulders rose and fell in time with his ragged breathing. He looked like a wild animal caught in a trap. A victim, not a killer.

I curled my legs inward and wrapped my arms around them like a shield. I stared at Matthew, my eyes asking the question I couldn't put into words. *Why?*

"Oh, my darling," he murmured. "I'm so sorry. I had a bad dream."

He reached a hand toward my face, and I flinched. He leaned away, and the mattress creaked as we separated, creating a buffer of space between us. Only hours before, our bodies had sought each other out in this bed; I'd felt safe and cherished in my husband's arms. Now I couldn't bear for him to touch me.

"It was more than a dream," I said curtly.

"I didn't know what I was doing," he said. His expression acknowledged it was a feeble excuse.

I tipped my head to the side so the lamplight fell on my neck, which still throbbed with the imprint of his fingers. I could tell from his anguished expression that he'd left marks. That he hated himself for what he'd done. Despite my apprehension, his misery tugged at my heart.

"You won't understand," he said.

"Tell me," I demanded.

Matthew's voice seemed to be coming from very far away. "I still see them. After all this time."

"Who?"

"The boys. From the trenches. The boys I was supposed to save."

The trenches. When Matthew had spoken of his time in the war—which was seldom—he was amusingly self-deprecating, making fun of the way he had nearly fainted at the sight of blood or made a mess of wrapping bandages. Stories of long ago, amusing escapades. That night, he finally told me the truth.

"You can't imagine the state of the bodies they brought into that field hospital. And I was expected to patch them up."

"I'm sure you did the best you could."

Matthew turned away, unwilling to face me while he dredged up his memories.

"There was one fellow," he began, "the one I dreamed of tonight. He'd been blinded by gas, and his body was oozing with burns. I'd studied biology for one year—I didn't have the faintest idea what to do! I pulled off the field wrappings, and layers of skin came along with it. He screamed and screamed. I wasn't treating him; I was torturing him. The sounds he made—I can still hear them. And to know it was all my fault . . ."

"Oh, Matthew."

"I'd had a few close calls before, when my hands wouldn't stop shaking, but that was the last straw. I covered his mouth and began raving like a madman, shouting at him to shut up. Tonight, in my dream, I was trying to make him stop."

Matthew took a deep breath that sounded like a shudder.

"The nurses had to pull me off him. The next thing I knew, I was invalided out. Couldn't talk above a whisper, my throat was so sore."

"Invalided?"

"Shipped home for what Mum called a 'rest cure.' Not that there was anything restful about it. I was visited every night by the bloody corpses of men I'd let die. Do you know what it looks like when your stomach's been ripped open?"

I didn't want to know, but I kept still as Matthew described horror after sickening horror, and the world I knew shattered. The poised, self assured man I had married was nothing more than a thin, brittle shell. Here beside me, shaky, was the real Matthew. The one who'd always been just beyond my grasp.

I was scared and furious and brokenhearted, all at once. My first thought was that I had been duped into marrying a man who might be insane. Then my mind flashed to images that couldn't be memories but had the clarity of truth. Ma's body slamming against the kitchen table. The glint of silver as she drove the knife into my father's stomach, over and over, until her hands were stained crimson. The slickness of the blood beneath my knees and palms, the shrieks and guttural groans. Maybe Matthew wasn't the only one who was broken.

Slowly, carefully, I inched across the bed until our shoulders touched. My toes sought out his feet under the sheet.

"The war's long over," I said. "You have to put it behind you."

"Don't you think I've tried?" The sharpness of his voice hit me like a slap. "Mum consulted the best doctors in the world! Not one of their treatments worked. I lied when I told you I'd been in Europe on business. I went back to France. It's a booming business, escorting tourists around the battlefields. I tried to make my peace with what happened, but the nightmares kept coming."

Dashing Matthew Lemont, strolling the deck of the *Franconia*, dazzling me with his confident smile. He'd been a figment of my imagination all along.

"Then I met you," he said. "I began looking forward to the future, for the first time in years, and the dreams went away. I thought I was cured."

"Is that why you married me?" A whisper.

Matthew didn't answer, which was an answer in itself. "It was rotten not to tell you all this before. I didn't know how."

My illusions about Matthew were shattered on that dismal Sunday night. But he could never know. As the shock wore off, I was overcome by a maternal affection for the suffering man beside me. *I made a promise,* I told myself. *For better or for worse.* If it was in my power to take away his pain, I would.

I clutched his hand and squeezed. "It's all right."

Matthew tried very hard to smile. His arms and chest shook with suppressed sobs, enough to make the mattress quiver. My liar's instinct told me he hadn't revealed the whole truth, that he was deliberating whether to confide the rest.

"There's something else," I said. As if I already knew.

Matthew released a breath with a drawn-out shudder. "Sometimes I see Aunt Cecily," he whispered. "Bleeding."

He sounded like a terrified child confessing a mortal sin that would damn him to hell.

"Mum mustn't know. She thinks I'm doing so much better."

"I won't say a thing. I promise."

My assurances seemed to soothe Matthew, though his eyes were still agitated, his muscles tense. I had to do something—anything—to distract him from his guilt-ridden thoughts. I slipped my nightdress up over my shoulders and head. It was the first time Matthew had seen me naked, in the light. I took hold of his hand and placed the palm flat across my bare chest.

"Do you feel it?" I asked. "My heart?"

Eyes fixed on mine, he nodded. How beautiful he was. How fragile.

"They're gone," I whispered. "Cecily and those poor boys. But I'm alive. I'm here."

Matthew's other hand reached out and caressed the curve of my breast.

"I'm here."

Matthew wrapped his arms around me, pressing his face into my neck. His stubble grated against my skin as he kissed me roughly. Desperately. His hands clutched at my waist and back, and I twisted and arched to accommodate him, responding in kind as his movements became more frantic. His teeth cut against my lips; his fingers dug into my hair as I squeezed his thighs and backside. For once, I didn't worry what Matthew was thinking or whether I was doing the right thing. I simply matched him push for push, moan for moan. Physical sensation silenced our troubled minds, and our bodies pounded together in a matching rhythm that left me gasping. My arms ached from the effort of holding him so tight.

At last, Matthew collapsed on top of me, sweaty and spent. I whispered that I loved him, and he whispered it back. I saw how tired he was, yet how unwilling to surrender to sleep, and I told him it would be all right. That I wasn't afraid.

"I'll make it up to you," he mumbled. "When work settles down, I'll take you on a proper honeymoon. Anywhere you want."

If Matthew was soothed by planning an imaginary vacation, I'd play along. "I've always wanted to see palm trees," I said. "What about Florida?"

"We can do better than that. Money's no object." Fatigue was making him slur his words. "Let's go far away. To the other side of the world."

"Africa." I don't know what made me say it. Heaven knows I'd never pictured myself as a safari type of girl, and the last thing Lakecrest needed was more stuffed animal heads.

"Africa," Matthew breathed. He entwined his fingers with mine and pressed his lips against my knuckles. Then, holding my hand like a talisman against his chest, he drifted into sleep. I lay beside him, disconcertingly awake, and stared at the thick pillars of our bed, the lumpy horsehair sofa, the heavy velvet drapes. We were surrounded by an old man's vision of grandeur. Was it any wonder Matthew felt tormented by the past?

I had a sudden, striking vision of Matthew and me lying in a field, staring up at the vast African sky. Sharing sights and smells and tastes that would be immortalized in shared memories. I held on to the thought like a beacon in the dark. Beside me, Matthew snored gently. At peace.

＝

As the newest Mrs. Lemont, I was the star attraction on the North Shore social circuit that fall. Through a whirl of dinners, card parties, and tea dances, I played the part of Poor Girl Made Good: grateful for my unexpected fortune, gushingly adoring of my perfect husband. Matthew's mother, seemingly resigned to the marriage, sorted through all my invitations, telling me which to accept and which to politely decline. I was also subjected to regular lectures on topics such as managing the help and where to summer. Following Hannah's orders was an easy way to maintain peace, especially since I couldn't keep all the people I'd met straight and didn't yet think of any of them as friends. Hannah could be bossy and high-handed, but she and I shared a common goal: Matthew's happiness.

My days arranged themselves into a predictable routine: A hurried early-morning good-bye to Matthew, followed by breakfast on a tray in my room. A morning walk around the estate, which I'd drag out by sitting on the rocks along the lakefront or watching the gardeners at work. A midday meal in the dining room with Hannah, during which she'd drone on about dull housekeeping matters, followed by an afternoon of reading or writing letters. Matthew usually caught the train that arrived in East Ridge at six o'clock, and his homecoming was the highlight of my day. After supper, we'd gather in the sitting room to play cards or checkers while Hannah went on about the "appalling manners of today's youth" or "that terrible noise that passes for music these days." I became quite expert at nodding while stifling a yawn.

Marjorie was rarely at home. I'd see her occasionally in the upstairs hall or front entry, trailing cigarette smoke, and we'd exchange polite but distant chitchat. She didn't discuss how she spent her days, and I didn't ask. Most evenings, she was out with friends. Hannah and Matthew didn't seem concerned by her frequent absences, but I wondered what she was up to on all those late nights out in the city. Was she really a dope fiend? Some evenings, when I heard the squeal of tires on the front drive and rowdy, slurred shouts as Marjorie was dropped off, I couldn't help feeling jealous. The weeks I'd spent with Matthew in Chicago had already taken on the heart-tugging weight of nostalgia, and I wondered if I'd settled for marriage too soon. On the nights Marjorie stayed in, the sitting room seemed brighter, and Matthew's laughter was easy and free. Marjorie brought a spark of life to those monotonous hours.

Christmas passed in a flurry of holiday parties, and then winter swept in. The invitations dried up, and Matthew disappeared along with the sunlight. Pleading work, he began sleeping at the downtown apartment on weeknights and carting home loads of papers on Friday. There were muttered hints about trouble at the office, though Hannah forbade business talk at the dinner table, and Matthew told me it would blow over soon enough. But I couldn't help worrying that he was pushing himself too hard. I've never been the kind of person who needs to fill every silence with chatter, so I was perfectly happy to sit quietly with Matthew in our room, both of us absorbed in our own tasks. But even on those occasions I had him to myself, he seemed distracted, caught up in thoughts he was unwilling to share.

"What's wrong?" I finally asked. "I'm no financial genius, but there must be some way I can help."

Matthew's face sagged into the weary, haunted expression I'd glimpsed on the deck of the *Franconia*. "You can't," he said.

What could possibly be weighing on him so heavily? From offhand comments Marjorie had made, I'd understood Matthew to be largely a figurehead at Lemont Industries. Hannah sometimes took calls from the company's business manager, and I suspected she had the final say in important decisions, which, given Matthew's mental state, seemed wise.

"You should be able to share your burdens," I said, squeezing Matthew's shoulder. "That's the point of marriage, isn't it?"

"It's my burden to bear, and I hate that I've worried you. What a disappointment I must be."

I protested that of course he wasn't, that I couldn't be happier, but my cheery words only made him look sadder. His nightmares had become more frequent—once a week or so—but I kept to our mutual agreement never to discuss them. When I was jolted from sleep by a sound or vibration of the bed, I shook Matthew awake and comforted him the only way I could, with fervent kisses and greedy fingers. When his eyes sometimes spilled over with tears, I pretended not to notice.

My life felt like the grounds of Lakecrest: trapped under a layer of frost, as lifeless as the bare trees that formed a stark tableau against the lake. From time to time, I took the train to Chicago to visit Blanche, but for the most part my excursions were solitary, to a tearoom in East Ridge or the town library to check out the latest mysteries. If the sky was clear, I'd pull on my boots and tramp through the soggy snow along Deertrail Road, the narrow lane that skirted other properties. Only once did I see anyone else outside, a figure on the front lawn of a Tudor-style mansion that had sold for a fortune a few months before. It was a woman—I could tell by the cut of the coat—but she didn't raise her hand in greeting or call out. She just watched as I trudged on, and I felt more alone and invisible than ever.

One Sunday in late January, as I was on my way to the kitchen for some tea, I heard shouting from the study. I paused outside the door, listening. I couldn't make out individual words, but I recognized Matthew's and Hannah's voices, his heated and demanding, hers curtly dismissive.

Suddenly, I heard Matthew from what seemed like inches away, his declaration crystal clear: "I'm my own man, not your puppet! When will you treat me accordingly?"

Surprise made me pull back, and just as well. The door flew open, and I barely had time to back into the Arabian Room, out of sight. Heavy footsteps stomped down the hall, followed soon after by the click of Hannah's heels. I hurried to my room, thinking Matthew might tell me what happened. But he wasn't there. Nor was he in the dining room that evening.

"Matthew's gone out" was Hannah's unsatisfying explanation. Her dour expression didn't invite further questions.

I went to bed alone, and though I stirred when Matthew slipped in beside me later, I was too tired to ask questions. Sleep held me so tight and fast that I didn't even notice when the unmistakable signs of a nightmare began. It wasn't until Matthew started screaming that I realized what was happening and dragged my exhausted body upright.

Placing a hand over his mouth to block the sound, I began my usual murmurs of reassurance, but Matthew was too lost in his delusions to hear me. He thrashed away, hitting me with a brutal kick to the stomach. Reeling from the blow, I grabbed his wrist and said his name sharply, a mother disciplining her unruly child.

It only infuriated him more. Lost in the throes of a monstrous vision, Matthew attacked me with punches and slaps, hands flailing wildly. I hid my face behind my arms, pleading, but I was no match for such an onslaught. It wasn't until I'd slid off the bed and cowered on the floor that the Matthew I knew emerged. He stared at me, his eyes wide with shock, as if I were the one who'd gone mad.

"Kate."

He looked devastated, and I wondered if he'd left marks I'd have to explain to Hannah the next day. I hiked up my nightgown, bracing myself to provide the usual comforts. But Matthew recoiled when I edged toward him, naked.

"No!" he protested, as if I disgusted him.

I covered myself with the sheet, burning with hurt and shame. Maybe I was no better than Ma, offering up my body so brashly. I turned away from Matthew, and tears slid silently down my cheeks and onto the cotton fabric. The top border was still crisp from Alice's daily ironing.

"What happened?" I whispered.

I didn't ask because I wanted to hear another account of mutilated young soldiers; in fact, I dreaded it. But if I ever wanted to put an end to this miserable night, I'd have to settle Matthew down by talking to him calmly and rationally.

"I can't," he said.

"Whatever it is," I said, "I won't love you any less."

I can be very convincing, when I have to be.

There was a very long silence. Finally, shakily, Matthew told me what he'd seen in his dream. Cecily lying on the grass. Her dress torn, breasts exposed. His hand reaching out to touch the dark-red stain on her gleaming white skin. His sticky palm, caked with Cecily's blood.

"It felt so real. Like I was there."

Carefully, slowly, I asked, "Were you?"

Matthew slammed his hand against the bed. "Of course not!" he hissed. "I've told you, I don't know what happened to Aunt Cecily!"

What's that famous quote about someone protesting too much? I couldn't believe Matthew would kill a woman he so obviously adored, especially since he'd been only twelve when she disappeared. But could those images be more than the invention of a shell-shocked mind? It was possible he'd seen something that was beyond his ability to understand at the time. He might have seen her die.

I kept such thoughts to myself, of course. I told Matthew he'd gotten things all mixed up in his mind, and I could tell he ached with regret for what he'd done. Yet he stayed on his side of the bed. The center—where we usually slept, a tangle of arms and legs—remained defiantly empty. It was the first time Matthew had rejected me in five months of marriage. And I couldn't help feeling he'd lost faith in my ability to help him.

That was the night I vowed to find out what happened to Cecily. Matthew's tortured dreams, I believed, were signs he'd never resolved himself to his aunt's loss. Only the truth would allow him to heal. Had Cecily died that night, inside the Labyrinth? I didn't see how it was possible. The police had searched the grounds and hadn't found a body or any evidence of violence. She could have been kidnapped, but there'd been no demand for ransom. Most likely, Cecily had chosen to leave, in which case I might be able to follow her trail.

It is possible for people to disappear, from places with unpaved streets and broken streetlights, where neighbors don't know each other's names and don't care to. But women like Cecily Lemont don't vanish without a trace. They take taxis and trains and visit banks and stores.

You can't lie low in a crowd when you're wearing silk and are used to being waited on hand and foot.

I suspected Hannah knew more about her sister-in-law's fate than she let on; a wolf's fur can't stay hidden beneath sheep's clothing forever. But she'd never admit to it if I asked. It was possible Cecily had confided her plans to a friend, someone who'd promised to keep them secret but might be convinced to talk after all this time.

I knew just where to start.

Mabel Kostrick lived in the Continental, a smart building that over-looked the southern edge of Lincoln Park. When I had phoned and asked to meet, she sounded cautiously friendly, and she greeted me at her apartment's front door the same way. Her smile was warm, her handshake tentative.

She led me to what she called the morning room, a cheery space with tall windows and chairs upholstered in bright yellow. A maid brought in a tray for tea, and superficial chatter took us through the pouring and serving. It was only once Mabel and I were seated at opposite ends of a sofa, cups in hand, that I told her the reason for my visit.

"I don't see how I can help." A protest, but her expression showed she was intrigued.

"That day we met, at the Temple, you told me you knew Cecily."

"Yes, but it was such a long time ago. We exchanged letters after I moved away, but I didn't see her for years."

"Can you think of any reason Cecily might have left Lakecrest without telling her family?"

"I truly can't. As I said, we didn't keep in touch."

"When did you first meet her?"

"Oh, I don't remember. Our families traveled in the same social circles, or what passes for society in East Ridge. Everyone in Chicago knew who she was. They were still talking about her debut when I came out, how she'd dazzled everyone and then sailed off to Oxford in a blaze of glory. It wasn't long after that I heard she was back at Lakecrest, declining all invitations. There were rumors of a breakdown. I do think she must have been through a dark time to be so understanding with girls like me."

Dark time. I thought of Matthew's unpredictable, mournful moods. The way his entire body could go limp with gloom.

"My mother was a very demanding woman, and I was awfully shy, with a terrible stammer," Mabel continued. "The more Mother berated me, the worse the stammer got, until I was convinced I'd never be able to speak normally again. Mother was terrified she'd never marry me off. When I heard Cecily had begun a salon for young female artists, I begged to go. Painting was the only thing I was any good at, and Mother agreed to let me stay for a month. It changed my life."

"How?"

Mabel looked away, thoughtful. Deciding how to answer. "Cecily was the first person who made me feel my opinions had some value," she said at last. "She gave us lessons each day—literature, art, that sort of thing—but she encouraged each of us to try new things. To follow our passions."

Mabel made it sound as if Cecily was running an art school. But I knew it had been more than that.

"Those buildings on the grounds, the Labyrinth and the Temple," I said, "were they part of this salon?"

"Oh yes." Mabel smiled, mentally reliving her memories. "Cecily believed very strongly in what she called 'the drama of place.' Certain sensations can only be felt in the appropriate surroundings. We'd stand in the Temple and toast each other in the moonlight or wade into the lake at dawn to recite lines from the *Iliad*. She'd tell stories of women who performed dazzling feats of bravery—it was all quite thrilling.

"You've heard of Theseus and the Minotaur? That was one of Cecily's favorites. On my last night, she sent me into the Labyrinth alone. I was terrified! I stumbled against this massive dark figure and saw two enormous horns looming over me. It was only a statue, but I didn't know that; I thought it was the Minotaur himself, coming to kill me. I punched and kicked as if my life depended on it, and it was utterly glorious, fighting back! Though my hands were bruised for days afterward."

Mabel looked pleased by the memory of pain. "To Cecily, we were all goddesses, capable of wondrous things."

Matthew had said something similar. I remembered the story collection, the emotions that pulsed across the pages.

"I still don't understand," I said. "The woman you describe was brilliant and strong and talented. Why did she keep herself shut away at Lakecrest?"

"I don't know," Mabel said softly.

She hadn't told me everything. I could tell by the way she looked down at her hands, the stiffening of her shoulders. There was some part of Cecily's story Mabel didn't want to share.

"I've read the *Twelve Ancient Tales*," I said. "It was clear from those stories that Cecily felt things very deeply. Did she have any"—I hesitated, trying to find the right words—"romantic partners?"

"Cecily talked about love a great deal," Mabel said. "The difference between eros and agape, physical and spiritual love. But she never confided any affairs of the heart to me."

"And she never married," I said. "I wonder why."

"Marriage isn't for everyone. Cecily relished her independence. She was answerable to her brother, I suppose, but he didn't take much interest in her escapades. She could do as she pleased."

What was it Matthew had once told me about his father? *A remarkable man. Smart as a whip, bursting with confidence.* Yet his wife, Hannah, never talked about him.

"How well did you know Jasper?" I asked.

"Oh, we exchanged pleasantries over the dinner table, but I can't say we ever had a conversation. Jasper struck me as very old-fashioned. Much stodgier than Cecily."

"Maybe she had a secret lover," I suggested. "They could have met in the Labyrinth that night and eloped."

Mabel's mournful expression made me suddenly ashamed of my lighthearted tone. "I hope to God that's what happened," she said. "That she's happy, somewhere."

"Do you think it's possible?"

Mabel shook her head. "I don't know."

This time, I knew she was telling the truth.

"Matthew's mother thinks Cecily killed herself," I said.

"Why? She had everything to live for!" Mabel's eyes welled up with tears. "No matter what her family says, she wasn't crazy. She was an angel, the kindest person I've ever known. You can't imagine how awful it is to see her reputation dragged through the mud. I'm sorry. I'm finding this all rather upsetting."

Dragged through the mud? Before I could ask what she meant, Mabel was standing up, making it clear the conversation was over. I thanked her for the tea, trying to hide my disappointment. Mabel escorted me to the front door, but just as I was about to walk out, she reached out and put a hand on my sleeve.

"I want an answer as much as you do," she said, apologetic. "I've kept in touch with a few of the other girls who stayed at Lakecrest with me. I'll write them and see if they remember anything."

"Thank you. I'd appreciate it."

"And one more thing—it's just occurred to me. My husband hired an investigator not long ago, when he suspected one of his accountants of cooking the books. It was all handled very quietly. I don't know how much a detective can track down after all this time, but I could give you his name, if you're interested?"

I was. I waited while Mabel phoned her husband at his office and wrote down the information on a monogrammed note card.

Sherwood Haveleck. The address was on the north side of the city, less than a mile away.

I had lunch plans with Blanche. If I told the driver I was going shopping afterward and sent him away for a while, I could catch a cab to Mr. Haveleck's office and be back downtown within an hour.

One meeting, just to see what was possible.

⌒

I was usually able to put on a cheery face for Blanche; we were both good at summoning an air of carefree fun. It didn't work that day. She quickly picked up on my preoccupied mood, and it wasn't long before I was confiding everything about my search for Cecily.

"She must be dead, don't you think?" Blanche asked. "Knowing for sure won't make Matthew any happier."

"You're probably right. But his nightmares are so terrible. I have to do something."

She looked at me with a concerned sympathy that reminded me of her mother, Aunt Nellie, sitting at my kitchen table during a long-ago visit. She'd come to the rescue with some of her daughters' hand-me-downs and a stack of dollar bills shortly before I left for St. Anne's, when Ma had been desperate enough to ask for help. Whenever the nuns at school talked about saints, I pictured them with Aunt Nellie's face.

"What's up, toots?" Blanche asked. "You don't seem like yourself."

"The weather, I guess. Not seeing the sunlight for weeks."

"It's not that. Or—not only that. Ever since you got married, you're so serious. Like the Lemonts sucked all the life out of you!"

She smiled and tilted her head to show she was teasing. But she wasn't, not really.

"It's harder than I expected," I said, "being stuck out there at Lakecrest. Matthew's so busy I barely see him. And when I do . . . well, he's not the same fellow who swept me off my feet." The admission felt like a betrayal, but it was a relief to tell the truth.

"I had no idea you were so unhappy."

I considered saying, *I'm scared.* Or *I think I made a terrible mistake.* But one confession would lead to another, and what would Blanche say then? *Serves you right?*

"Any girl who gets married has to make adjustments," I said, stoic. "I do have one thing to look forward to. Matthew has promised we'll go to Africa for a delayed honeymoon."

"What a hoot! Imagine you, a big-game hunter!"

"Hardly. I'll be admiring the lions and elephants from a safe distance, I promise."

"When are you going?"

"April. Hopefully."

"You can't wait that long to have some fun! Why don't you two come to the club? I'll make sure you get a prime table. Champagne, if you want it. The real deal, from France. The maître d' has connections."

"Oh, I don't know. Matthew's always so tired."

"It's only . . ." Blanche turned away and back, the very picture of indecision. "My boss, Mr. Pitz, moved me up from coat-check girl to hostess because of you. He wants to class up the place, get the word out that Mr. and Mrs. Matthew Lemont have been coming to Pharaoh's. It would really help me out if you stopped in. Just once."

I was grateful she'd trusted me with the truth and immensely sad that she'd had to do it. How unfair for Blanche to be put in that position, when she was the only person in Chicago who couldn't care less that my last name was Lemont.

"Of course we'll come," I said. "It's been forever since Matthew took me dancing."

"Thanks for being so nice. I feel awful, having to ask."

"I'm happy to do it."

"I don't know how I can possibly return the favor, but if there's anything you ever need, don't forget that I'm on your side. If that mother-in-law makes you miserable, call me up and complain, and I'll listen for hours. All right?"

I never would have said I loved Blanche before that moment, but I did, just then.

"Let's make this a weekly date," I said. "You and me, for lunch. What do you say?"

Blanche nodded happily.

"And I insist on paying. I've got the money, so why not?"

"I've always wondered how that works. Does Matthew give you an allowance?"

"I can buy whatever I want on credit, and the bill's sent to the Lemonts. I never have to carry a penny. Matthew's bank even sends a monthly payment to my mother. He's hoping she'll visit, when she's up to it." The story of my mother's lingering illness couldn't be dragged out much longer, and I wondered if Blanche knew it was a lie.

"Can't blame him for being curious." Blanche said. "Isn't it strange to think that your husband has never met your mother?"

"The thought of her in the same room as Hannah is enough to give *me* nightmares!"

We laughed, and I felt such a rush of warmth toward my cousin that I reached out and squeezed her hand.

"I'm so lucky to have you," I said. "Someone to trust with all my secrets."

Most of them, anyway.

"We're family," Blanche said. "That counts for something."

"That counts for everything."

I had recently discovered the novels of Agatha Christie, and I expected Mr. Haveleck to fit the Hercule Poirot model: a stickler for details with a precise but soothing manner. The man who greeted me after I tapped on his glass office door looked so disheveled that I doubted he could find his own cuff links, let alone Cecily Lemont. Uneven streaks of pomade cut across his black curly hair, and his shirt was creased, the collar askew. Had he slept in his clothes?

"To what do I owe this pleasure?" he asked, ushering me in. He pushed a stack of papers off a chair so I could sit down. The one window in the room overlooked an alley, but I was grateful for the gloominess. It hid the full extent of the mess.

"I'm sorry to barge in like this, without an appointment," I said. "My name is Kate—that is, Mrs. Matthew Lemont."

He made a good show of hiding his surprise, nodding and forcing his smile wider. But I'm good at reading people. I saw his eyes widen. The slight shift of his body as he sat up straighter.

"I'm sure you've heard of the Lemont family," I said, hoping he wouldn't start groveling. "I've come on a matter concerning my husband. Can I count on your discretion?"

"I wouldn't be much of an investigator if I couldn't keep a secret," he said smoothly.

"My husband's aunt, Cecily Lemont, disappeared from the family's estate in 1912. No one has heard from her since, and everyone assumes she's dead."

Mr. Haveleck sat stone-faced; none of this was news to him.

"I thought you might be able to find out what happened."

"It was a long time ago." Mr. Haveleck eyed me doubtfully.

"I've been in touch with one of Cecily's friends, and she's helping me track down other women who knew her. But I can't start questioning the servants or the neighbors. My mother-in-law would not approve."

"I'll bet. Well, Mrs. Lemont, with the greatest respect, I don't think I can help."

I was so surprised by the rejection that it took me a minute to recover.

"I'm prepared to pay whatever it takes," I said, indignant. "I'm sure there are other detectives who'd be only too happy to take my money."

"So if I say no, you'll go to my competition instead?"

"If I have to."

A slow smile. "I can't make any promises."

"Then I won't expect any," I said. "Now, I believe it's standard procedure to make a deposit in advance. Will this do?"

I pulled five twenty-dollar bills from my pocketbook. They fluttered between us for a few seconds before he reached out and took them.

"Here's how it works," he said, sliding the money into a desk drawer. "I have a team of guys who do the legwork, but it takes time. Especially this kind of job. There may be some travel involved."

"I understand. If it's a matter of money, I can pay whatever you need to hurry things along. My husband . . ."

My husband is a very sick man.

My husband sees Cecily, bleeding, in his dreams.

"My husband and I would be grateful for anything you find out. Would it help if I told you what I know about Cecily?"

"Sure."

It took a half hour to tell my story: Cecily's mysterious change from bright, creative artist to sickly recluse; her abruptness with Matthew on the night she disappeared; the last sighting of her heading toward the Labyrinth. Mr. Haveleck jotted notes without ever seeming to look at the paper in front of him. He listened with intense, unwavering attention, and I began to understand why businessmen like Mabel's husband trusted him.

"This is a good start," he said at last, putting down his pen. "Plenty of possibilities to explore."

"Do you have any theories based on what I've told you?"

As I'd suspected, Mr. Haveleck wasn't able to resist a demonstration of his deductive skills. "Given what I know of human nature, and the circumstances of Miss Lemont's life, I'd say there's a good chance she ended up in an asylum."

Mabel had insisted Cecily wasn't crazy. But they hadn't seen each other for a long time. How could she know for sure?

"Someone like Cecily Lemont wouldn't be locked up in the county hospital, but there are some other places, more private, where she might have been admitted. Most likely under a different name."

Mr. Haveleck began rummaging through a pile of books and papers next to his desk. It made no sense. Mabel had said Cecily was answerable to her brother, but if Jasper had his sister committed, why would he call in the police to search for her? If he was worried about being publicly shamed, he could have put out a story about her being sick or going abroad.

Mr. Haveleck slapped a folder down in front of him. "I'm not saying that's what happened. It's one avenue I'll explore, among many others."

I thought of Cecily, locked away for more than fifteen years, and felt queasy.

"You all right, Mrs. Lemont?"

"Fine," I said, but not nearly as confidently as I'd intended.

"How about I get you a glass of water?"

I nodded, and Mr. Haveleck hurried out. I gazed at the folder on the desk in front of me, then pulled it into my lap. Gingerly brushing off the dust, I pulled out a stack of pamphlets.

St. Claire's Retreat

Lake County Rest Home

Chicago Clinic for Nervous Disorders

The front of the Chicago Clinic brochure had a sketched illustration of a wide stone town house. Flowers were planted in neat beds along the front. I flipped the pages, skimming flowery descriptions of the hospital's services. Something nagged at me, and I slowed down to read more carefully.

> *The Chicago Clinic for Nervous Disorders is a haven for those suffering from melancholia, mania, and other disorders of the brain. We take pride in our ability to treat patients in a soothing atmosphere conducive to a restful mental state.*

All very reassuring, if you weren't the one stuck there.

> *Great strides are being made in the understanding of the human brain, and we are pleased to offer the latest advances in modern medicine, tested and approved by the finest experts in the field. The Clinic was the first institution in the United States to offer the Millchen Cap, with impressive results, and we continue to seek out promising new therapies. Every patient is given a personalized course of treatment, tailored to her particular needs.*

Her needs. Of course. Were men ever diagnosed with "nervous disorders"?

There was a picture of a nurse wearing a crisp cap and sturdy shoes, holding the hand of a smiling young woman wrapped in a dressing gown. Another photo showed what looked like a recreation room, with card tables and a piano and a seated figure in the corner fitting together a jigsaw puzzle. It could have been the common room of a college dormitory or a ladies' social club. The Clinic, it seemed, was intent on not looking like a hospital, at least in its advertising.

My eyes wandered to the text at the bottom of the page.

For a private consultation in complete confidence, please contact our Medical Director, Dr. Ernest McNally.

An address on South Blackstone Avenue. A telephone number. And then, in tiny letters at the very end: *Est. 1870. Founder: Dr. Martin Rieger.*

I'd seen the name before. Heard it.

Then I remembered. Rieger was Hannah's maiden name. Dr. Rieger was her father.

CHAPTER SEVEN

I'd read novels about innocent young women being carted off to insane asylums by evil stepfathers or jealous relatives out for an inheritance. I'd imagined what it would be like to be tossed into a dingy cell and left to rot. I told myself not to get caught up in such melodramatic nonsense, but I couldn't help wondering if that had indeed been Cecily's fate. And the more such thoughts consumed me, the harder it was to wait for Mr. Haveleck's official report. He'd shown a flicker of interest when I told him the Chicago Clinic for Nervous Disorders was founded by Hannah's father, but he didn't seem to take the connection as seriously as I did.

"A thorough investigation takes time, Mrs. Lemont," he'd told me as I rose to leave. "You must be patient."

I didn't think I could wait. And so I headed to the Clinic a week later, telling myself not to get my hopes up, that I'd most likely find out nothing at all. The most important thing was to find a convincing reason for this sudden excursion to the south side of Chicago. I was pretty sure Hank, the driver, reported all my comings and goings to Hannah.

Hank rounded a corner and announced, "Blackstone Avenue." Brick apartment buildings filled most of the block, with a few houses scattered in between.

"You can drop me off here," I said. "My cousin swears by this Italian woman, says she makes the most exquisite lace handkerchiefs. I'd love to surprise Mrs. Lemont with one, so I hope we can keep this visit between us?"

Hank's broad, dark face was set in its usual blandly pleasant expression, and it was hard to tell whether he believed me. Suddenly, I had an idea. I knew Hank had a wife and children who lived somewhere called the Black Belt, south of downtown; he stayed with them on Sundays, his day off. Hannah had told me Hank had come up from Mississippi to work in a factory during the war, but Negros weren't welcome on the assembly lines after the white boys came home. "And it all worked out for the best," she'd concluded. "Hank has the right temperament for domestic service."

"Does your family live in this part of the city?" I asked.

"A few miles from here," Hank said cautiously.

Strange that I'd spent so many hours sitting a few feet behind him, yet I didn't even know the ages of his children or if they were boys or girls.

"Why don't you stop by and visit?" I suggested. "Come back in an hour or so. It'll be our little secret."

Hank considered my offer and nodded. I'd all but promised not to tell Hannah where he was going. Hopefully, he'd do the same for me.

I waited for the car to drive away, then walked to the end of the block. The Chicago Clinic for Nervous Disorders looked exactly like the picture on the pamphlet: a somber, respectable building that did nothing to draw attention to itself. Three rows of evenly spaced windows crossed the stone façade, and a doorbell at the top of the front steps was marked with a small brass plaque that said simply, "Visitors."

I rang the bell. A middle-aged nurse in a starched white dress and cap opened the door.

"May I help you?"

I stepped confidently into the entryway. A narrow hall ran straight through the center of the building, with closed doors along either side.

"I'd like to speak to the director, Dr. McNally."

"Do you have an appointment?"

"No."

"He's very busy. If you let me know what it's about, I'll see if one of the other doctors is available."

"I do apologize for the inconvenience," I said. "Only it's very important, and I simply must see him. Please?"

I fingered the mink stole around my neck and made a show of inspecting my diamond-inlaid watch. The nurse looked me over, calculating what my clothes must have cost. Apparently, I was worth making an effort for, because she invited me in and said she'd see what she could do. She indicated a sitting room to the right where I could wait.

I glanced around. There wasn't much furniture, just a row of wooden chairs lined up against the walls. In the corner was a desk, and I strolled over to take a closer look. A visitors' log—no entries for today—and a pile of letters. A few blank forms labeled *Patient Information.* Was it worth rifling through the drawers? It was unlikely they'd keep anything important out here, in a public space.

I heard the clatter of heels in the hall and moved back from the desk. Expecting the nurse, I was surprised to see someone else enter, a woman in an old-fashioned, shabby dress. She walked with a slight hunch and the overall weariness of someone in bad health. But she smiled brightly and seemed eager to chat.

"Hello! Here for the visiting hours?" she asked.

I shook my head. "I'm meeting one of the doctors."

"I'm usually the only one here on Tuesdays. It's a shame. So many patients get no visitors at all."

Patients. So there were people living here.

"I just popped off to the washroom, but I heard the bell, and I tell you, it's a pleasure to have some company on such a gloomy day. I come see my sister Lizzie every Tuesday and Thursday. Holidays, too, when I can. She may not know what day it is, but she deserves a Christmas present and something on her birthday as much as anyone else. It makes a difference—I know it does."

"Is she well cared for here?"

"Oh, they've been wonderful, under the most trying circumstances. We couldn't keep Lizzie at home, not after she started hearing voices. I had my children to think about. She scared them something awful—not meaning to, she'd feel terrible afterward, but my husband finally put his foot down and I can't blame him. I'm grateful he's willing to pay the fees. She'd be at the state asylum otherwise."

"How long has your sister been at the clinic?"

The woman looked up at the ceiling as she did her mental calculations. "Eleven years, just about."

Eleven years! Then it was possible Cecily had been here even longer.

"They've done what they can," the woman went on. "She'll never get back to normal, but she has good days, now and then."

I heard approaching footsteps, and the woman reached out to pat my hand. "It's the hardest thing in the world, sending someone away. I'm sorry if that's what you're going through."

The nurse walked up to us, all brisk efficiency. "Dr. McNally will see you," she said to me. "Mrs. Wilson, if you don't mind waiting a bit—Lizzie's had a difficult morning, and we'd like her to settle down before you see her."

The nurse escorted me to the doctor's office across the hall. It was appropriately imposing, with a vast cherrywood desk, Oriental carpet, framed diplomas and letters, and a bookshelf filled with medical texts—all designed to show off the importance of its occupant. Dr. McNally himself was a wiry, short man with thick glasses and thinning white hair. Full of fidgety nervous energy, he shook my hand. I introduced myself as Mrs. Douglas Marshall (Aunt Nellie's married name), and he ushered me toward an armchair. The doctor took a seat next to me instead of sitting behind his desk. Was he trying to put me at ease? Or examine me more closely?

"What can I do for you, Mrs. Marshall?"

"Thank you so much for seeing me on such short notice." I smiled brightly. "I've heard about the wonderful work you do here. How you've helped so many sick women." I leaned in toward him, dropping my voice. "I've been told you have a connection with the Lemont family?"

Dr. McNally looked wary.

"I meant"—I was grasping for the right words—"I'm told your hospital caters to the right sort of people. The support of a family like the Lemonts reflects very highly on your establishment."

The appeal to vanity was the right approach; I watched as the doctor puffed up with pride. "Hannah Lemont is the daughter of our founder, Dr. Rieger. A great man. Very influential in the field."

"Really? How so?"

"Well, Dr. Rieger called himself a scholar of madness. He was very well-read, not just in medicine, but history, philosophy, literature—anything that shed light on the workings of the human brain. In his view, mental disorders are a reflection of the society in which they appear. As we move into a modern age, our treatments must adapt accordingly. Many of the methods he pioneered here have been adopted by hospitals all over the country."

"How marvelous. You trained under him, I suppose?"

"Yes. Though he is no longer with us, I like to think I am continuing his work exactly as he would have wished." Dr. McNally gave me a concerned smile. "Are you here on a family matter, Mrs. Marshall?"

I brushed my fingers against the sleeve of his white coat and pretended to blink away tears, just to be sure I'd snagged him.

"I'm here on behalf of a friend. A dear person, but she's been going through a difficult time. Brooding, refusing to eat, that kind of thing. I was hoping I might have a tour and learn about your various treatments."

"It would be my pleasure. I can explain our work along the way."

I'd imagined cell-like rooms and lunatics in straitjackets. What I hadn't expected was for the Chicago Center for Nervous Disorders to feel like my old Catholic boarding school. The corridors were dark, and the doors were equipped with sturdy locks, but the rooms were bright and spotless. It was one of those frigid winter days when the sky turns an almost blinding shade of blue, and the sunlight streaming through the windows made every surface gleam.

We walked into the common room I'd seen in the brochure. A teenage girl was picking out "Three Blind Mice" on a grand piano, and women who didn't look the least bit insane sat reading and sewing, watched over by nurses. We peeked into what looked like perfectly normal bedrooms on the second floor, all with pictures on the wall and immaculately folded blankets. The rooms could be bolted from the outside, I noticed, but there weren't any restraints in sight.

"How many residents do you have?" I asked.

"A dozen or so, at any given time. Most of our residents are with us a few months."

"A woman I met in the visiting room said her sister had been here eleven years."

"Yes, poor Lizzie Welcher. An unusual case. The majority of our patients recover sufficiently to be sent home. Shall we make our way downstairs? The kitchen and dining room are on the lower level, and we pride ourselves on serving high-quality meals."

"What about that way?" I pointed up the stairs, toward the third floor.

"Our Severe Cases wing. I'd prefer those patients not be disturbed. They could be quite aggravated by a strange face."

I knew it was highly unlikely—impossible, really—that Cecily would be locked up there. But I felt a sudden, overwhelming need to see for myself.

"I'd like to have a look," I said firmly.

I turned away from the doctor and began walking confidently upstairs. A nurse at the top barred the way, but stepped aside when Dr. McNally caught up and indicated with a flick of his hand that I was free to go.

The doors on this floor were made of metal, with small glass observation windows. I heard scuffling sounds. Indistinguishable words. I glanced into a room that at first appeared empty. Then I saw a figure tied to the bed, straps connected firmly at her shoulders and knees. She was asleep, with her tongue lolling out from her mouth. I turned to the room opposite, drawn by an odd rustling that reminded me of the mice that used to rummage through Ma's pantry. An old woman with roughly chopped-off hair was rubbing her hands together. They were encased in bulky mittens, the ends secured with twine. I wondered why until I saw the woman desperately paw at her face. Her hands slid along her greasy head, and she grimaced in frustration. Without the mittens, I slowly understood, she would be clawing her own cheeks, pulling out her hair. Destroying herself.

The final room was what did me in. I peered inside and instantly pulled back in shock when another face appeared, mirroring mine. It was an image from a nightmare: a gaping mouth; wild, bedraggled hair; eyes that were the definition of madness. She screamed, and I screamed, and those sounds set off a chorus of shrieks and yelps from the surrounding rooms. I ran past the scowling nurse, past Dr. McNally and his disapproving frown, and down the stairs to the main floor landing. The doctor caught up with me soon after, as I gulped mouthfuls of air to steady my breathing.

"I'm so sorry," I said, looking down in embarrassment.

"You can't quite understand until you see for yourself," he said sadly. "Despite our best efforts, there are some we cannot save."

His dejection was so real, so honest, that I berated myself for my dark suspicions. Dr. McNally, by every indication, was a devoted doctor, not the kind of man who'd lock away a difficult woman in exchange for a hefty payment. And I'd gotten a look at all the "severe cases." None of them bore any resemblance to Cecily Lemont.

"Would you like to see the rest of the building?"

I shook my head. I already knew what it would look like: meticulously neat and clean, with a lingering scent of bleach. I wanted to leave. To breathe fresh air.

"I've taken up enough of your time," I said.

"It was my pleasure. I hope I can be of help to your friend."

"I hope so, too."

Almost frantically, I pulled at the front door, dimly aware of the nurse hovering behind me. The assault of bitter cold made me gasp, but I pressed my face down into the mink, anxious to move, to get away. A walk around the block would clear my head; I didn't care if my feet went numb and my eyes watered from the stinging wind.

But I'd gone only a few steps before I saw the black Packard parked at the corner. I hadn't expected Hank to be back yet; hopefully, he hadn't seen me come out from the Clinic.

"Have a good visit?" I asked breezily, as Hank got out to open the door.

"My wife was still at work," he said. "But the girls were glad to see me."

There was so much I could have asked. What did his wife do? How old were his girls? But I felt awkward prolonging the conversation. *Lemonts aren't overly familiar with staff*, Hannah liked to say. I waited until Hank was settled behind the wheel before I spoke again.

"How long is the drive back, do you think?"

"Usually an hour and a half or so."

"Usually?"

We stopped at a red light on Michigan Avenue. Hank turned around to face me.

"When I take Mr. Lemont."

"I don't understand."

Hank looked confused. Then his face relaxed into its usual inscrutable expression, and he looked back toward the windshield. Carefully, he guided the car forward.

"I thought you knew, ma'am," he said flatly, reverting to his role as the invisible, inconsequential chauffeur. "Mr. Lemont goes to that building all the time."

I couldn't bring myself to ask Matthew. What would I say? *I've been investigating Cecily's disappearance because I was afraid you were involved in her murder, and I thought it would be a good idea to snoop around a loony bin in case she'd been locked up for the past sixteen years. And by the way, what are you doing there?*

The longer you avoid a subject, the harder it becomes to discuss. One day went by, then another. I stared at Matthew across the dinner table and saw the gray shadows under his eyes. I pressed my face into the curve of his neck as we huddled together under our covers each night, warming each other inside the frigid sheets, and still I said nothing. The only logical reason for Matthew to visit the clinic would be for some kind of treatment, which meant he was even more disturbed than I'd thought. Even worse, he was too ashamed to tell me. All the more reason for me to continue my search for Cecily.

I waited as long as I could before calling Mr. Haveleck. Lakecrest's only telephone was tucked in an alcove off the front entry, and though

I'd made sure Hannah was out, I spoke in a near whisper in case one of the maids was eavesdropping.

"Nothing to report yet," Mr. Haveleck said.

"But it's been nearly a month."

"Patience, Mrs. Lemont. This is not the kind of undertaking that can be rushed. I assure you, my men and I are hard at work, and I'll notify you as soon as I have news. In the meantime, try not to fret."

I wasn't very good at following his advice.

I started lingering in Cecily's bedroom, moping around as if I expected her ghost to appear and explain everything. Which was pointless, because every trace of her had been scrubbed away. There was no armoire full of gowns to rifle through, no silk pillows that carried a trace of her perfume. One day in late February, I sat on the window seat that looked out over the estate, trying to calm my swirling, maddening thoughts. A brief warm spell had melted all evidence of the previous months' snow, and the landscape had transformed from white to gray-ish green. I wondered if she'd sat in that same spot on her last night at Lakecrest, if this was where she'd formulated a plan to escape. Suddenly, I caught a flicker of movement in the distance. Someone was walking along the path that led to the north edge of the estate, the path that ended at the Labyrinth.

I'd never been inside; I'd never wanted to before. But suddenly, I felt an overpowering urge to go. I rushed out of the room, down the stairs, and pulled on my coat and boots. I had the strange sensation that the apparition I'd seen was Cecily herself, luring me. I'd heard so many stories, but the woman herself was still a hazy blur: strong yet sickly, brilliant but crazy. If I walked the same twisted passageways that she once had, would I be able to summon her essence? Figure out who she really was?

I slipped out the kitchen door. The temperature had jumped from fiendishly bitter to simply cold, and I walked with my scarf hanging loose around my neck rather than twisted around my head. In the summer, this part of the estate had a certain wild beauty, but without the wildflowers and tall, swaying grasses, the landscape looked stark and unwelcoming.

When I arrived at the Labyrinth, I called out, "Hello?"

There was no answer.

The walls loomed over my head. Scraggly weeds crowded around the base, and tendrils of frostbitten ivy looked ready to push through the mortar. I could see cracks in the brick, gaps where pieces of masonry had crumbled away. It was a sad, desolate place, and I suddenly felt like a fool. Of course no one else was out here. Why would anyone want to be?

And yet I didn't turn away. I pushed aside my distaste and walked inside. Immediately, I was faced with a choice. Left or right? Left, I decided, then right. It was important to have a system to avoid getting lost. I'd alternate directions at each turn and see where it got me.

Where it got me was nowhere. I covered a good distance, but all I saw was one narrow passage after another. There was no way to tell whether I was making progress toward the center or simply wandering in circles. I didn't panic, but I hated the disorientation, the uncertainty of not knowing where I was. I felt stupid, not heroic. Cecily would have urged me to *surrender to the magic*, or some other gibberish, but my mind simply didn't work that way. For all my curiosity about her, I'd never really considered how different her mindset was from mine, how we might not have liked each other at all.

Just as I had the thought, I heard a rustle behind me. I froze, spooked. The noise continued, getting steadily louder, then Marjorie thumped around a corner in green rubber boots, swathed from neck to knees in a fur coat.

"What are you doing here?" I demanded, annoyed.

I hadn't even known she was home. Lakecrest was so huge that you could spend all day inside without hearing anyone else—one of the many reasons I hated it.

"I saw you march off across the lawn," she said. "You were gone for so long, I thought you might need help."

Was she the person I'd seen walking toward the Labyrinth? No. That figure had been wrapped in a dark, heavy coat, not fur.

"I'm lost," I admitted.

"Follow me." Marjorie turned back the way she'd come. "It's easy when you know the patterns."

Sure enough, within two turns we had entered an oval-shaped clearing. Stone benches sat at either end, and in the middle was the Minotaur statue Mabel Kostrick had described. It struck me as more odd than frightening: a muscular man's body topped with the head of a wild bull. If I'd seen it pop out of the darkness without warning, though, I probably would have been scared witless.

"Rather delish, isn't he?" Marjorie said. "I'm not sure how he figured into Aunt Cecily's raging orgies—or whatever went on out here—but I feel sorry for him, stuck here all alone."

She walked over to the statue and ran her palm along the figure's muscular arm. The icy marble made her hand tremble.

"Aunt Cecily used to call me Artemis and Matthew Apollo. Do you know the story?"

I shook my head.

"She was the goddess of the hunt, and he was the god of light. The divine twins."

Marjorie said the phrase with a smirk, but it struck me as an apt description. She and her brother did have an aura that set them apart from ordinary folks, something more than good looks or the elegant crispness of their voices. They carried themselves with an easy, serene aloofness that seemed at times otherworldly.

"Were you and Matthew very alike as children?" I asked.

"Were we ever!" Marjorie said. "Sometimes it felt like I could read Matts's mind." She glanced at me, smiling. "Don't worry. I can't anymore. The secrets of your married life are safe."

"I don't know what you mean." I was so prim that I might have been Hannah herself.

Marjorie laughed. "I have a feeling you aren't the prissy little miss everyone thinks you are. No girl could keep Matthew's interest for more than a few weeks before you came along. You must have a few tricks up your sleeve."

"I love him," I said defiantly.

"Do you?" she asked, as if I'd just declared a belief in unicorns or fairies. I remembered Matthew telling me how mothers had pushed their daughters at him. He'd never had to pursue anyone, and his loyalty had never been tested. Was he capable of sticking out a marriage through thick and thin? I wasn't sure.

"You don't have to pretend with me," Marjorie said. "I know what you're up to."

For one terrifying moment, I thought she'd figured it out and that I'd be revealed for who I really was.

"You're out here because you want to solve the great family mystery, don't you?" she asked. "The fate of Cecily Lemont! Tempting, I know. But it's a waste of time."

Relief washed over me. "Why?" I asked.

"Because there's no answer."

Marjorie's bitter tone took me aback. She reached into her coat pocket and pulled out a cigarette. She smoked with an elegant grace that made the puffs of white an extension of herself, a billowing caress that swirled around her slender body and framed the angles of her face.

"I loved Aunt Cecily, I really did. She was quite magical. She could turn an afternoon at the beach into a pirate adventure, and before long, you'd be digging like crazy for a hidden chest of gold. But there were other times . . . times she'd stay in bed, refuse meals. I'd take up her tea, and she wouldn't say a word when I walked in or even look at me! It was cruel."

I thought of Matthew, skulking away to the office after supper, as he'd done off and on for weeks. The door was ajar one night, wide enough for me to peek inside and see Matthew at his desk, head in hands. Not a paper in sight. I'd tiptoed away, feeling helpless.

"There was one time I'll always remember," Marjorie went on. "Not long before she vanished, Aunt Cecily had a terrible fight with my father. She was shrieking like a madwoman, and I thought she really had gone bonkers. She locked herself in her room and stayed there for two days. I knocked and knocked and begged to come in, but she never answered."

Matthew had told me something similar, about Cecily acting odd around the time of her disappearance. But he'd said nothing about a fight with Jasper, and Mabel had made it sound as if he tolerated Cecily's activities.

"When I heard Aunt Cecily was gone, I was sad, of course," Marjorie was saying, "but it was also a relief. I spent so much time *worrying* about her. It's very hard on a child, living with that kind of uncertainty."

"I know."

It came out unthinkingly, and Marjorie gave me a curious look. For a moment, I thought she was going to ask me what I meant. Anyone else would have. But Marjorie wasn't much interested in stories that didn't center on her.

"Come this way," she said. "I want to show you something."

Marjorie led me through an opening in the opposite direction from where we'd walked in. A shadowy ribbon of cigarette smoke floated alongside us as we turned enough corners to make me thoroughly confused. After a few minutes of what felt like aimless wandering, Marjorie stopped in the middle of a passage that looked as if it stretched the entire width of the Labyrinth.

"It's here somewhere," she mumbled, stepping aside and running her hands along the wall. She pushed and prodded, then let out a self-satisfied grunt as she pried one of the bricks loose.

"Can't have a maze without a secret passageway." She pulled out the brick and nodded toward the empty space where it had once sat. "There's a hook in here, and once you unlatch it . . . presto!"

A section of the wall swung out, away from us, and I could see the wintery gray expanse of water beyond. We stepped outside, onto a promontory overlooking the lake. The vegetation here was nearly knee-high, but looking down the hill abutting the shore, I could see the remains of a trail leading downward.

"Does anyone else know about this?" I asked.

Marjorie shrugged. "I've never brought Mum here for a picnic, if that's what you mean. Matthew and I used to come sometimes. Not for ages, though."

I glanced toward Lakecrest. The Temple blocked most of the view; all I could see was the house's roofline, which meant no one there could see us.

My mind swirled with possibilities. Hannah had told me the beach was Obadiah's creation—using sand carted in from Indiana—but that the water was relatively deep along the rest of the coastline, and I should never go swimming off the rocks. A boat could have met Cecily here that night. Or was it possible she'd rowed away on her own?

"Marjorie," I said, heart racing, "Cecily could have slipped out of the Labyrinth here, to escape without being seen."

"Escape? From what?"

I couldn't say.

"Besides," Marjorie said, "she'd never run off in the middle of the night with no luggage. Aunt Cecily was as spoiled as the rest of us."

Marjorie flicked her eyes backward, toward the walls. "I've been begging Mum to tear this down for years. The Temple, too. They're only standing because Matthew doesn't want to betray Aunt Cecily's memory. What does it matter? She's dead! She must be."

Marjorie tossed the stunted end of her cigarette to the ground and crushed it under her heel.

"They dragged the lake, you know. Looking for her body. I snuck away from Nanny and heard the policemen talking about water currents. They said if she'd done herself in, she'd wash up on shore in a few days. I avoided the beach for quite some time after that."

"You don't really think she killed herself, do you?" I asked.

"Whatever happened to Aunt Cecily, she's not coming back. So it's no use agonizing over it."

Marjorie turned her face toward the bleak horizon. Casually, as if discussing the weather, she said, "You may be surprised to hear this, but I do like you."

I flushed at the unexpected compliment. "Oh?"

Marjorie nodded, confident in the rightness of her approval. "You're good for Matthew. You keep him calm."

"I'm worried his nightmares are getting worse," I said. Hesitant.

"Why?" She gave me a troubled look.

"He sees Cecily's body. Covered in blood."

I'd assumed Matthew confided everything to his sister, but it was clear from Marjorie's reaction that she hadn't known.

"Poor Matts."

She looked so sad, so stricken, that I found myself reaching out to touch her shoulder. She twisted away. How like Marjorie to offer the possibility of friendship and then tug it back.

"I'm doing everything I can to make him better," I said.

"You can't," she muttered.

"I have to try. He's my husband."

"Yes. But you'll never be able to understand him, not the way you want." Marjorie looked toward Lakecrest. "You have no idea what it means, to be a Lemont."

I am a Lemont! I wanted to taunt her. But I wasn't. Not yet.

"We'd better go back," Marjorie said flatly. "Mum will send out a search party if we're late for afternoon tea."

I scurried to keep up with Marjorie's long, decisive strides. We made our way back to the lakefront path in silence, and I thought the conversation was over. As we approached Lakecrest, Marjorie stopped and turned around.

"I meant what I said earlier. I like you." Her brittle tone undercut the compliment, but I faked a grateful smile. "The best thing you can do for Matthew is to be a devoted, obedient wife. Have a pile of gorgeous babies and host luncheons and don't meddle in matters that don't concern you."

Always one for dramatic exits, Marjorie left before I could respond. Her words echoed through my head, and something she'd said revived a fear I'd been trying to quash. As soon as we arrived back at the house, I snuck away to phone Blanche.

Two days later, in the consultation room of the doctor Blanche recommended, I discovered my suspicions were correct. I was pregnant.

CHAPTER EIGHT

Matthew and I had agreed to wait. I'd taken the necessary precautions, and I figured we'd have a few years to travel and enjoy ourselves. Sure, I'd missed my monthly in January, but I'd skipped once or twice before, when I was wound up tight with worries, and it had come back with no problems afterward. It wasn't until I counted up the weeks and realized I hadn't bled for two months that I felt uneasy.

And now I knew for sure.

I made my way home from the doctor's office in a shocked daze. For the first time since I'd moved to Chicago, I wished my mother lived nearby. She was the only person who would understand why this supposedly happy news filled me with dread. Then I thought of Blanche, who must be wondering why I'd turned to her for help when I had my pick of Lemont family doctors. I could count on my cousin for straight advice.

Blanche was about to go to work when I called, so I agreed to meet her at the club. She greeted me with a kiss on the cheek and led me to a table in the corner. The Pharaoh's Club had a sad, neglected air in the midafternoon, like a party dress that dazzles only when it's worn.

Without people, without music, the gold tablecloths and sapphire-blue walls looked garish, and I could see stains on the worn carpets. A lingering aroma of smoke and spilled champagne hung in the air.

"Are you sure it's all right?" I asked. "You're not too busy?"

"Naw, Mr. Pitz is thrilled you're here." She rolled her eyes toward the manager, who had hovered over us when I came in.

Darling Blanche. I'd taken her for granted during those weeks we shared a room, those giddy days when all my thoughts were tangled up in Matthew. Only a few months had passed since then, but I felt ages older in my squeaky new shoes and expensive wool coat. Blanche looked different, too. Her lighthearted manner seemed forced, part of the uniform she pulled on at the club rather than natural high spirits.

"What's going on?" she asked.

"I'm going to have a baby."

Blanche worked her features into a smile. "Congratulations. You must be over the moon."

"I'm not. That's what's so awful. Matthew and I were going to Africa . . ." A tent under the night sky. I longed for that imaginary vision so much it ached. "We can't go if I'm pregnant. He'll be so upset."

"You haven't told him?"

"Not yet. I can't. I'll have to pretend to be thrilled, and I'm not."

Blanche blinked quickly. Were those tears? She rubbed at her eyes with the heel of her hand.

"Blanche, what is it? Please tell me."

She started to laugh, but it came out as a sob. She turned away and took a deep breath.

"Well, aren't we a pair of perfect saps," she said. "Kate, I know it's a surprise and all, but don't you see how lucky you are? You've got a husband who loves you and a beautiful house and soon you'll have a baby—what's there to complain about? You have everything a girl could ever want."

"Oh, Blanche." I was stung by my utter denseness. "You'll have babies, too, one day. I know it."

"Will I?" She looked at me, anguished. "The problem is, I've found my guy, the one I want to live happily ever after with. But it's never going to happen."

"Why not?"

"Because he's married, that's why. It doesn't matter that his wife is a shrew who makes his life hell or that he loves me as much as I love him. We're stuck. I have to see him here every day, and we have to pretend like nothing's going on, and I don't know how much longer I can stand it."

I remembered Blanche chattering about a good-looking saxophonist who'd joined the club's band. She'd talked about him a few times, giggling, when I asked her if there was any special man in her life. Then she'd stopped. I thought it meant things had cooled down; now I realized she'd gotten secretive because things had heated up.

"He can get a divorce, can't he?" I asked. "No one holds that against a musician."

"His wife will never agree. He's committed adultery, even admitted it to her, but she won't let him out of the marriage. She'd rather make him suffer."

Blanche's shoulders slumped, and she covered her face with her hands. I pulled my chair over and put an arm around her shoulder.

"I'm so sorry," I said. "I had no idea."

She nodded. "I know. I shouldn't have sprung this on you."

"No, I'm glad you did," I said. "Listen, why don't you come up to Lakecrest this weekend? My mother-in-law is having a big supper on Saturday, and I'd look forward to it a lot more if you were there."

"Really?"

"Really. Stay overnight. Bring your fellow—no one needs to know he's married. It will shake things up, having a jazz player around."

"Oh, Billy can be real smooth," Blanche assured me. "I'd love for you to meet him. He's just the greatest. You know what it's like, falling in love so fast your heart hurts."

"Sure I do."

That was enough of an opening for Blanche to let loose with all the feelings she'd kept sewn up, and I let her go. I listened and nodded and smiled. It was enough, for a while, to distract me from what was to come: sharing the news that the Lemont family was about to welcome its newest addition.

I'd prepared myself for Matthew to be disappointed and sink into one of his moods, but in the end he surprised me. Though it took him a moment to understand what I was saying, he seemed genuinely happy, wrapping me in his arms and swearing he couldn't care less about Africa. The only things that mattered were the baby and me. At the dinner table that night, Hannah reacted with genuine delight, squeezing my hand and looking at Matthew with adoring, misty eyes.

Marjorie shrugged. "I should have guessed," she said. "You have been looking chubby, Kate."

As Hannah and Matthew chattered and Marjorie sulked, I found myself strangely silent. The momentous news really had nothing to do with me. It was all about the baby, Hannah's first grandchild. There was talk of names and decorating the nursery and pulling out Matthew's old christening gown, and suddenly it was all too much.

"Kate?" Matthew pushed back his chair and stood up. "Are you all right?"

"A bit light-headed, that's all."

"You mustn't push yourself," Hannah ordered. "Perhaps I should cancel the dinner party on Saturday. It might be too much."

"No, please don't," I said.

"If you're sure," Matthew said.

I nodded. "I invited Blanche," I said. "Hope that's all right."

"Of course," Matthew asked. "One more won't hurt, will it, Mum?"

"Two more," I said. "She has a beau, Billy. They could stay for the weekend."

Marjorie snickered. "Why not invite the whole Pharaoh's Club revue?"

Hannah uttered a sharp tsk. "If Kate would like Blanche and her gentleman friend to stay, then they're welcome." She patted my hand. "Whatever you want, my dear."

She was practically groveling. That might be the one bright spot of this pregnancy.

Blanche and Billy arrived late Saturday afternoon, in time for a quick tour of Lakecrest before the rest of the guests arrived. With his dark hair and dark eyes—echoes of Rudy Valentino—Billy made a dashing impression, and he was friendly and good-natured, perfect for Blanche. I genuinely hoped things would work out for them.

Billy's eyes got wider and wider as we entered each new room. "I can't believe you live here!" he exclaimed.

"I can't believe it, either."

"It's swell. Like something out of the pictures." His cheerful enjoyment made me less self-conscious, and I liked him even more.

Marjorie, not surprisingly, made straight for Billy when she joined us later for drinks.

"Shame you didn't bring your saxophone," Marjorie told him. "Wouldn't that be a hoot, jazz in the sitting room?"

"I'm glad to have the night off for a change," Billy said.

Despite Marjorie's flirtatious banter, Billy stuck by Blanche's side as the rest of the guests trickled in. A good sign. The group Hannah had assembled was a ragtag assortment of East Ridge society and Lemont Industries managers and their dowdy wives, none of whom did much to liven up the conversation. Blanche and Billy were the only guests

younger than forty until the final couple arrived, not long before supper was announced. A husband and wife, cheeks flushed from the cold,
apologizing as Hannah made quick introductions.

"Mr. and Mrs. Victor Monroe. Our new neighbors."

Matthew extended his hand. "So you're the ones who bought the
old Finley place. How's it suiting you?"

"It's a palace!" Victor said, his voice as powerful as his handshake.
"You get so much more land for your money here, compared to New
York."

I looked at his wife. Small frame, mousy hair, delicate features. I
remembered the woman I'd seen standing forlornly in the snow from
the road. She didn't seem to recognize me, but why would she? I'd been
so far away.

"Kate Lemont," I said. "Nice to meet you."

"Eva. Thank you for having us."

"How are you settling in?"

Eva spoke quietly but precisely, like someone who carefully considered each word. "All right, I guess. We've got three little ones, and our
old nanny didn't want to move, so I've been busy hiring a new staff.
Training the maids how we like things done. You know how it is."

Did I?

"Please let me know if there's anything I can do to help," I offered.
I couldn't imagine she'd ever need anything from me, what with all that
staff, but it seemed like the polite thing to say.

Before I could come up with any more stilted conversation, I saw
Hannah beckon me over and excused myself.

"Kate, this is Dr. Westbrook," she said, indicating an elderly
bearded man. "He's a specialist in obstetrics at Northwestern."

Obstetrics? Hannah had told me not to talk about the baby, saying
it was bad form to acknowledge my condition so early.

"An old friend of my father's," Hannah explained.

Nodding at me, the doctor said, "You're too young to have known Dr. Rieger, of course."

"Oh, I've heard a great deal." I'd let Hannah wonder what I meant by that.

"A giant in his field," Dr. Westbrook said. "I wonder what he'd say about all the nonsense that's taken over in recent years."

"What do you mean?" I asked.

"The blather about dreams. Blaming all psychoses on terrible mothers."

"So you don't subscribe to Dr. Freud's theories?"

"They're quite dangerous!" Dr. Westbrook exclaimed. "Anxiousness, melancholy—these conditions have a physical cause, and they demand a medical solution. It's very dangerous to suggest otherwise."

"Dr. Westbrook," Hannah interrupted, "given our families' long friendship, there's something I wanted to ask. Dear Kate recently informed us she is *expecting*"—the last word whispered, with a conspiratorial raise of the eyebrows—"and I hope you'd do us the honor of looking after her."

"It would be my pleasure," Dr. Westbrook said.

"I already have a doctor."

"Nonsense," Hannah admonished. "Dr. Westbrook has delivered hundreds of babies. You're a very lucky girl."

Dr. Westbrook reached into his jacket and pulled a calling card from the inside breast pocket. "Phone my office on Monday to make an appointment."

"Don't forget," Hannah told me. "I want you to receive the very best care."

After all, I was carrying the next Lemont.

At supper, I was seated next to Luanne Handleman, the ancient president of the East Ridge Ladies' Club. Luanne, who was nearly deaf, kept asking me to repeat what I said, leaving me little time to get to know Billy, who was seated on my other side. Occasionally I'd hear

Marjorie's laugh float above the general monotone of conversation, giving the night a charge, a sense that anything might happen.

Hannah liked to run her parties the traditional English way, with the ladies and gents separating after the meal. As the maids cleared the dessert plates, Hannah rose from the table, but instead of escorting the women out, she walked over to Matthew and put her hand on his shoulder.

Matthew stood up. "I'm afraid I must excuse myself," he announced. "I have some pressing business to attend to. Harry, Jerome—come with me to the office, and the other fellows can have their cigars in the billiards room. Ladies, if you'll excuse us?"

Business? On a weekend? Even more surprisingly, Hannah followed Matthew, leaving the hostess duties to Marjorie and me. Eva Monroe asked to use the phone to check on her children, and I escorted the rest of the women to the sitting room, wishing I could trudge upstairs to bed instead.

Most of the ladies gathered at card tables to play bridge, while Luanne and another old biddy settled into armchairs across the room and looked half-asleep. Marjorie stood by the fireplace, smoking and flicking the ashes over the grate. Blanche was nowhere to be seen; most likely, she'd snuck off with Billy. I couldn't blame her.

I watched a few hands of cards, trying to look interested. If only I could pick up a book instead.

Eva came in, her lips pinched tight.

"I'm so sorry, but I'm afraid we'll have to be going," she said. "My littlest has so much trouble settling down if I'm not there, and it's possible she has a touch of fever."

"Of course, I understand," I said. "I'll pass on your regrets to Matthew and his mother."

She smiled gratefully and hurried off. I sank down onto a sofa, and Marjorie tossed the end of her cigarette into the fire and came over to join me. She crossed one slim leg over the other and slid a finger in her hair, pulling a straight blonde chunk back and forth against her jawline.

"That's what you have to look forward to," she said.

"What?"

Marjorie smirked and eyed my stomach. "Mothering. Worrying about Junior having a touch of fever."

I glanced around, but no one seemed to be paying attention.

"I do find it strange," Marjorie said. "I'd have thought you'd be happier about the baby."

"Maybe I'm still getting used to the idea."

"Well, it's gotten you in Mum's good graces. Isn't that what you wanted? Even Matthew seems pleased, though I can't imagine why. I never thought he was much for children."

"Who's not much for children?" Matthew had walked into the room so quietly that I didn't hear him until he was perched on the arm of the sofa.

"You, dear brother," said Marjorie.

"Oh, they're not so bad," he said with a smile. "Maybe it's time we had some little ones around to cheer us up."

"Oh yes. I'll be so much cheerier with a screaming baby in the house."

"You'll change your mind one day," Matthew said. "When you have children of your own."

"What if I don't?" Marjorie's glare was icy. "What if I have no intention of popping out grandchildren for Mum?"

The card players glanced over at the sound of her rising voice.

Quietly, but with an edge to his voice, Matthew said, "If you're in a bad mood, that's no reason to take it out on me and Kate."

"Oh, goodness no, not Kate. Your perfect little wife."

If only you knew, I wanted to hiss, but I kept silent. There was an undercurrent of danger in Marjorie's expression, and I sensed another, wordless conversation taking place between her and Matthew. An exchange of looks that made me worried.

"Margie," Matthew pleaded. "Please."

"Good God, Matthew, when did you get so *old*? You're as bad as Mum. I can only imagine how dreary you'll be once you're a *father*."

She stood up. "I'm going to find that divine Billy. He's the only person here worth talking to."

A wave of lethargy tugged at me, and I slumped against Matthew.

"I'm sorry, darling," he said. "She loves creating a scene. It's got nothing to do with you."

Of course it did. Marjorie had been acting like a jilted lover ever since I told her about the baby. But I'd gain nothing by pointing that out, or by mentioning that I'd seen something glittery and unfocused in her eyes.

"Would it be all right if I went to bed?" I asked. "I'm so tired."

"I'll walk you up."

Matthew, sweetly protective, pressed his palm against my back as we went up the stairs. Once in our room, he turned on the bedside light as I pulled off my dress and tossed it on a chair. I'd gotten spoiled enough that I didn't think twice about leaving my clothes for the maids to wash and put away.

I sagged down onto the bed. "Marjorie said I looked unhappy," I said. "About the baby."

It was a test, an opening for Matthew to admit he'd noticed the same thing. He laughed and kissed me on the nose.

"Don't mind her. Aren't you curious why Mum dragged us off after dinner?"

"Sure." I'd almost forgotten.

"The board of directors finally agreed to set up Lemont Medical as a separate company. Mum's been pushing for it for years. With so many new medicines coming to market and hospitals being built, it's the perfect time . . ."

I leaned against him and let my eyes drift shut. For so long, I'd wished Matthew would confide in me about his work. Now I was too tired to care.

". . . to ask me if I'd do it."

"Do what?" I asked, jerking myself upright.

"Run the new company. It'll be a sacrifice, of course. I'll be traveling, meeting with bankers and doctors. That's why this baby is such good news." He gave my belly a pat. "Something to keep you busy while I'm gone."

"Oh, Matthew." I tried very hard to look happy. Inside, I felt almost sick with worry. How could Hannah think Matthew was ready for such a responsibility?

"Don't you worry," Matthew said. "Mum will look out for you. She'll take care of everything, I promise."

He was more right than he knew.

Within a week, I was spending every morning on my knees in the bathroom, quivering with nausea. I spent most days in my room, while Hannah and the maids hovered, trying to tempt my unpredictable appetite with crackers and warm milk. One afternoon, when I was feeling strong enough to walk downstairs and listen to the radio, I heard Hannah on the phone, turning down an invitation on my behalf.

"I'm afraid Kate's not well. I'll pass on your best wishes. Thank you. Yes, we couldn't be more pleased."

You'd have thought *she* was the one expecting.

"Who was that?" I asked, walking into the entrance hall. Who cared if I was caught eavesdropping? Hannah had no right to take my calls.

"I informed Luanne that you will not be attending any Ladies' Club luncheons for the foreseeable future."

It was no great loss; the club's gatherings were an irritating mix of gossip and one-upmanship. But I was furious at not being allowed to make the decision myself.

"I thought it was vulgar to talk about my condition until I was further along," I said.

"In normal circumstances, yes. But I'm afraid it can't be helped, given your delicate state. Now, what are you doing out of bed?"

"I feel fine," I said. "I was going to listen to the *Thursday Mystery Hour*." Then, with a certain defiance, I added, "If you don't mind."

Hannah took me by the crook of the arm, as if I were an invalid. "Of course not. I'll get you settled. It's time we had a talk about what's expected of a woman in your condition."

And that's when I learned the baby didn't just mean I wasn't going to Africa. It meant no more solitary walks along Deertrail Road. No dashing off to lunch dates in Chicago whenever I pleased. For the next seven months, Hannah would determine what was suitable and what wasn't. Thanks to the baby I hadn't planned for and didn't want, my mother-in-law was now in charge of my life.

CHAPTER NINE

It was a wetter than usual spring. Everyone said so. The rain poured down in torrents, soaking the landscape until water bubbled up from the ground. Puddles as big as ponds filled the front drive and back lawn, and the sky never changed from a dull, blank gray. Winter in Chicago is what most people complain about—the cold, the wind—but January and February had been crisp and bright, with swaths of snow glittering under clear blue skies. Spring felt desolate in comparison, and the few brave tulips that burst from the sodden flower beds were hardly enough to raise my spirits.

Hannah insisted I choke down a horrible tea each morning, which helped with the nausea, but her constant attention made me want to scream. She told me when to eat, what to eat, and when to go to bed. I hadn't been so closely watched since school, when Sister Agatha and the other nuns were always eyeing us girls for signs of sinful behavior.

I wasn't allowed to leave the house except for my monthly appointment with Dr. Westbrook, who asked nosy questions about my feelings on motherhood and marital relations with my husband. I was convinced everything I told him would be reported back to Hannah, so I put up with his poking and prodding and smiled demurely when he lectured me for not wearing a maternity corset. The only time I ever missed having morning sickness was in his office. What I would have given to vomit all over his pristine white coat!

Good Lord, I was bored. Denied my rambling walks outside, I paced the halls of Lakecrest instead. The rooms felt clammy and oppressive, with a lingering smell of wet plaster, and I began to hear the steady drip of leaks throughout the house. It was as if tiny rivers were trickling inside the walls, just out of sight. Even with a heavy cardigan pulled over a wool dress, the damp cold seemed to seep through my skin.

Matthew went off for a week to Boston, then for another to New York, and Marjorie tagged along to visit friends. My only visitor during their absence was Eva Monroe. I came close to asking her about the time I'd seen her standing alone in the snow; even from so far away, I'd sensed her loneliness. But Eva had a wariness to her, reminding me of a cat that scurries under the bed if you approach it too quickly. Confidences would have to wait.

Besides, I never knew when Hannah would swoop in. She had an unnerving way of inserting herself into our conversations, as she did one day when Eva and I were having tea in the morning room. I'd asked Eva how she was adjusting to country life, and she gave me a tight, wistful smile.

"I'd have been perfectly happy in an apartment in the city," she said. "Victor's the one who wanted to live out here. He thought the little ones needed space to roam."

"So they do."

Hannah was standing in the doorway; I hadn't even realized she was home.

"It's lovely out here in the summer," she continued. "We have a beach, down by the lake. You and the children are welcome anytime."

"Oh, that's so kind. We'd love to."

"I should warn you, the water's freezing. Even in August."

Eva smiled and shook her head. "I don't think they'll mind. My Rosie loves swimming so much, she's practically a mermaid."

With Eva, every topic veered to the same destination: her children. They were the center of her world, the only subject on her mind. Would I be like that one day? I couldn't imagine it.

I heard the irritating leaking again that night, when Hannah and I took our usual spots by the sitting room fireplace after supper. To pass the seemingly endless hours before bedtime, I'd begun reading aloud from a family history commissioned by Obadiah Lemont while Hannah worked on her embroidery. The author, one T. L. Blythe, must have been well paid, because he laid on the gushing praise with a heavy hand.

The book began with the Lemonts' supposed descent from French royalty, the ultimate flattery for a nouveau riche American family. Then came a few chapters on Henri, the fur trader who traveled across the northern territories and created supply routes seemingly single-handedly. The rumor of his marriage to an Indian princess—more royalty!—was described in a single sentence. That section was followed by the exploits of Henri's son, George, who somehow managed to be present at all the major events leading to the founding of Chicago. It was George who coined the family's Latin motto, *Factum est* ("It is done"), words that were now inscribed over Lakecrest's front door. His wife was described briefly as "a Talbott of Philadelphia." Another prize claimed by the ambitious Lemonts.

The second half of the book was centered on Obadiah himself: buying up land in the wake of the Great Fire, socializing with Rockefellers and Vanderbilts, expanding shipping routes throughout the Great Lakes, and establishing his family as one of the richest in the Midwest. The man portrayed in the book was half business baron, half frustrated artist, someone who could demand a meeting at the White House one day and buy the contents of a French chateau the next. A man who always wanted more.

Mr. Blythe outdid himself in his obsequious description of Lakecrest:

> *The crown jewel in the Lemonts' empire, the mansion stands as a monument to the indomitable American spirit, a new world forged from the ashes of the old. In its noble turrets and soaring archways, we witness man reaching toward the heavens and achieving a small measure of its perfection here on earth.*

Obadiah must have loved that part, I thought. And then I heard it: the same incessant dripping that seemed to follow me throughout the house. It was impossible to tell where it was coming from; the sound seemed to echo from the ceiling to the walls to the card tables.

"There it is again," I said to Hannah. I'd been pestering her about the leaks for days.

Her gaze remained focused on her stitches.

"Can't you hear it?" I asked.

It was such a little thing—a few drops of water, here and there—but it had begun to nag at me. How was all that water getting in? Where was it going?

"Old houses settle," she said, maddeningly calm. "You have to get used to the odd bump or creak."

Drip. Drip. The noise seemed to taunt me. I looked back at the book and saw a reproduction of a painting I'd noticed in a forlorn corner upstairs. A woman with a long neck, her slim shoulders emerging from a low-cut ball gown. The caption identified her as Leticia Lemont, Obadiah's wife. She was beautiful, of course. She'd have to be, to produce a daughter like Cecily and grandchildren like Matthew and Marjorie. Her profile and posture were the very definition of elegance.

I flipped through the pages. Other than noting her marriage to Obadiah, the author had nothing else to say.

"What was Leticia like?" I asked. "Jasper and Cecily's mother? I know she died before you moved to Lakecrest, but you must have heard stories."

"Jasper never talked about her. She was sickly, I think."

Another wife ignored by the Lemonts' own history book. No wonder Cecily was so determined to support female artists. In this family, the women were always overlooked.

It wasn't long afterward that I decided to create a shrine to the Lemonts' forgotten women. I'd turned the bedroom adjoining mine into a dressing room, and Matthew agreed to move his portrait of Cecily there. Next to that, I added the portrait of Leticia and one of Lucy Talbott Lemont, Matthew's great-grandmother. She looked severe in an unflattering lace cap and black dress. I even put up a painting I'd found in an unused bedroom of a woman in an Indian headdress. It wasn't the fur trader's wife—the picture was dated 1855—but I pretended it was. The Indian princess deserved a spot among the others.

They've all survived this, I told myself. *They married Lemonts and had children and continued the family line. I can do it, too.*

I did attempt domesticity, at least for a while. I tried knitting baby booties, which ended in snarled failure. I built elaborate houses out of playing cards, and I worked my way through the works of Charles Dickens, giving up midway through *David Copperfield*. I sent a letter to Mr. Haveleck, asking if we could meet.

I received his curt response a week later: *Nothing to report yet. I appreciate your patience.*

March gave way to April, with no relief from the rain. Matthew went to Minneapolis and Detroit; Marjorie escaped to a school friend's winter home in Palm Beach. Although I invited Blanche out to Lakecrest for lunch—no drives into Chicago, Hannah had informed me curtly—she canceled three times in a row and began crying when I asked about Billy. I felt the physical distance fraying our friendship, and the occasional tea with Eva couldn't take its place. Even Hannah seemed to disappear, spending entire days at the offices downtown. Is it any wonder I began roaming the halls, desperate for some kind of distraction?

All right, snooping.

I wandered for hours, dipping in and out of drawers and poking through closets. I hoped to find a treasure trove of Cecily's possessions tucked away in the attic, but a day rummaging through old furniture and storage trunks revealed nothing other than a few of her landscapes—pleasant but unmemorable—and a scrapbook of old newspaper clippings. A list of debutantes, with Cecily's name prominently featured, descriptions of parties she'd attended, a mention of her in a story on the latest style in hats. The last clipping in the book was a society column, Mrs. Whatchacallit's Whispers, dedicated to Miss Cecily Lemont's upcoming, soon-to-be-triumphant journey to Oxford:

The noted beauty and linguistic prodigy will be the first American woman to sit for the university's ancient languages exam. Asked about her prospects, Miss Lemont said, "I plan to make my hometown and my country proud." Accompanying her on the month-long excursion will be her father, Mr. Obadiah Lemont, and her tutor, Dr. Martin Rieger of the University of Chicago.

Dr. Rieger? It seemed odd that a doctor would be teaching ancient Greek in his spare time. There were no handwritten notes or captions on the pages, no way to know who'd put the scrapbook together. I put it back on the shelf where I'd found it.

I discovered a few more traces of Cecily in the office closet, which was filled with boxes of Obadiah's papers. Not surprisingly, he was a pack rat who saved what looked like every piece of mail he'd ever received. Most were of absolutely no interest, but I pulled out anything that mentioned Cecily.

A note to the housekeeper, Mrs. Briscoe:

> *Staffing for the upcoming year: Two additional gardeners and one stonemason to complete the enclosed plans drawn up by Miss Cecily Lemont. The gardeners to be hired by Mr. Hutchins, under Miss Lemont's supervision . .*

Attached were sketches of the Labyrinth and the Temple, along with a page of expenses for their construction. The stonemason, apparently, had been brought over from Italy and was given his own apartment in East Ridge. When this was added to the shocking amounts Obadiah spent on Lakecrest and his collections, it was a wonder the family had any money left at all.

A pamphlet touting a "rest cure" at a California hot spring seemed like an odd man out, until I saw a note in Obadiah's handwriting enclosed inside:

> *Cecily,*
> *Might this be of interest? Stimson's wife found it helpful. Jasper is much in favor of you going, which may be a*

*point against it in your eyes. No matter to me if you go or
stay, only that you get well.*

A letter from the editor of the *Chicago Literary Review*, dated June
8, 1895, was buried in a stack of social correspondence:

Dear Miss Lemont,
*Thank you for sending the story "Artemis and Actaeon"
for our consideration. It shows remarkable talent in style
and execution, and we would be delighted to publish it
in our winter issue. The* Review *has always been a cham-
pion of the fairer sex, and we believe your voice would
be a welcome addition to the literary circles of our city.
Please find enclosed a payment of $2.00, our standard
fee for a story of this length. I also encourage you to pay a
visit to our offices at your earliest convenience. It would
be a great pleasure to meet you in person.*

I didn't recognize the title from Cecily's *Twelve Ancient Tales.*
Annoyingly, there was no copy of the magazine itself, and I made a
mental note to see if I could find one somewhere else in the house.

The most intriguing discovery was the draft of a letter Obadiah had
written to Jasper. Had he rewritten it later? Or simply never sent it?

*I have neither the time nor the inclination to insert my-
self in women's squabbles. Cecily has been on at me about
the changes at Lakecrest, and I have told her in no uncertain terms that Hannah—as your wife—has the final
word. You'd best heed that advice as well. Do as you wish
in your city lodgings. I have never condemned your activities, as long as they are kept within the usual bounds.
However, I urge you to show more respect to Hannah*

*than you do your sister. I have indulged your childish
games far too long, to my great regret.*

What "activities," I wondered, should be "kept within the usual
bounds"?

I tried to imagine Hannah as a newlywed, walking through these
same rooms. Ignored by her husband, looked down on by her sister-
in-law. To my surprise, I felt a twinge of sympathy. Had Hannah worried about Obadiah the same way I worried about her? I thought of
Marjorie and her jealous stares whenever I clung onto Matthew's arm
and wondered if Cecily shot the same kind of looks at Hannah. There
were photographs of Jasper all over the house, some as a dashing young
man-about-town and others as an older, distinguished businessman.
But Hannah hardly ever mentioned him.

"What are you doing?"

I looked up and saw Hannah staring at the mess of papers around
me. Appalled.

"I . . . I was curious," I stammered, "to know more about the family's history."

"So you decided to go through our confidential papers?"

Honestly, she was acting like she'd caught me digging around in
her jewelry box. *My last name's Lemont,* I wanted to say. *Don't I have a
right to know what's going on?* But I held back and summoned a meek,
helpless expression. "I didn't think you'd mind."

"Oh, bosh. You knew exactly what you were doing. Sneaking
around behind my back. I'm on to you, my dear. And I can make things
very unpleasant if you stir up trouble."

Hannah had often made me feel self-conscious or irritated. But I'll
always remember the way she glared at me that afternoon, full of self-
righteous fury, because it was the first time I truly felt scared.

Drip. Drip. The sound kept mocking me, in my bathroom, in the morning room, in the halls. The dankness seemed to have settled into my very bones, and my throat grew raspy from a cough I couldn't shake. Lakecrest was a Frankenstein's monster of architectural castoffs, and the miserable weather seemed to bring it to life. The windows rattled and groaned with the wind, and steam hissed from the bedroom radiators in a steady, eerie shriek. The house's damp, moldy odor, as inescapable as the leaking water, added to the overall impression of decay, as if the building was rotting away from the inside.

The gloomy library was one of my least favorite places in the house, but at least it was warm. There were no windows to let in a draft, just shelf after shelf of dusty books. Though I'd never felt like curling up and reading on its moth-eaten couch, I found myself lingering there one afternoon, as I searched for another book of Lemont family lore to read with Hannah.

The library was one of the least-used rooms in the house, so it was a surprise to hear footsteps approaching as I was crouched in a corner, examining a shelf near the floor. I'd just pulled out an intriguing volume titled *The Ways of Madness*, written by Dr. Martin Rieger himself, when I looked up to see who'd come in. Edna was halfway through the room before she saw me. She stopped abruptly, sending dishes clattering on the tray in her hands. I stared, eyebrows raised.

"Mrs. Lemont." She said the name crisply when she spoke to Hannah, but with me, she dragged it out grudgingly. As if I didn't deserve it.

"What's going on?" I asked.

"It's nothing to do with you," Edna muttered.

"Oh no?" I usually bent over backward to be polite to the servants, as people who haven't been raised with help often do. But not that day. My voice was terse. "I do live here."

"You'd better speak to the senior Mrs. Lemont," Edna said, turning aside.

I reached out and put my hand against the tray to stop her. "It's Mr. Matthew you should be worried about, not her. If he were to find out you were up to any funny business . . ."

It was enough. Edna had been raised in the real world, just like me. She knew when alliances needed to shift.

"All right, then," she said gruffly. "But she doesn't need to know I've told you."

I slipped the book into my sweater and cinched my belt tight to secure it, watching as Edna walked around the couch to the back of the room. She tapped a foot against the bottom of a bookshelf, and it swung outward with a creak, revealing a set of wooden steps. *Of course,* I thought. Obadiah would have insisted his mansion be built with a hidden room or two.

Edna clicked a switch at the top of the stairs, and a dim light filtered upward. I walked down into a narrow, cramped chamber that smelled of wet dirt; the only thing I could see was a dark-gray metal door. A root cellar? Edna nudged past me and pulled a key from her apron pocket. She unlocked the door and pushed it open, then stepped back so I could enter first.

It was a prison cell, or what I'd always imaged one would look like. A single bed sat lengthwise against the wall, with a porcelain chamber pot peeking out from underneath. A wooden chair had been tipped sideways onto the floor. Next to the door was a small table covered with bottles that gave off a tangy, medicinal smell. I saw a figure on the bed, nearly covered by a thin gray blanket. Not moving. I took a step forward, then two. That's when I realized the person lying in front of me was Marjorie.

She seemed to have aged a dozen years. Matted chunks of hair clung to her cheeks, and her skin had a sick, grayish tint. Her eyes stared at me, blank.

"Kate," she said. No emotion.

It took me a few seconds to find my voice. "What happened?"

Marjorie erupted with a sharp, barking laugh that echoed against the walls.

I turned around to look at Edna, standing in the doorway. "What's going on?"

She walked past me without answering. She picked up the knocked-over chair and retrieved a bowl and cup from the floor. Both tin, I noted. Unbreakable. She set down a fresh, identical set of dishes next to the bed, then poured out a spoonful of dark-pink liquid from one of the dozen bottles clustered on the table. Marjorie gulped the medicine down with a wince.

Her duty completed, Edna said she'd wait outside. After she'd closed the door forcefully behind her, I pulled the chair over to the bed and sat down.

"I don't understand. Your mother told me you were in Palm Beach."

"Did she? How clever." At least the tart sarcasm was recognizably Marjorie.

I held out a hand. "Would you like to sit up?"

"No. Makes my head swim."

The stink of urine and sweat hung in the stale air. I took a deep breath—through my mouth, not my nose—and tried to keep from gagging.

"Marjorie, what are you doing here?"

She rolled onto her back and pulled one leg out from under the covers. A thick leather band was strapped around her ankle; she shook her foot, and I heard the rattle of a chain. Twisted coils of steel ran to an anchor in the wall.

"Your mother did this?"

"For my own good. I believe it's referred to as 'drying out.' You didn't hear about my latest escapade?"

I shook my head.

"Nearly killed myself with a mix of cocaine and home-brewed bourbon at Ramsay's. Can you imagine *le scandale*?" She looked pleased at the thought of causing a fuss. "I guess Mum paid the right people to keep it out of the papers. Not for my sake, of course. For hers. Saving what's left of her precious reputation."

"So she's locked you up? That's absurd!"

"Isn't it?"

The Marjorie I knew would be furious. Raging. The woman lying listlessly on the bed in front of me was a pale imitation of my sister-in-law, drained of the fire that made Marjorie so captivating.

"You'd think Mum would understand," Marjorie said. "After all the pills and potions she's forced on me. There was this horrible paste I had to spread all over my face to fade my freckles. Another cream to whiten my complexion—that one stung horribly. Syrup to help me sleep after Cecily left and I was afraid the devil was coming to snatch me in the night. It worked; it really did. I wish I still had some, but Mum cut me off.

"Isn't it funny how Mum would love to get the whole country swallowing Lemont Industries' magic pills, but she sneers at me for trying out anything else? Cocaine's not nearly as bad as they'd have you believe. Hard to find these days; you have to make friends with real lowlifes to get the good stuff, and that's what gets me in trouble. Oh, I have stories. I only wish I could remember half of them."

"Marjorie," I said abruptly. "This is crazy! You have to get out of here!"

"Crazy?" Her words had started to sound slurred. "We're all crazy. This entire damned family." She stared at me, eyes dulled of all feeling. "You'll go crazy, too, if you stay."

I felt sick.

"Get out," she mumbled. "Leave me alone."

My hands were shaking as I walked out of the room. Edna locked the door behind me, and we walked back upstairs.

"That room," I said, as we emerged into the library. "Marjorie. It's not right."

"Mrs. Lemont decides what's right," Edna said. "She's who I take my orders from."

Not forever. I flashed Edna a look, and she was sharp enough to understand what I meant.

"You agreed not to tell," Edna said. Defiant, to cover up her fear.

"I won't."

There was no point confronting Hannah anyway. Matthew was the one who needed to know. When he heard what Hannah had done to Marjorie, he'd understand why I didn't trust his mother. It might even be the first step in convincing him to move away from Lakecrest. Matthew was in Detroit, but I'd call his office; they'd know how to reach him.

Trembling from the cold—or was it nerves?—I rushed toward the telephone in the entryway. My heels echoed through the Arabian Room as I ran across the painted tile floor, and then suddenly, I was flying. My feet slid out from under me, and I fell with a disorienting thud onto my side.

For a moment, I couldn't breathe. My whole body was tense with shock as I made a mental inspection of the pain. Ankle, knees, shoulder, head. An odd pressure in my belly. God help me, what I felt first was relief. If something happened to the baby, I'd be free.

That thought was followed immediately by crippling guilt. What kind of person would wish for something so awful? Jerky sobs swelled up and out. I told myself it was Hannah's fault for locking Marjorie up. And Matthew's fault for not being there to comfort me, as I'd comforted him so many times in the dark. Most of all, it was Lakecrest's fault, this mausoleum filled with shadows and dark corners and leaks that never,

ever stopped. Lakecrest itself had reached out and hurled me to the ground, a punishment for my hatred.

Or maybe the house really had driven me crazy.

It felt as if I lay there forever, wretched and alone. In fact, it couldn't have been more than a minute or two before Alice came in. She was young—no more than eighteen—but had a touching desire to please that made up for her inexperience, in my eyes at least.

"Oh, Missus!" she cried, hands fluttering. "Are you all right?"

I gingerly moved one leg, then the other. My stockings were wet, for some reason, and my left ankle felt stiff and sore. Alice took hold of my upper arms, and I managed to stand. Wincing, I shuffled to the nearest chair, a ridiculous silk-upholstered eyesore Marjorie jokingly called the sultan's throne.

"I'll get Edna," Alice insisted. Though I dreaded facing the cook after our recent confrontation, I was grateful for her efficiency once she arrived.

"I'll call Dr. Gordon," she said. "He's very well regarded in East Ridge. Won't take him long to get here. Then I'll bring in some tea. Alice, you inform Mrs. Lemont; I believe she's in her dressing room upstairs. But clean that up first."

I looked to where she was pointing. Water had seeped through the bottom of the French doors that opened onto the terrace. Though the puddle extended several feet into the room, it was almost invisible in the dim light. I watched numbly as Alice brought in a mop and began swabbing. All those tiny drips making their way through the nooks and crannies of this house had gathered here. Waiting for me.

"Is this yours, Mrs. Lemont?"

Alice held up the book I'd taken from the library. It must have tumbled out of my sweater when I fell.

"Yes. You can take it to my room when you're finished."

Alice was giving the floor a final inspection when a stocky man walked in carrying a toolbox. He paused when he saw me and tipped his head.

"Mrs. Lemont."

I knew he was the caretaker, and his name was Karel, but we'd never spoken. Hannah seemed to like him—as much as she liked anyone—and she'd trusted him enough to leave him in charge of Lakecrest while the family was abroad. Though I knew I should say something polite, I was distracted by his dark, baggy coat and lumbering walk. I'd seen someone else move in that same distinctive way, leaning from side to side with each step. So much for my ridiculous illusion that Cecily herself had lured me out to the Labyrinth; it had been Karel all along, inspecting the property. Doing his job.

"Over here," Alice told him.

Karel pulled off his coat and neatly folded it before joining her on the other side of the room. He watched Alice finish up, then examined the doors.

"I've heard leaks all over the house," I said.

"Of course is water." He had a strong, guttural accent, but spoke confidently. "Not well built, this house. Always repairs."

I was surprised to hear one of the staff criticize the place they depended on for their livelihood.

"I thought Mr. Lemont—that is, Mr. Obadiah—hired the best workers money could buy."

"Good workmens, yes. He make them do job too fast. Always hurry, hurry. Not careful, you understand?"

I nodded. Karel didn't have the deferential manner of the maids, or even Edna, and I sensed he took great pride in telling the truth, even when it wasn't what his employers wanted to hear.

"Did you know Mr. Obadiah?" I asked. It was hard to tell Karel's age from his weather-beaten skin, though he looked to be in his sixties.

"Long time ago," Karel said. He grunted and pressed his finger into a section of spongy wood at the bottom of the doorframe. "Here the water is coming. I will fix how I can, bring new wood tomorrow."

He pressed a rag into the narrow gap at the bottom of the door. As he was securing it, Edna bustled in with a tray and announced the doctor was on his way. She hovered over me while Karel gathered his things and left. It was frustrating, not being able to ask more questions, but I planned to seek him out as soon as I was better. Karel had known Obadiah, which meant he'd also known Cecily. He might have seen or heard something on the night she disappeared.

Or was I just desperate to talk to someone who hated Lakecrest as much as I did?

Soon enough, the grandfatherly Dr. Gordon arrived. He pressed around my stomach and asked if I had any pain or cramping. I told him no.

"I do feel something strange, though. Like bubbles popping."

"Why, it's your child, Mrs. Lemont! Is this the first time you've felt it move?"

I nodded.

"Well, fancy that. He wants you to know he's all right."

Having been assured by the doctor that my ankle was twisted rather than broken, Edna and Alice helped me limp upstairs, where I lay in bed and pretended to be asleep when Hannah came to check on me. I really was asleep when Matthew crept in sometime in the middle of the night.

"I'm sorry, darling. Didn't mean to wake you." He leaned over and kissed me on the forehead. "How are you?"

My ankle was still throbbing, but not as much. "Better. No harm done. What are you doing here?"

"I caught the first train home. I had to make sure you were all right."

I was so touched I nearly cried. Matthew laughed and tousled my hair. "You'll get the royal treatment tomorrow," he said. "Just because you're stuck in bed doesn't mean I can't spoil you."

Stuck in bed. The words sparked my memory: Marjorie, her leg chained to the wall. The terrible blankness of her expression when she told me to leave. Frantically, I told Matthew what I'd seen, but the more I talked, the less interested he seemed. There was no anger, no outrage. Only resignation.

"I'm sorry you had to see her that way," he said at last.

"You knew?" I felt the same jarring shock as when I'd hit the floor. Matthew nodded.

"You told me Marjorie was in Palm Beach! You lied!"

"To spare you this kind of reaction. Don't worry. It's for her own good, and Mum has everything in hand."

His mouth and eyes were set in an expression I'd come to know well, one that meant a conversation was over.

Then, lightly, he said, "Jock Halverson was warning me the other day how emotional women can be when they're expecting." A smile. A fatherly pat on the cheek. "He said I should buy you flowers every week, but I've done him one better. I picked up a little something for you during my trip."

Matthew reached into his jacket pocket and pulled out a small velvet bag. I pulled it open, and a stream of diamonds slipped into my hand. Matthew picked up the necklace and brushed my hair aside to fasten the clasp. He brought the hand mirror from my dresser so I could see the gems form a cascade of light against my skin.

"Do you like it?" he asked.

"It's gorgeous."

Matthew looked as happy as if he'd designed it himself. Hadn't I always dreamed of wearing diamonds? And about a dashing husband who'd give them to me?

Matthew started talking about Jock's new racehorse and whether I'd like to visit the Halversons at Saratoga one day, and I found I had nothing more to say about Marjorie. Matthew was the one I needed on my side, not his sister. He'd rushed home when he found out I'd been hurt, and his presents were getting more and more lavish. What else mattered?

I didn't consider until later how much Marjorie's fate was tied to my own. If Hannah didn't hesitate to lock up her own daughter, what would she do to me if I ever crossed her?

CHAPTER TEN

What is madness?

Attempting to formulate a concise answer to that question risks an onset of the very disorder under study. Madness has taken a multitude of forms through the course of human history. At times, it has been as revered as it is now maligned.

My own approach is a psychological-cultural one, examining the methods by which deviations from behavioral mores have been described and treated in the medical and humanistic literature of their time.

Honestly. You'd think a book about lunatics would be a little more fun.

On Dr. Gordon's advice, I'd been sentenced to a week in bed. Matthew had gone back to Michigan, and I was hoping Dr. Rieger's book might lead to some revelations about Cecily. Judging by the introduction, it would be more useful as a sleeping aid.

Bored, I flipped ahead, stopping at the occasional pictures. Illustrations of the human brain. An engraving of a medieval madhouse. A painting of women in flowing gowns cavorting in a field. I stopped and looked at the chapter title: "Madness as Divine in Ancient Greece." I skimmed the text:

In his Phaedrus, *Plato ascribed to Socrates the belief that madness can be inspired by the gods. As such, it arises in four distinct forms: the madness of love (caused by the machinations of Eros and Aphrodite), the madness of artistic inspiration (the Muses), the madness of prophecy (Apollo), and the madness of mystical rite (Dionysus). The Dionysian rites, in particular, offer persuasive evidence that madness does not always spring from a physical cause. It was a state that could be achieved through particular actions and thus could be discarded afterward with little effect on the memory. Such madness has been given no place in our modern world, but we reject it as a relic of the past at our peril. Unleashing that madness can serve a larger social purpose, and we might all benefit were we to rediscover and adapt those ancient mysteries to our own times.*

That caught my attention. I read on, enthralled, as Dr. Rieger described a play where women ran around in leopard skins as they were initiated into a secret sisterhood. When they discovered a man spying on their rites, they tore him to pieces. It almost made me regret my lack of a classical education; the stories were as melodramatic and blood soaked as the tawdriest horror novel.

Ancient sources record countless instances of women obtaining cathartic release from episodes of "madness" that bear little relation to the disorder as it is understood to-

day. However, the particular elements of each rite were lamentably undocumented by its practitioners, secrecy being essential to such groups' convictions. In the absence of such knowledge, preposterous theories could spread unchecked. Scenes such as Pentheus's death in The Bacchae *cannot be held up as historical evidence, for it may be no more than a playwright's attempt to shock his audience. Whatever such rites entailed, the madness of Dionysus was widely accepted as a religious practice. Indeed, it was one of the few ways women were able to obtain a measure of freedom in an otherwise limited public sphere.*

Was this where Cecily had gotten the idea to wander the grounds, spouting poetry in the middle of night? From what Mabel had told me, Cecily's rituals were odd, but harmless. I turned the page and stopped at a photo of an ancient Greek vase featuring painted female figures pulling a man apart, their expressions grim.

I thought of Matthew's dreams. Cecily's blood.

It didn't make sense. Cecily couldn't have been the victim of some murderous frenzy. There had been no acolytes at Lakecrest that evening, no rites at the Temple. No evidence of anyone coming to a bloody, tragic end.

I skipped past chapters on medieval asylums, the Enlightenment, and the rise of modern psychology. The final page had a photograph of Dr. Rieger holding what looked like an inverted metal bowl attached by wires to a small electrical box. Probably the infamous Millchen Cap I'd been hearing about. I saw a resemblance to Hannah in the doctor's stiff, upright posture and narrow nose. But it was impossible to tell what he really looked like behind the bushy mustache and thick glasses.

I turned the final page, ready to hide the book back in my nightstand. There, pasted inside the back cover, was a handwritten note.

To my dear Cecily, my muse and inspiration for a most divine madness. May your work heal others even as you spur mine on to greater heights.

Then, annoyingly, a few lines I couldn't read in what looked like ancient Greek, followed by a signature:

Yours ever, M. R.

I closed the book, letting my mind wander. Girls gathering on the lakefront. A stone temple and white robes. But what did it have to do with Cecily's disappearance? I fidgeted and fretted and realized I'd be driven crazy myself if I didn't get out of the house. Mr. Haveleck still hadn't told me what he was doing with my money, and I had every right to demand an answer in person.

Gingerly, I stood up. My ankle was still sore, but I could walk without too much of a limp. I got dressed and leaned out the doorway of my bedroom. The house was silent. Clutching the banister for support, I made my way downstairs to the telephone, holding *The Ways of Madness* in my other hand. Checking one more time that I was alone, I called Mr. Haveleck and told him I was bringing something that might help in his search for Cecily. Informing someone of a visit—rather than asking for permission—was a tactic I'd learned from Hannah.

I rang the bell for Alice and asked her where Hannah was.

"Ladies' Club luncheon," she said.

Perfect. Hannah would be gone for hours, and Luanne usually picked her up and dropped her off. That meant I wouldn't have to take the train downtown.

"Call for Hank, would you?" I said. "I'm going out for a bit."

Hank pulled up at the front door a few minutes later. He stepped out and walked around to the passenger door, looking uncertain.

"I going to the North Side," I told him. "Clark and Fullerton. Mrs. Lemont doesn't need you for anything, does she?"

"No, ma'am," Hank said. Then, hesitantly, "Sure you're feeling all right? Heard you had a fall."

"Oh, it was nothing, really. I'm fine."

Hank pulled the door open, and I saw a flash of concern as he watched me climb in. Stone-faced Hank, worried for me? I was touched.

"It shouldn't take long," I said. "Just a quick meeting with a friend."

Mr. Haveleck wasn't a friend, of course, and he didn't look particularly glad to see me when I arrived at his office. I passed him Dr. Rieger's book, pointing out the note inside. Mr. Haveleck looked a little taken aback by my description of drunken women running wild across the estate, and he shook his head when I asked if he could read ancient Greek. He took a quick look through the book, but soon handed it back.

"Mrs. Lemont, I pride myself on my honesty," he said. "Some people in my line of work string along their clients and milk them for what they can get. That's not how I do business."

He pulled a folder from the chaos on his desk. *Lemont* was written across the top right corner. The pile of papers inside was disappointingly small.

"I'll tell it to you straight," he said. "I don't know what happened to Cecily Lemont, and I don't think anyone ever will."

I'd known it was a long shot, but that didn't stop the crush of disappointment.

"I'll tell you what we did find," he said. "Maybe it will help, a little. We tracked down a few servants who used to work at the house and neighbors who knew her. Nobody noticed anything out of the ordinary in the weeks before she disappeared.

"Now, that's what we got from doing face-to-face interviews. But we always follow up on unofficial stories, too. The gossip that goes around, someone passing on what they heard from their barber or the lady next door. And that led us to a Mr. Patrick Donnelly. He was the overnight ticket agent at the Bluffside train station. He sold a ticket for the earliest train to a woman who wore a scarf around her hat so he couldn't see her face. When Cecily Lemont's disappearance became big news, he told his boss about it and got the brush-off. A fancy lady like that wouldn't walk all the way to Bluffside in the middle of the night when she could have gone to the East Ridge station less than a mile from her house. But maybe she did, if she didn't want to be seen. Maybe she caught the train to Union Station. What then? Hundreds of trains leave Chicago every day. If she wanted to disappear, she could."

"I see," I said, trying hard not to show my disappointment. "Well, thanks. I appreciate your efforts. I guess we should settle the bill?"

"The deposit you paid covers it."

"That hardly seems right. I'm sure you and your men went through a lot of trouble . . ."

"We're square." Mr. Haveleck stood abruptly and walked around to the front of his desk, eager to show me out. "I'm sorry I wasn't able to help you in this matter, but I hope you can put it all behind you. Look to the future, not the past."

He shook my hand firmly and pulled open the door to his office, wishing me the best as I walked out. I clutched the book to my chest as I left the building and stepped back into the car.

"Where to?" Hank asked.

"Home, I guess."

Disappointed and glum, I gazed out the window. The rain had let up at last, but the city seemed drained of all color. Men and women scurried along the sidewalks in dark coats and hats; the streets and houses were a blur of brown and beige and gray.

Suddenly, I saw something that made me shout out, "Stop!"

Hank pressed the brakes and pulled over.

"I won't be a minute," I said, so eager to get out that I opened the door myself. I rushed back toward a sign I'd spotted on a wide brick building: "Academy of Arts and Classics." Inside, there was a familiar smell of chalk dust and warm bodies confined together in small spaces. A dour-looking man in an old-fashioned black jacket and waistcoat peered out from a door labeled "Office." A schoolmaster, from the look of him.

"May I help you?" he asked. I could hear chanting from down the hall, dozens of children's voices reciting their multiplication tables.

"Can you read ancient Greek, by any chance?" I asked, followed by a flirtatious smile.

The man looked momentarily confused, then self-satisfied. "Yes."

"I wonder if you might help me." I pulled out the book and showed him the writing on the note. "What does this say?"

He uttered a few words of what sounded like gibberish, then added in English, "'Ever shall the wine of wisdom flow.' Plato, I believe. Or was it Aristophanes?"

"Thank you. Most obliged."

As I turned and hurried out, I heard him spluttering behind me, "Madam? Madam?"

Hank raised his eyebrows in a silent question when I arrived back at the car.

"No more stops," I said, suddenly exhausted. I sank into the backseat and tossed Dr. Rieger's book to the side. Why had I gotten my hopes up, thinking this would be the clue that solved the case? *The wine of wisdom.* What a lot of hooey. Wasn't the whole idea behind Prohibition that alcohol led to the very opposite of wisdom?

The dull, ashen lake seemed like the perfect reflection of my mood as we drove northward. Had I really wanted to know the truth about Cecily for Matthew's sake? Or had I simply wanted to get the upper hand on my mother-in-law by proving she'd been involved? It didn't matter anymore. Cecily was most likely a disturbed woman who ran away from home and died anonymous and alone. And I'd never be able to fix Matthew's broken heart.

As we drove beyond the city limits, through Evanston and Wilmette and Winnetka, the clouds miraculously thinned and faded, bathing trees and houses in a glow of late-afternoon sunlight. Tulips and irises and daffodils filled the well-tended flower beds of the North Shore, and my dreary mood began to lift. As we came up the front drive of Lakecrest, my heart didn't sink with the usual dread. I saw, for the first time, the building's peculiar charm, its potential for greatness. Take away the gargoyles and columns, make the doors and windows a uniform size, and it might even be beautiful.

Look to the future, Mr. Haveleck had urged. As I got out of the car, I gazed up at the words carved into the front archway. *Factum est.* Could it be done?

I'd hoped to get back before Hannah realized I was gone, but I wasn't that lucky. She was standing in the front hall when I stepped inside.

"Where have you been?" she demanded. Livid. "I've been worried sick!"

"I'm fine. I had to do a bit of shopping."

"I gave clear orders to Hank," she fumed. "He wasn't to drive you anywhere."

So that's why he'd been wary about taking me to Chicago. I felt a childish satisfaction that he'd disobeyed her.

"May I be excused to get ready for supper?" I asked. Sweet as pie.

Hannah nodded brusquely. "Matthew's taking the five-thirty train from Union Station. We'll be eating at seven."

Less than an hour before I'd have to face her again. At Marjorie and Matthew's insistence, Hannah had reluctantly agreed that formalwear was no longer necessary for family dinners, but I was still expected to change out of my day dress into something more appropriate for evening. Upstairs, I stripped down to my slip, then washed my face and hands in the bathroom. I pulled my makeup pouch out from a shelf in the cabinet, hoping a line of kohl around my eyes might distract from the bags underneath. Red lipstick, too, rather than my usual light pink, to show Hannah I wasn't cowed by her bullying. I reached toward the back of the shelf, searching for a particularly gaudy shade Marjorie had given me for Christmas.

I pulled out the slender gold tube, and a brown paper–wrapped package slid out alongside it. The package fell to the floor, flapping open on its way down, and a dozen flat white tablets scattered onto the floor.

Irritated, I scooped them up. The only benefit of pregnancy so far was that I no longer had to deal with this particular precaution, one I'd discovered in the *Family Limitation* pamphlet Blanche kept hidden underneath her mattress. She had blushingly admitted she'd bought a pessary, just in case, and I'd said who wanted to fuss with fitting it in the right spot when you could just stick a pill up there? Blanche thought sticking a pill *up there* couldn't possibly stop a baby, and I told her it looked easy—all you had to do was wait for it to dissolve and did whatever it did to the man's *you know*—and we'd doubled over giggling and thought ourselves very daring.

So much for my faith in modern methods.

I flushed the suppositories down the toilet, then picked up the wrapping. Something about the way the pills had fallen nagged at me, and I held up the paper, feeling at the edges. It had been new, unopened. Was it my imagination, or was the tape that held it together barely sticky? The usual label was attached from a small clinic in Chicago; Blanche had bought them for me so I'd be spared any gossip. The pills inside had looked the same as usual, but how could I be sure?

No method was foolproof. I knew that. But my thoughts raced on anyway, as I imagined how easy it would be to swap one white pill with another—especially if you had access to a factory that manufactured medicine.

I didn't have to fake my nausea when I called for Alice and said I wouldn't be down for supper. I scrubbed the kohl off my face and collapsed on the bed. Once the thought had lodged in my brain, it was impossible to think of anything else. *It wasn't an accident. Someone wanted me to get pregnant.*

There was a gentle knock at the door, and Matthew peeked inside. "Are you all right?" he asked.

"Tired," I said, which was true enough. I was tired of carrying around all this suspicion. All this fear.

"Can I bring you anything?"

I shook my head and turned away. Matthew slipped out and quietly closed the door behind him.

I was jumping to conclusions, presuming the worst. But I couldn't stop picturing the tape, the wrapping, the pills scattered across the floor. Matthew and I had never really discussed the measures I took to avoid a pregnancy; he left what he called "the arrangements" to me. But he was the only one who knew where I kept my supplies. And hadn't he been surprisingly happy about the baby? As if he'd wanted one all along.

By the time Matthew came back after supper, I was jittery with suspicion. When he asked how I was feeling, I threw the packaging toward him and demanded to know what he'd done. If he'd been so desperate for a child that he'd tricked me into getting pregnant.

"Do you really think I'd do that?" he asked. Wounded.

That was the problem. I wasn't sure.

"Tell me the truth," I said. "That's all I want."

Matthew hesitated, and I saw the two sides of my husband battle for control: gentle, kind Matthew, who wanted to protect me, and steely Mr. Lemont, who'd let me provoke him only so far.

"The truth," he said at last. "All right, then. I've put on a happy face for your sake, but I don't want this baby any more than you do. I was thrilled you agreed to put off having children. What's done is done, and we have to make the best of it. But there are times I dread becoming a father. What kind of parent do you think I'll be, when there are days I question my own sanity?"

Matthew looked at me warily. Bracing himself for my reaction. "There you have it," he said. "The truth."

I could have matched his honesty with my own, but I was more eager to place blame.

"Well, I can think of someone else who's desperate for a baby. Your mother."

"Every woman her age wants a grandchild! Honestly, Kate, you're being ridiculous."

Matthew pulled a cigarette from the silver case on his nightstand, lit it, and took in a slow, deep breath. He used to smoke only occasionally, but his habit had picked up since he was put in charge of Lemont Medical. The leisurely way he held the match, the drawn-out inhaling and exhaling—it all seemed calculated to distance himself from the conversation.

"Why shouldn't I think the worst of your mother?" I sniped. "She keeps her own daughter chained up in the basement!"

"Marjorie's better," he said. "Mum sent her off to the Kendricks' in Palm Beach."

"Oh really? Why should I believe you this time?"

"You don't understand." Matthew spoke slowly, as if lecturing a child. "You talk about my mother as if she's some sort of villain, when she's done everything she can to help Marjorie. And you."

"Oh yes, it's very clear she enjoys being in charge, which is why I don't put anything past her. She controls your life, and now she's trying to do the same to me!"

"You'd never manage here without her. Do you ever think how lucky you are? How many girls dream of living in a house like Lakecrest? You'd be serving drinks at the Pharaoh's Club if I hadn't married you!"

It stung. Exactly as Matthew had intended.

"I wish you'd stop smoking in the bedroom," I said, brushing the white puffs away from my face. "You know it makes me queasy."

Flopping down on the bed, Matthew sucked in another mouthful of smoke and blew it upward. I was losing his attention, losing him. He was retreating into the poised, detached shell that had become his second skin.

"I know I'm being ungrateful," I said. Not quite ready to touch him, I sat on the side of the bed, close enough for him to reach me, if he wanted. "I'm doing my best to get along with your mother. Honestly."

Matthew sat up, stubbed out his cigarette, and slid toward me. "Look at things from her side. I know she can be chilly, but she's kept this family and the company together. Without her, I don't know where we'd be."

"I wonder if Marjorie would agree."

"Marjorie's sick."

"Then she should have been sent to a hospital, not a cell in the basement."

Matthew sighed. "It's not that bad."

"How would you know? You weren't the one locked up there."

"I was. When I came back from France."

When Matthew had talked about being invalided out, I'd pictured him recovering at an expensive rest home, the kind of country place with a wraparound porch and views of nature. But, no. Matthew had been here, imprisoned in the basement of Lakecrest.

"It wasn't so terrible," Matthew said, seeing my stricken face. "I don't remember most of it, to tell you the truth. I came out all right, without making a public spectacle of myself."

"It didn't cure you, did it?"

"The doctor said I might never be cured. I'm better than I was. Perhaps that's the most I can hope for."

"I know about the clinic," I told him. Might as well get it out in the open; if I expected the truth from Matthew, I had to do the same for him. "Your visits to Dr. McNally."

"Who told you?"

I didn't want to make trouble for Hank. "I hired an investigator," I said. "He's the one who told me about the clinic."

"An investigator?" Matthew demanded. "Why in the world would you do that?"

"For your sake!" I shot back. "Because I was desperate to help you."

"You don't understand," Matthew said brusquely. "It's a business matter."

"Business?" I'd have been less surprised if he admitted Cecily was locked in the hospital's attic.

"We're testing out a formula," Matthew explained. "A treatment for nervous hysteria. It's made one woman's mania vanish almost entirely. Others carry on conversations, perfectly calm, when before they'd just babble . . . I've tried it, Kate. It works."

I realized with a start that it had been weeks since Matthew woke me in the middle of the night. I'd been so caught up in my own unhappiness that I'd entirely overlooked the fact that Matthew was sleeping peacefully for the first time in our married life.

"This medicine could be the making of Lemont Medical," Matthew said. "*That's* my terrible secret, Kate."

"I had no idea."

"No, you didn't, because this kind of thing must be kept completely confidential until we release our results. We can't risk our competitors finding out about it, and that means we're all bound to silence, even with our own families. I was going to tell you, as soon as I could, but instead you chose to snoop and spy. What did you do, go through my papers? Follow me to the clinic?"

"Of course not," I said. "It was my idea to go there to learn more about Dr. Rieger's work."

If I'd been less flustered, I might have come up with a better lie. Matthew stared at me, uncomprehending.

"Grandfather Rieger? Why are you interested in him?"

I didn't have an answer. Not one I wanted Matthew to hear.

"What happened, Kate?" he asked. Defeated. "Don't you trust me anymore?"

"What happened? I'm living in a house I hate with a mother-in-law who will never think I'm good enough for her son. I barely see my husband, who spends all his time at work but tells me nothing about it. I am constantly terrified of not living up to my new family's expectations. And I can't stop wondering what the Lemonts have done to make everyone talk about them so much!"

I could hear my voice, shrill and accusing, and I hated the sound of it. But I couldn't stop. "I'll tell you the real reason I went to the clinic. I thought I might find your aunt Cecily there."

The name struck Matthew like a curse. He stared at me, horrified.

"Isn't it possible your mother packed Cecily off to an institution? You said yourself she'd do whatever it took to save the Lemonts from scandal." The words were like a poison, my body expelling them against my will. "Hannah could have killed Cecily for all I know!"

"Kate!" Furious. "That's crazy!"

I remembered Marjorie's words: *We're all crazy. You'll go crazy, too.*

Ever since I'd gotten pregnant, emotions had bubbled up unpredictably, almost against my will. The self-control I'd spent years perfecting crumbled against the force of my anger. "Whatever happened to Cecily, she's lucky!" I shouted. "She made it out of this miserable house!"

"Stop it!"

Matthew lunged at me, grabbing my shoulders and squeezing until I winced. He leaned down, and his face came within inches of mine. His skin was taut with suppressed fury.

"You want honesty, Kate? I'll tell you something I've never told another living soul. Sometimes, in my dreams, I watch Aunt Cecily

bleed to death in front of me, and I look down and see my hands dripping red, and I know that I killed her. I feel the guilt of it, ripping me
apart."

His hands twisted into my hair and jerked my head back.

"If my mother's capable of murder, what about me?"

I whimpered, and Matthew let go. He stumbled backward and
sunk into an armchair. I could almost see the ferocity leave his body as
his shoulders slumped and his face fell into an expression of appalled
misery. I felt dizzy, bewildered.

"Kate . . . ," he began, weakly.

"Get out."

My heart pounded as Matthew stood and walked away. When his
hand reached for the door handle, I imagined the fingers coated in
blood. Had I heard a confession, disguised within a dream? Even after
the door closed firmly behind him, fear tingled along my skin like an
electric current. I was frightened of Matthew, frightened of Hannah,
and frightened of what Lakecrest was doing to me. The leaks and smells,
the eerie creaking that kept me awake at night—they were all meant
to torment me, just as memories of Cecily twisted my husband into
someone I barely recognized.

The bedroom that had once been my haven suddenly felt like a
trap. Was it possible our voices had carried down a hidden pipe in the
walls? That Hannah might have overheard us? *Ridiculous,* I told myself.
Yet I felt shaky and unsteady. If I stayed in this house, I might disappear,
too. I needed to clean Lakecrest's musty odor off my body, to think in
peace without jumping at every strange sound. And there was only one
place I could think to go, only one place Hannah wouldn't be able to
track me down.

Home.

With fumbling fingers, I packed a bag. I slid *The Ways of Madness*
into a side pocket, along with a copy of the *Chicago Literary Review*

I'd ordered from the magazine's offices; Ma would have something to say about Cecily's strange obsessions. I tiptoed down the hallway and back staircase and out a side door, and hurried along the curved drive. I was already on Deertrail Road, making my way to the East Ridge station, when I realized I couldn't catch a train because I had no money. Everything I bought when I went shopping was charged to the Lemonts' account, and I never had to pay for taxis or bus fare.

Though I was richer than I'd ever been, I didn't have a penny to show for it.

I could sneak back into the house; most likely, Matthew and Hannah hadn't even noticed I'd left. But the thought of returning made me feel sick. The baby squirmed inside my stomach, urging me forward. I looked along the dark road ahead. Only one light shone in the distance, from the porte cochere of the Monroes' house.

Eva and I had never shared more than polite conversation; we were more acquaintances than friends. But something told me she'd be sympathetic. Her marriage, from what I could tell, was not a particularly happy one. She might understand how it felt to have a terrible fight with your husband. She might even lend me the money to get home.

I knocked on the door, worried I'd cause a stir by arriving so late. To my relief, Eva was the one who answered and let me in. She looked at me, surprised and concerned, and I tried to explain what had happened, but all that came out were sobs. She took my bag and wrapped her arms around me in a tight hug. I was dimly aware of hovering figures around us—servants she whispered orders to as I let out all my fear and frustration and pain. Once I'd gained control of myself, she led me upstairs to a guest room, a feminine oasis of pink and white, and insisted I stay the night. I still hadn't told her what Matthew and I had fought about, and she hadn't asked.

"Should I call Lakecrest?" she asked. "Let them know you're here?"

I shook my head. "No. Please. I need some time on my own to sort things out."

"Can I get you something to eat? Soup?"

Eva gave me a sympathetic smile, and for a moment I thought she was going to tuck me into bed. I'd mocked her obsession with motherhood, but now I realized how lucky her children were to have her. How would I have turned out, if Ma had had half of Eva's warmth?

"I'm not hungry," I said, "but would it be all right if I sent a telegram?"

Eva looked surprised, but said she'd get me the number for Western Union. The message I dictated from the hallway telephone—and charged to the Lemont account—was short and to the point.

COMING TO VISIT. ARRIVE TOMORROW NIGHT.

Though I was mentally and physically exhausted, I couldn't settle down, even after changing into my nightgown and washing my face with the warm water a maid brought in a basin. I slipped between the flannel sheets and flipped open the magazine I'd ordered, the one that contained the story that wasn't in Cecily's book. It had arrived in the mail that morning, but I hadn't had a chance to read it yet.

As I began the tale, it felt as if Cecily herself was whispering in my ear.

ARTEMIS AND ACTAEON

BY CECILY LEMONT

There once lived a brother and a sister, two blessed children of the god-king Zeus. The boy, Apollo, was bold and golden as sunlight, his perfect features and imposing stature a model for male perfection. His sister, Artemis, was no less lovely, but her beauty was cloaked in modesty, hidden by her own reticence. When they were young, they were so close they shared the same soul, the same heartbeat. But time steered them along different paths, leading Apollo into the world and Artemis away from it.

Artemis chose the male arts of hunting and warfare over those deemed suitable for womankind. She learned to carve wooden swords and sharpen spears and how to follow tracks through dense woods and open fields. She spent countless hours with bow pulled taut, waiting for the moment to let her arrow fly. Her hands had none of the qualities praised in a woman; they were not soft or fragile or kind. Artemis's hands hauled dead rabbits and skinned deer; they were calloused and rough and nearly as strong as her will and her heart, a heart that softened only for Apollo, the one person she loved without reservation.

As Artemis aged from girl to woman, her freedom grew ever more constrained. Where once she had hours to wander the forest in peace, she was now urged to stay inside, to be watched over rather than the one who watched. On rare visits to the wilderness she loved, branches ripped her silk gowns and her sandals slid in the mud. All she had trained for threatened to be snatched away forever.

Artemis sought out her father and threw herself at his feet, a humbling posture for such a proud daughter. She begged Zeus to grant her the life she longed for: the life of a huntress free to explore in peace. She did not crave glory or gold. No, she would be content as a goddess of the shadows.

"Such a wish can be granted," Zeus told her, "but you will pay a heavy price. In exchange for your freedom, you must vow to remain a maiden of pure virtue. You will never marry, never feel a man's touch. You will renounce, forever, any chance at love."

Artemis agreed. She forswore the palaces of the gods and lived off the land, content with the earth's riches. She dressed for ease, not the eyes of others, in a leather tunic and thick-soled, sturdy boots. She was joined in her travels by a faithful band of fellow virgins, all sworn to protect each other's honor in a fellowship of trust. It was an idyllic life, until one man nearly destroyed it.

Actaeon was a hunter—some said the greatest of them all. As tales of his exploits spread, he dared boast he was better than Artemis. When such whispers reached her ears, Artemis did not refute them; better she remain an unseen threat than a face-to-face rival. Silently, she tracked Actaeon's whereabouts and shadowed him as he stalked a boar. She saw the attributes that made other women swoon: the arms strengthened by bouts with wild animals and the proud strut that signaled mastery. But Artemis was never one to lose herself in a man's looks. Her only male companion, Apollo, was the epitome of male beauty. How could any other man compare?

No, it was Actaeon's skill she admired. He brought his dagger down with such precise aim that the boar was felled with a single blow. She wondered what it would be like to hunt alongside such a man rather than hide from him, to have a partner who matched her own talents. But she kept her distance. Not knowing was the price of the life she led.

As she stole away, Artemis's thoughts were so caught up in Actaeon that she made a fatal mistake. For once, she did not focus all her senses on her surroundings, and she did not notice that Actaeon had begun tracking her. He followed her deep into the forest, eager for a glimpse of the mysterious huntress at work. He heard voices, laughter, and the splash of water. Carefully, silently, he slipped forward and stole a glance from between the trees. There, he beheld an amazing sight: Artemis, naked, bathing in a secluded pond. Actaeon was instantly, tragically entranced. For the mighty huntress who could kill with her bare hands was also a goddess, the sister of Apollo, and her loveliness was a wonder to behold. Actaeon gasped, and the sound froze Artemis with horror.

Shame, dark and fierce, swept over her, and any pleasure she might have taken in Actaeon's admiration was quickly smothered by fury. So quickly it appeared but an instant, Artemis's handmaidens covered her nakedness and stood at the ready with bows and arrows in hand.

Weaponless, but no less fearsome, Artemis called on all her divine powers and cursed Actaeon for looking upon what no man should see. With one enraged glare, he was transformed into a stag. Horrified, Actaeon stared at his reflection in the water. The boastful hunter had become a beast. He turned and ran, leaping around the trees in search of escape, but all too soon he heard the zealous barking of his own hounds, set upon his scent. They raced after him, hungry for such a prize and well trained by the man they chased. They nipped at his legs, then leapt up and sank their teeth into his flesh. Actaeon fell and was torn apart by his most faithful companions.

With his last breaths, he felt the torment he'd brought upon so many other creatures.

Artemis stood over the bloody remains of the man who'd come close to stealing her prized innocence. She looked up and saw her brother beside her. He had come to offer the rescue she did not need.

"Let this death be a lesson to all," Artemis vowed. "The rage of a woman shamed shall know no bounds."

Apollo stared at his sister, the quiet girl who had begged to join his excursions and listened obediently to his pronouncements. For the first time, he saw the powers of destruction at her command, and he did not know whether to be frightened or proud of the woman she had become.

I remembered that Cecily called Matthew and Marjorie the divine twins, but they hadn't even been born when she wrote this story. Had Cecily imagined herself as the virgin huntress, content in her solitude? Was Jasper the brother, horrified by his sister's brutal powers?

I shut the magazine and turned off the light. Eventually, I drifted into a dream where I was running through a forest, chased by howling creatures I couldn't see. Ahead was a clearing. Safety. In a swirl of color and sensation, I saw chunks of flesh spread across the grass, the rotting remains of a bearded man. Obadiah? A sticky layer of blood pressed against my bare feet. The screams rang out again, and I realized with a sudden, sick certainty that it wasn't wolves or dogs. It was a horde of women, coming for me.

I woke with a start, heart pounding. Light poured through the windows; I'd forgotten to pull the drapes the night before. I heard distant footsteps, children chattering. Hurriedly, I got dressed and smoothed my hair. If I caught one of the morning trains from Union Station, I'd get to Cleveland before dark.

"Eva!" I called out from the top of the stairs. No answer. I walked down, into the deserted foyer, and followed the sound of voices toward the back of the house. Peering through the doorway of a large sitting room, I saw Eva on a couch, holding her littlest in her lap. One of the other children was running back and forth with a rubber ball. Eva saw me and stood, shifting the baby to her hip. Her eyes darted toward the part of the room out of my view.

I hadn't realized until then that she had a guest. Hannah.

CHAPTER ELEVEN

"Come along," Eva said, shooing her children out. As she passed me, she murmured, "I had to call. I knew they'd be worried."

It was jarring to see Hannah amid the hobbyhorses and wooden blocks, all the messy trappings of family life that would soon be mine.

"Time to get you home, Kate," she said coldly. "Matthew's very upset."

She said nothing else. Not when I left to gather my things or when I gave Eva a sullen good-bye or when I stepped into the car. Hank kept his face toward the windshield; there'd be no friendly greetings today. It wasn't until we arrived back at Lakecrest that Hannah finally spoke.

"Matthew's in the morning room."

I'd braced myself for a lecture, even a full dressing-down. But Hannah marched up the stairs, leaving me to face Matthew alone.

He'd made an effort to pull himself together. He was wearing one of his immaculately tailored suits, and his hair was smooth with pomade. But his matinee-idol features sagged with exhaustion, and his eyes, which I'd last seen wild with fury, looked at me with almost tearful relief.

"Kate."

I hesitated, but Matthew didn't. He practically fell forward, capturing me in his arms, pressing me close, and dropping his head into the curve of my neck. He pulled me toward a love seat so we sat side by side.

Matthew squeezed my hand. "I'm glad you're all right. I was so afraid."

Guilt made my response sharper that it should have been. "I should have left a note." A pause. "I didn't know what to say."

"It's all right. I figured I'd lay low and sleep in one of the guest rooms. But I tossed and turned, and when I came to check on you, I realized the bed hadn't been slept in. We've been searching the house and grounds all night."

Just like when Cecily disappeared. It had never occurred to me how terrible it would be for Matthew to go through that again.

"Thank God Eva rang this morning," Matthew said. "Not that I blame you for leaving, after what I said."

What I said. The cautious man beside me didn't seem capable of raising a hand in anger to anyone, let alone killing the aunt he loved. But what he told me would have to be addressed somehow if our marriage was going to survive.

Matthew clutched my knee, reassuring himself that I was really there. "I have a proposition. Since you've already got your bag packed, why don't we get away for a bit? We can stay at the apartment downtown. See a show, take Blanche and Billy out for dinner—whatever you want."

"What about work?"

"I've already canceled my meetings. I'm yours through the weekend."

His hand brushed my cheek, and my apprehension melted. When was the last time Matthew and I had fun together? The last time I felt young?

Matthew reached out, carefully, and patted me on the stomach. It was that touch, more than anything he said, that made me believe in him. In us. From the day I'd found out I was pregnant, I'd thought of the baby as a burden. Now, for the first time, I allowed myself to picture the child who would be born in four months. Would it be a daughter for Matthew to spoil? A son he'd one day send off to Yale? The thought of Matthew holding a baby—our baby—filled me with a sudden, sharp ache, and I surprised us both by bursting into happy tears.

I told Matthew I looked ridiculous, stepping out around town with a belly that bulged against my dress. He laughed and said I was more beautiful than ever, and strangely enough, I believed him. Though I felt pudgy and clumsy, I giggled my way across the dance floor at the Pharaoh's Club with Matthew holding me firmly in his arms. We drank gin fizzes with Blanche and waved to Billy in the band. All around us, it seemed, people were talking fast and walking even faster, living at a pace I'd long since left behind. I tried to put on an air of nonchalant elegance by smoking a cigarette through a holder, and when I gave up, coughing, Matthew kissed me, breathing in the smoke from my mouth to his.

"Don't try to be Theda Bara," he said with a grin. "I like you as you are."

We stumbled back to the apartment, giddy with alcohol and laughter, kissing in the elevator and pulling off each other's clothes in the hall. My skin warmed as Matthew's hands ran over my slip, but I started feeling self-conscious when his fingers wandered underneath, along my swollen stomach. Ever since the baby, he'd been careful how he touched me, as if I were a fragile piece of china, and I wished we could get back to how it used to be, without that barrier between us.

I kissed Matthew's neck, then pressed my teeth against his skin and grabbed the hair at the back of his head. He gave me a mischievous look.

"Feeling naughty?" he asked.

"Very."

With a tantalizing smile, Matthew threw one arm around my back and the other under my knees. He lifted me up and began carrying me to the bedroom, but I shook my head and whispered, "The sofa."

Our next kisses were harder, rougher. His hands pushed and pulled as I egged him on with suggestive whispers. Matthew's unpredictability had often left me scared and confused, but that night, I finally understood I'd always been attracted to the danger beneath his calm surface. It was what had intrigued me about him from the very beginning. The terrible things we'd said to each other weren't forgotten, but they no longer mattered. I was swept up in the sensation of Matthew's hands and mouth on my skin, and I didn't want it to stop.

Curled up afterward in bed, Matthew began apologizing again, and I told him not to worry.

"Your dreams are just that. Dreams. I know you wouldn't hurt Cecily." Gently, I ran my lips along the rise of his collarbone. "Or me."

Relief loosened the muscles in his shoulders and neck. "It's so hard to explain what it's like, to wake up and not know what's real." His hand rounded the curves of my shoulder, my waist, my hip. "It's more frightening than the dreams, sometimes. But when I see you, I know I'm safe. It makes me love you even more."

"I don't want to lose this feeling," I said. "You and me, together."

"Me neither."

Matthew flashed one of his dazzling smiles. The kind that would have tempted me to kiss him if I hadn't been so intent on what I wanted to say.

"Do you promise we'll always come first with each other? I'll do my best to get along better with your mother, but if she keeps bossing me around, I want to know you'll take my side."

Matthew nodded. "I will."

"Lakecrest's part of the problem, too. You know it is. It's your home, but it's never felt like mine."

"Well, how about we bring the place into the twentieth century? Buy some new furniture, fix up our room however you like. Would that help?"

"It might."

"Marjorie will have some ideas. She has quite an eye."

Of course, I thought. *Something else she's good at.* Matthew must have sensed my irritation, because he propped himself up on one arm and looked at me intently.

"About my sister," he said. "Don't judge her too harshly. We used to be inseparable, and it's been hard for her since I married. If only she'd find a nice fellow to settle down with . . ."

I remembered what Marjorie had told me in the Labyrinth: *Sometimes it felt like I could read Matts's mind.* The wistful way she'd said it.

Matthew wrapped his arm around my shoulders and squeezed.

"You remember our wedding vows? For better or for worse? Well, we've gotten through the worse. When I think how terrified I was to tell you the truth about my dreams, all that skulking around to the clinic—God, it's wonderful to be past it all. To know we can be completely honest with each other."

He ruffled my hair with his fingers and pulled me close for a deep, lingering kiss. With a sudden twist in my chest, I realized I loved him—really loved him, with a deep, unshakeable certainty. Whatever Matthew had done, whatever his weaknesses, I wanted to live with him, raise children with him, grow old by his side. And I could lose it all, forever, if I gave him what he wanted. Total honesty would mean telling him the one thing guaranteed to shatter his trust, that I was no better than all the other girls who set out to catch Matthew Lemont. It didn't matter that my feelings for him had changed; he would never forgive the betrayal. I buried my face in Matthew's chest, afraid he'd see the regret etched across my face.

"Don't go to sleep just yet," he said, nudging me gently in the ribs. "There's something I need to tell you."

I turned to face him, forcing what I hoped was a convincing smile.

"Redecorate all you want. See if it helps. After the baby's here, if you're still miserable at Lakecrest, we'll move. Buy our own house."

"Really? What about your mother?"

"It's not her decision. From now on, you come first."

I didn't have to fake a smile this time. "I'm the luckiest woman in the world."

And I meant it.

—

Our lovestruck mood lingered after we returned to Lakecrest, but I should have known I couldn't escape my past forever. A few weeks later, as I sat on the terrace reading a magazine, I heard a distinctive voice drift out from the conservatory.

"Lemonade! Divine!"

Ma always did have a mouth on her.

Matthew, who'd been fiddling with a puzzle next to me, popped up his head and looked at me expectantly. "Surprise!" he said.

I was shocked and furious, in equal measure. Before I could say a word, there was my mother, done up in an enormous hat and a gaudy floral dress, grinning at me like a gambler who's won the pot. Marjorie and Hannah stood close behind, their expressions unreadable.

Matthew took charge, and thank God. I could barely think where to start.

"Mrs. Moore, such a pleasure to meet you at last. Looks like our little scheme was successful—Kate had no idea you were coming!"

"Aren't you a trickster," Ma gushed. "I can't tell you how happy I am to be here." She squeezed his hand, then turned to me.

"Look at you!" She threw her arms around me and let out a sound that was half sob, half giggle. "My little mama-to-be!"

"It's good to see you," I managed, as I extracted myself from her embrace. She felt and looked healthily plump, hardly the invalid I'd made her out to be. "I hope you're feeling better? After being sick for so long?"

"What a trial, you can't imagine," she said. "I prayed for deliverance, and what do you know? I feel *quite* healed. Oh my heavens, look at this view! Right to the water!"

"Please, sit down, Mrs. Moore," Matthew said.

"It's Mary to you, dear. I already think of you as my own son."

Looking irritatingly self-satisfied, she told me how Matthew and she had arranged the visit in secret. As if I'd find it charming. I knew the real reason she hadn't told me she was coming: she knew I'd find a way to stop her.

Gerta came in with a pitcher of lemonade and a platter of tea cakes. Ma took four and began popping them in her mouth whole. Hannah allowed herself a brief scowl of disapproval, and Marjorie, amused, leaned forward.

"Is this your first visit to Chicago?" she asked.

"Yes, it is. My responsibilities to the Fosters leave precious little time for travel."

"The Fosters?" Marjorie asked.

"Mr. Joseph Foster, my employer, and his widowed mother."

There was a long, uncomfortable silence. Hannah looked as if she felt sick. Ma, with her usual disregard for social graces, went on to make things worse. "I do appreciate the money you've sent, but it's not enough for a poor widow to build up a nest egg. Besides, the Fosters are practically family. The old dear depends on me utterly."

How proud she looked, how unaware of the Lemonts' disdain. It was one thing for Matthew to marry a girl with no money, but quite another for her mother to still be working as a servant. If only they knew the rest of the story: that Ma shared Mr. Foster's bed. That she was hoping he'd marry her after the death of his mother (the "old dear" she usually referred to as the "old bitch").

To my enormous relief, Alice stepped into the room and asked to speak to Hannah. I took the interruption as an opportunity to change the subject and began asking Ma about her trip. Not long after, Hannah came over, looking concerned.

"There seems to have been a mix-up at the station," she said. "The trunk your mother brought is labeled O'Meara, not Moore."

Ma raised her eyebrows at me: *Shall I handle this, or you?* I felt my face flush.

"It's my trunk, all right," Ma said, perfectly serene. "O'Meara was my married name, but I don't need to tell you how some people can be close-minded when it comes to the Irish. As soon as my Katie started school, I changed our name to Moore. I didn't want anyone to think she was good for nothing more than scrubbing floors or taking in laundry."

And just like that, a subject I'd avoided and fretted over—my real name—was dealt with and discarded. Swiftly, expertly, Ma chattered on about her struggles to raise an honest girl in an evil world. It was all so noble and inspiring that she even managed to dredge up a few genuine tears.

"She's a good girl, my Katie." A sentimental shake of her head, a dreamy-eyed expression. "One in a million."

"That's exactly how I feel," Matthew said.

Ma's story was a pack of lies, but I realized with a jolt that her feelings were real. I *was* the culmination of all her dreams. Matthew looked at me adoringly: his charity project, the deserving youngster he had saved from poverty. Marrying me made him feel like a better man.

"It's lovely to see how much pride you take in your daughter," Marjorie said. "So many children are a great disappointment to their parents."

Ma was the only one who didn't notice the sly insult to Hannah. "Oh, I've known Katie was special ever since she was a little girl. That's why I scrimped and saved to send her to St. Anne's. Get her mixing with the right people. At college, she was rushed by all the best sororities."

"Mother, please . . ."

"Had her choice of dates to the dances," Ma went on, oblivious to my embarrassment. "We had some good laughs about it, didn't we, Katie? Who'd have believed my little angel would be courted by someone like Randall Bigelow?"

No, no, I had to make her stop. But how, when I felt too nauseous to speak? Hannah looked thoughtful, as if she were trying to place the name. Maybe she knew his family. All rich people met eventually, at one summer resort or another.

"Randall Bigelow?" Matthew asked me with a grin. "Should I be jealous?"

I took a deep breath, calmed my breathing. "You can't expect me to keep all my admirers straight," I said lightly. "There were too many to count!"

Matthew laughed along with me, and even Marjorie joined in. Not Hannah. She knew something was wrong.

"What room will Mother be staying in?" I asked her.

"The Yellow Room."

"You'll love it," I said, grabbing Ma's hand. "Why don't I take you up and show you around?"

Ma followed eagerly; I knew she was dying to get a look at the rest of the house. I waited until we were upstairs, with the door closed, before letting loose.

"What were you thinking, coming here with no warning?"

Ma pretended to look contrite. "It was Matthew's idea. He sent the money for my fare and begged me to come. He said you needed cheering up, though I can't imagine why."

I sat down on the bed and ran my palms over the silk coverlet. I tried to see Lakecrest through Ma's eyes. How all this luxury must dazzle her! No wonder she was confused by my unhappiness.

So I laid it all out, telling her about Hannah's suspicious watchfulness and Marjorie's jealousy, about Cecily and the strange hold she still had over the family. How every time Hannah smiled at me, I worried she was planning to drive Matthew and me apart.

"Good gracious." Ma had never been one for cuddles and sweet talk; life had wrung her dry of sentiment. "So what if you've got a bossy mother-in-law and live in a house you don't like? Half the women in America are in the same boat!"

"It's more than that," I said. "It's Matthew. He has terrible dreams, where he sees himself killing Cecily. I don't think he hurt her—I truly don't—but still, it scares me. There's something wrong with him, and I can't fix it."

"Since when has a woman ever been able to fix a man?"

I could tell by the way Ma stared at me, fierce and direct, that she was talking about my father. About herself. We'd never really talked about that night in our run-down tenement, about the knife she'd plunged into Binny O'Meara's stomach. I'd never dared ask.

"Most women get worn down by beatings," she continued. "They lose their fight. You and me, we're different. Your father did his best to crush my spirit, but he couldn't. He pushed and he pushed, and in the end . . . I cracked."

Ma shrugged, as if she were admitting to a minor lapse that shouldn't be held against her. "The judge sent me to the asylum rather than having me hanged for murder, because people lined up to testify about your father's rages. Not one of them faulted me for what I did.

"Your Matthew, now . . . I'll admit I hardly know him. But it's plain as the nose on my face that he adores you, and *your* misery is making *him* miserable. He doesn't hit you, does he?"

I remembered Matthew's twisted face as he thrashed against me in bed. His wild eyes as he wrapped his fingers around my neck. I shook my head. The creature who hurt me wasn't Matthew.

"Then what in the world's got you so spooked?" Ma asked.

"The Lemonts have this motto, 'It is done.' It means they always get their way. Hannah looks at me sometimes like she's biding her time until the baby comes, but after that, who knows? They have this cell in the basement, and she could lock me up, anytime, without anyone knowing. She's got all sorts of doctors in her pocket who could declare me crazy and clear the way for a divorce."

Ma blew out a breath. Her body looked as tough and resilient as ever, but her face had a resigned weariness that was new. She'd expected to be married by now, living off the Fosters' money. But old Mrs. Foster was still alive, Mr. Foster kept up his excuses, and here Ma sat, without a ring on her chapped hands.

All I needed was reassurance. Understanding. Until I realized my mother had none to give.

"It's the pregnancy that's got you thinking so strange," she said. "Once you've got that baby in your arms, you'll see. All these worries will go away."

Ma didn't want to hear I was unhappy, because it went against everything she'd raised me to believe: a good-looking husband plus a pile of money equals a perfect life. Even if it wasn't true, I'd damned well better act like it was. The feelings I'd poured out scattered and evaporated. There would be no more confessions, not to her.

"We'd better set down the terms of your visit," I said, all brisk practicality. "How long are you staying?"

"Matthew suggested a week," Ma said. Her eyes were asking me for more.

"A week," I agreed. "But only if you're on your best behavior. If I hear one more word about Randall, you'll be on the first train home."

"I'm sorry. I wasn't thinking."

"No, you weren't."

"No harm done, though?"

I thought of Hannah, following the conversation like a huntress who's caught a glimpse of her prey. Was I safe? I'd tried so hard to forget what happened, but Randall would always be there, haunting my past. A reminder of the time I, too, had cracked.

⌇

I'd enrolled at the Teachers' College of Ohio, but unofficially I studied the fraternity boys at Ohio State, deciding which of them would be my future husband.

There were a few who said they loved me, and one who insisted on introducing me to his mother. But none were quite good enough. I held out for better, and it all paid off when Randall Bigelow asked me to the Alpha Delta dance at the beginning of my senior year. Randall was flashy and funny, and it didn't take much effort to stare at him adoringly. I knew right away he was the one. His father owned hotels all over the state, and the family was flush with money. There was a flurry of proposals in the spring before graduation, and I figured I'd be next.

What I didn't know was that Mr. Foster, a traveling salesman, liked to stay at the Bigelow family's hotels and had struck up a friendship with Randall's father. At some point, with Randall and me all but engaged and Mr. Bigelow boasting about the sweet young girl from Cleveland who was likely to be his new daughter-in-law, my name was mentioned. And Mr. Foster recognized it, right away. Ma always did love to brag about me.

I don't know exactly what Mr. Foster told Mr. Bigelow or what Mr. Bigelow told his son. I only know it was enough to send Randall barging into my dormitory, raging drunk, at three o'clock in the afternoon. I'd never seen him blotto, but he was grinning in a way that didn't look happy as he flung open the door and stood there, hands pressed against either side of the doorframe. Swaying.

"Kate, Kate," he murmured, and I didn't say anything, not even when he came inside and closed the door behind him.

He did the talking, and he had plenty to say, about my mother and her whoring and whether I, too, was a whore. I saw very quickly that everything hung in the balance. I could be a good girl and kick him out and accept it was over. Or I could make one last-ditch effort to keep him. Maybe my father's blood rose up in me at last, because I decided to take a gamble. I blinked up some tears, threw myself into Randall's arms, and told him it shouldn't matter. Not when I loved him with my whole heart. I'd show him how much I loved him, I said, and he couldn't have hated me too much, because he sure was eager to get his hands up my skirt.

It all moved much faster than I'd expected. From what I'd heard from under the table in our apartment, Ma put on more of a show. With Randall and me, there were a few minutes of groping and some clumsy adjustments of arms and legs as we fell back onto my bed.

Randall unbuttoned his trousers—he didn't even push them down off his hips—and then he was on top of me, shoving my knickers to the side.

I let my muscles go loose, and Randall murmured, "Good girl."

It was the only thing he said, other than a few grunts as he thrust into me. It hurt, as I expected it would, but not nearly as much as the thought of having to start all over with a new fellow. I thought I'd done the right thing.

When he was done, Randall rolled off and straightened his clothes without looking at me. Was that when I knew? Or was it when I said his name and he shook his head in disgust? In a matter of seconds, I lurched from relief to panic. Randall's shifty eyes, his hurry to get out—I knew what it meant. His words only made it official.

"I was right. You are a whore."

At least my mother got paid, I thought, the words jabbing like a dagger. *You got what you wanted for free.*

I'd always prided myself on being smart. Good at schoolwork, but also good at knowing which way the wind was blowing, which way to shift when disaster loomed. I looked at Randall's smug face, and hate welled up like a fever, goading me into action. My arm shot up, and I clawed at his cheek, my nails ripping into his skin. Then I started screaming.

The commotion attracted a few girls from down the hall, the ones who'd pretended not to notice when Randall came into my room. The housemother was there a minute later. Randall gasped and clutched his bleeding face as I told the story of his vicious attack and how I'd only just managed to fight him off. I cried on my next-door neighbor's shoulder so I wouldn't have to watch Mrs. Llewellyn march Randall out.

I never saw him again.

Rules were rules. I was reprimanded for allowing a man in my room and lost my evening passes for a month. An example had to be made for the other girls, Mrs. Llewellyn said. Later, she told me she'd decided not to report Randall to his fraternity or the university—better to keep things quiet, for both our sakes. I'd made a mistake letting him in, he'd made a mistake getting drunk and "frisky" (her word), and I'd taught him a well-deserved lesson. It was all best forgotten, with only two months left until I graduated.

It wasn't enough time to land myself a new husband. Once I left school, I had to start over from scratch.

I wondered where I'd be now if I'd put my mind to teaching. Really worked at it. But I hadn't. Ma had set me on my course, and I'd stuck to it. But I'd never forgotten Randall's face when he looked at me as if I were a piece of trash. I couldn't risk Ma slipping up and saying too much about her past or mine. It would destroy me to see that same look on Matthew's face. To know that love could turn so quickly to hate.

CHAPTER TWELVE

Ma was on her best behavior during the rest of her stay, charming Matthew with her salt-of-the-earth, plain-talking style. I'd never seen him laugh with such genuine warmth. When Hank pulled up the front drive on her last day, Matthew looked genuinely sorry to see her go.

"Mary, there's something I'd like you to have," he said, pressing an envelope into her hands. "This should be enough to set you up in your own place, and I've made arrangements with the First Bank of Cleveland so you'll have a regular monthly income. I don't want you to worry about money ever again."

Ma looked ready to choke up. She grabbed Matthew's arm and pulled him close so she could kiss him on the cheek.

"You're a blessing and a saint. A dear, dear boy, and I couldn't be prouder to call you my son."

I rode with Ma to the East Ridge station and sat with her on a trackside bench while we waited for the train to arrive. Ma was still clutching the envelope, like she couldn't believe it was real unless she had it in her hands.

"Did you put Matthew up to this?" she asked.

"It was all his idea," I said. "But I agreed, wholeheartedly. You can't stay at the Fosters' anymore."

"I always thought he'd make an honest woman of me, one day."

"Well, he hasn't."

It came out more harshly than I'd intended, but it was well past time she faced reality. "Everything you do reflects on me and the whole Lemont family. You've got to keep your nose clean and stay out of trouble."

Ma smirked, and I could tell she was considering a snappy comeback, something about trouble finding her no matter what. I glared at her and then at the people who'd begun to crowd around us as the train pulled in.

"This might be just the push Mr. Foster needs," she said. "Once I'm no longer under his roof, he'll stop taking me for granted. I wouldn't be surprised if we're married by Christmas."

Poor old Ma, still hoping a man would rescue her, too. We stood, and she gave me a fierce hug. "The next time I see you, I'll be a grandmother!"

I thought with a pang of everything Ma had done, raising me on her own. I'd have nurses tending to my baby day and night. I'd never have to feed my own child or wash out a filthy diaper or worry where the next dollar was coming from. Ma had done her best, and I found—to my surprise—that I was going to miss her. Her matter-of-factness and common sense had been an antidote to all my vague suspicions.

Which isn't to say a certain weight wasn't lifted from my shoulders as Hank drove me back to the house. I'd spent days on edge, bracing myself for Ma to make a crude joke or otherwise embarrass me. Now, it felt as if I'd been set free. It was May, four months until the baby was due. Four glorious months I'd be excused from boring social obligations, and I intended to enjoy them.

The Lemonts were always saying Lakecrest was at its best come summer, and finally I understood why. Outside, the landscape beckoned:

the blue of the lake, the plush green of the lawn, a rainbow's worth of flowers blooming across the estate. Sure, I slowed down as my belly filled out; I got tired more easily and took to lounging on the terrace rather than walking along the lakefront path. But my fears about spooky old Lakecrest seemed like a distant memory, especially with Hannah bending over backward to keep me happy.

Hannah and I never talked about my escape to Eva's, just as Marjorie and I never talked about what I'd seen beneath the library. Hannah's unorthodox cure appeared to have worked; Marjorie seemed calm and good humored, and she only rarely poured drinks from the silver flasks she had stashed around the house. She spent most mornings at the East Ridge Tennis Club ("The pro's a real looker," she told me with a grin) and afternoons at one private beach or another with what she referred to as "the usual crowd." Though Hannah was always telling her to wear a hat, Marjorie's face soon had a burnished glow that made her hair look even more golden in contrast.

There were tiny warnings that life at Lakecrest wasn't as idyllic as it seemed, things that formed an ominous pattern only when I examined them later. Marjorie whispering intently to Matthew on the yacht when she thought I was below deck. Telegrams Hannah would read with a concerned frown and immediately rip into pieces. Matthew's evasions when I asked to take a Sunday drive to look at houses for sale.

"Plenty of time for that later," he'd say, or, "Let's not get ahead of ourselves."

I didn't push. As the pregnancy soothed me into a state of contented lethargy, I slept late, took afternoon naps, and browsed through books I couldn't seem to finish. What little energy I had was focused on the summer fête at the end of July. This was the event the Lemonts were known for, and I decided to embrace a public role in it, despite my condition and Hannah's objections. I insisted my name be added to the invitations as cohostess, spent hours sketching designs for a new dress, discussed the menu with Edna, and memorized the family tree of every Chicago socialite on the guest list. When I'd come to the party last summer, I'd been a nobody, underestimated and ignored. This time would be different.

I remembered Ma's stories of the boat trip from Ireland when she was a girl, how she believed that in America people could create their own destinies. I thought of Blanche, a small-town girl putting all her hopes in big-city dreams. Of Hannah, a doctor's daughter who married one of the richest men in town. They'd all invented new versions of themselves—why couldn't I? The Lemonts' fête would be the debut of a new, sophisticated version of Kate Lemont, the kind of wife no one would look down on.

I was nervous on the day itself, of course, and self-conscious about my size and whether I looked ridiculous in my lilac cotton dress. But it wasn't long before I was showered with unexpected—but very welcome—expressions of goodwill. Guests smiled at my round belly and gave me congratulatory hugs. Elderly neighbors cooed over me, Matthew's friends joked about whether I trusted him to hold a new-born, and elegant young mothers commiserated about swollen feet and backaches. "Poor thing," I heard one of Marjorie's friends whisper as I walked past, but she said it with an air of kindly concern rather than disdain. A vast improvement on how I'd been treated before.

"Will you be having the baby at home?" Eva asked as I mingled on the terrace. "I imagine the Lemonts are very traditional that way."

"Oh no," I said. "Lake Forest Hospital."

"Thank goodness!" Eva's sister Violet—tiny, reddish blonde, peppy—was visiting from New York. Her eyes crinkled as she smiled. "I don't know what I would have done without ether when I had my Gracie."

"Make sure you have a modern doctor," urged another woman. Lois? Yes, that was it. The wife of one of Matthew's friends from Yale. "Some of the older ones still think childbirth is supposed to be painful. Our punishment for Eve's original sin and all that."

"As if we don't endure enough as it is!" Violet said. "It took Eva nearly two days with Tommy, isn't that right?"

Eva nodded solemnly. "I was in bed for weeks afterward. Barely able to walk."

"No one ever warns you about"—Violet glanced around, then continued in a whisper—"what happens to your nether regions. I wouldn't let Stewart touch me for months!"

The women burst into laughter, and I managed a nervous smile. Inside, I felt queasy.

"Stop scaring Kate," Eva ordered. She turned and placed her hand on my arm. "You'll be fine. My nanny has a friend looking for a place. Used to work for one of the Armors. I'll send you her references."

"You won't need a nanny for the first year at least," Lois interjected. "A night nurse and a day nurse for babies—that's what works best."

As the women's chipper voices chattered on, I couldn't help but remember an earlier version of myself, looking at a group like this and thinking I'd never belong. Now, these same women were welcoming me into their sisterhood.

I saw Matthew through the crowd and tried to catch his eye, but he was looking straight ahead, walking determinedly toward the lakefront path. I wouldn't have thought anything of it if I hadn't seen Marjorie scurrying after him, her expression pained. I'd been craving a cold drink, and I waved over one of the waiters Hannah had hired for the day.

I sipped my lemonade and wondered why Matthew would walk away in the middle of the party. Marjorie stumbled at the edge of the terrace and swayed as she tried to right herself. Had she been drinking? Matthew headed north; if he knew Marjorie was behind him, he gave no indication. I watched their figures drift out of view.

". . . so generous," Eva was saying. "What do you think, Kate? Will you join me and the children at the beach tomorrow?"

"Excuse me." I put down my glass. "I'll be right back."

I told myself I wasn't spying. I was just curious about where they were going. My tight shoes and bulky midsection slowed me down more than I expected, and by the time I arrived at the Temple, Matthew and Marjorie had disappeared. The baby wriggled inside my stomach, a sensation that always took me aback. I stepped inside the Temple and looked up at the carvings that ran around the perimeter. I thought of Dr. Rieger's book, of crazed women who'd kill to protect their secrets. There was nothing sinister about the figures I was looking at: they were dancing, playing flutes, enjoying themselves. This, I realized, was the most joyous piece of art at Lakecrest.

I was about to turn back toward the house when I saw Matthew on the bluff; he must have walked up from the lake. Marjorie followed soon after, shouting his name. He stopped suddenly, and she careened into him, her hands reaching out to clutch his arm and waist. She pulled herself closer. She raised her face and pressed her lips against his in a passionate, ravenous kiss.

Later, the thought of it sickened me. But at the time, as I watched it happen, my first thought was how perfect they looked together. Artemis and Apollo, the golden twins. How could I ever compete with such perfection?

Matthew wriggled out of her embrace and ran a hand across his face. Marjorie was talking, and Matthew was shaking his head, stepping backward, trying to get away. The path they were on led past the Temple, and I realized with horror that they'd see me any minute. The only way to avoid them was to run in the opposite direction. Toward the Labyrinth.

I stumbled off, my thoughts racing. I told myself whatever I'd seen was Marjorie's fault, that she'd tricked Matthew into it. He'd stopped her.

But not right away. Not nearly fast enough.

I began to run. The Labyrinth, for once, didn't scare me. It was a refuge, welcoming me in. I careened along the passageways, all my effort spent on moving forward. To escape from what I'd seen. My shoes pinched my toes and cut into the backs of my feet. The baby wriggled, nagging me to slow down. All I could think of was reaching the center, resting on one of the benches until I could decide what to do next.

On I went, along paths that grew darker as the sky above turned an ominous gray. The ground was uneven and overrun with weeds; I stumbled into a wall, and the jagged brick surface scraped a bloody trail down my arm.

"Damn!"

The sound rang out, a jarring break in the silence. There was no buzz of insects, no birdcalls. No sign of any other living creature.

When the first drops of rain fell, I tried to walk faster, but the ground became more treacherous as it softened into mud. Soon I was drenched: hair flattened against my cheeks, soaked dress clinging to my legs. I pulled off my painful shoes and flung them aside, hobbling forward in my stockings. Each fruitless step brought me closer to panic. Surely I'd walked the entire Labyrinth twice over by now? At last, I saw an arched opening in the wall ahead. I passed through it into the clearing at the center, where the Minotaur beckoned me in.

I sank onto a bench. The narrow walls had offered some protection from the elements, but now that I was in the open, the ferocious wind made me gasp for breath. The violent gusts, the relentless rain, the pasty mud—it felt as if nature itself was raging against me. *All that's missing is fire,* I thought, and in response a streak of lightning cracked across the sky. For a moment, the Minotaur lit up, its eyes staring straight ahead. Then, with a wrenching groan, it tore free from the ground and attacked.

Screaming, I slid off the bench and cowered like a child. It took a minute to realize the statue wasn't moving; its base had crumbled after years of neglect, and one powerful burst of wind had been enough to topple it over. The wind howled in triumph and delivered its next blow: a massive onslaught that tore bricks from the crumbling walls and sent them toppling around me. I curled into a ball as the baby kicked. When the thudding stopped, I pushed the dripping hair from my eyes and saw that the entrance I'd just walked through was now blocked.

Tears streamed down my face, mingling with the rain. I had to get out, before the whole place collapsed around me. I stumbled toward the opposite side. Marjorie had shown me the way out months ago, but I couldn't even remember the first direction she'd turned. Silent weeping gave way to desperate, gasping sobs. I screamed for help until my throat ached, but there was no response. Who would hear me? Back at Lakecrest, the guests would be gathered in the ballroom, tut-tutting about the nasty weather. Had Matthew even noticed I was gone? Or were his thoughts too concerned with Marjorie?

I had never felt so alone. So hopeless. I moved through the darkness in grim defeat. Every corner led to another; each path that seemed promising led back where I'd started. Bricks fell at random around me as the ancient mortar gave way. *It's just like Lakecrest,* I thought. Hallways that circled back on themselves, doorways that led nowhere. The creations of unhinged minds, designed to drive me insane.

I heard a faint thumping in the blackness, and for one terrifying moment, I thought it was the Minotaur. I froze and listened. Footsteps. A faint voice calling out, "Mrs. Lemont!"

"Help!" I shouted. My voice was raspy and weak, not nearly strong enough to carry outside. Desperate, I began to wail, cries that were beyond words. With an oddly clear certainty, I knew I'd die if I stayed.

The steps quickened and grew louder. A lantern glimmered in the darkness, and soon I saw Karel walking toward me. His face told me all I needed to know about what kind of state I was in. It was all I could do not to rush into his arms and hug him in relief. I could hear Hannah's voice—*Lemonts are never overly familiar with staff*—and felt an irrational urge to laugh.

Blessedly, he didn't ask what I was doing there. He simply said to follow him, and I stuck close behind as he led me out. It felt as if I were moving in a strange but welcome dream as we stepped out of the Labyrinth a few minutes later. I'd been so close to the entrance—why hadn't I been able to find it?

The storm had died down, and golden hints of sunset peeked out from behind the drifting clouds. I'd have sworn it was midnight, but it couldn't have been later than eight o'clock. Time had moved differently inside, as if it were endless yet also didn't exist. Even as I walked away, the heaviness I'd felt inside lingered, a shadow on my soul. If the point of a maze was to test your wits and resourcefulness, I'd failed. And I couldn't help feeling the Labyrinth had wanted me to fail.

My muddy feet slipped on the gravel path. Karel put his hand under my arm and helped me along.

"The kitchen door," I muttered. "I don't want anyone to see me."

Karel nodded solemnly. He had one of those faces that's best described as wooden: his features were locked in an unchanging sulky expression, and frown lines were carved around his mouth. But his strong arms and confident walk were comforting, and I began to calm down. While he seemed perfectly content not to talk, it didn't seem right to leave without acknowledging what he'd done. As we approached the house, I thanked him for helping me.

Karel nodded. "You no go back there," he said. An order, not a request.

"Goodness, no." I had no intention of entering the Labyrinth again.

"Kate? Is that you?"

Marjorie's voice rang out across the lawn. As I'd guessed, the party had moved indoors, and I'd counted on the terrace being empty. But there was Marjorie, walking across the flagstones. Behind her, the doors to the Arabian Room stood open, and people were beginning to drift back outside.

Karel dropped my arm. If I hurried, I could make it around the side of the house before Marjorie reached me. But I hesitated, long enough for Marjorie to get a closer look.

"Gracious!" she cried out. "Where have you been?"

People were staring and whispering, waving to others inside so they could come out and gape. Why wouldn't they? There was Mrs. Matthew Lemont, bedraggled and wet, with dirt-caked legs and blood smeared along one arm. Marjorie escorted me straight into the lion's den. The Arabian Room was a swirling haze of colors and patterns, and I narrowed my eyes against the onslaught. Dimly, I heard voices: "Is that Matthew's wife?" "What on earth?" All I could see was Hannah, striding through the crowd with barely contained fury. Matthew was right behind her.

He looked upset, and I thought with an ache of the kiss, of Marjorie pressed against him. I wanted to slap him, and at the same time I longed to bury my face in his chest. The self-control I'd summoned for Karel began to crumple. It shattered completely when Matthew ran past his mother and grabbed my hands.

"Oh, my darling, are you all right?"

"Matthew." Hannah's voice was terse, but I knew what she was saying with that one clipped word: *You're making a scene. Get her out of here.*

I clung to Matthew, my shelter in the storm. He patted my head, my back, my shoulders. Reassuring himself I was still intact.

"I thought you were resting upstairs," he murmured. "What happened?"

"I got lost. In the Labyrinth."

"The Labyrinth?" Matthew asked. Bewildered. How could I possibly tell him the reason I'd gone inside?

"The storm," I tried to explain. "Bricks were falling down all around me, and the Minotaur—the statue—it crashed over, and the entrance was blocked and I couldn't get out . . ."

The words came faster and faster in a tumble of nervous release. Hannah's face tightened with impatience, and I realized the room had become utterly still. All conversation had stopped, and every single face was watching me. Marjorie looked coolly amused—enjoying herself!—and I turned my head to the floor to avoid the others' looks of sympathy and concern. They'd all heard me, rambling like a lunatic. Whatever hope I'd had of proving myself a worthy Lemont had been toppled as surely as the Minotaur itself.

I'd believed I could remake myself. But the Labyrinth had shattered that faith. It had shattered *me*.

"That's quite enough," Hannah muttered, pulling me from Matthew, smiling at her guests in a vain attempt to convince them this was only a minor disturbance. I followed obediently, a ragged puppet with no will of my own. She barked out orders, telling Alice to draw me a bath and the violinists in the front hall to play something lively. I staggered up the stairs, half dragged by the force of her grip. I was a naughty, disobedient girl being sent to bed without supper. And then, when I felt about as low as I'd ever been, I heard Matthew's voice echoing against the marble of the entryway.

"Kate!"

A year ago, I'd made a spectacle of myself, instigating a fight on the beach to get Hannah's attention and earn Matthew's trust. Tonight, Matthew was the one making a grand gesture, putting his loyalty to me above his reputation and his mother.

"I'll put an end to it, Kate!" he shouted. "That damn Labyrinth is coming down!"

━

I'm sure Hannah tried to stop him. Whatever she said to Matthew, it didn't work, because the workmen arrived the following afternoon. I watched them march across the grounds, holding pickaxes and sledge-hammers. The following day, a steam shovel rumbled along the lake-front path, spluttering smoke and pressing muddy grooves into the grass. It puttered around a bend, out of sight, and I tried to imagine the

Labyrinth in ruins. I didn't need to watch its destruction; I only wanted to know it was gone.

Matthew convinced me to join him on the terrace after lunch, luring me out with the promise of an ice cream sundae. I could hear the dull roar of the excavator in the distance, but Matthew seemed determined to ignore it. He talked cheerily about the weather (glorious) and the chances of taking the yacht out the next day (very good). Seagulls glided over our heads, and Lake Michigan glittered. At some point, the mechanical buzz of the excavator stopped.

I noticed a flash of movement in the distance. One of the workmen, running. Matthew stood up as the man drew closer. His face was flushed, and his chest strained against the buttons of his tight-fitting shirt as he fought for breath.

"Mr. Lemont!" he gasped. "We found something. Something in the maze."

Matthew ran. By the time I arrived at the site, he was standing by a skull that lay atop a pile of dirt. As we trudged back to Lakecrest, silent with shock, neither of us said what we knew in our hearts.

It was Cecily. She'd been buried in the Labyrinth all along.

CHAPTER THIRTEEN

Even the Lemonts couldn't escape an official inquiry. The police were called; investigators sifted through the heaps of rubble where the Labyrinth had once stood. The gates at the end of the front drive were pulled shut and locked, and Matthew told Hank to watch the fences in case an enterprising reporter tried to climb over. Matthew, Marjorie, Hannah, and I huddled in the sitting room, barely talking, barely eating. The only time anyone left the house in the following days was when Matthew and Hannah went to the police station to identify the remains.

"Was it her?" I asked Matthew when he returned. I couldn't bring myself to say the name out loud.

"There was a ring Mum recognized. The body . . ." He shook his head, shutting me out. "I'm sorry. I can't." The devastation on his face broke my heart.

The police agreed to question the family at home to avoid a circus at the station. That morning, Marjorie had Alice go into East Ridge to buy the latest newspapers. The words "Lemont Scandal!" were splashed across the top of the pile that Marjorie tossed onto an end table.

"We shouldn't have that trash in the house," Hannah said, but without her usual force. She looked older than I'd ever seen her.

Marjorie appeared both exhausted and exhilarated, as if she couldn't decide whether to collapse in bed or relish the drama.

"I'd better make myself presentable before our friends arrive," she said. "I'm supposed to charm them, aren't I, Mum?"

When the policemen arrived less than an hour later, Matthew answered the door. Three officers and a secretary walked into the front hall, all of them trying to hide their awe of the marble opulence. The tallest of them seemed to be in charge, with the others hanging slightly behind.

"Chief Powell," he said. "Lake County Police."

Matthew reached out his hand, but the chief kept his arms firmly at his sides. His dark eyes, black mustache, and intent stare gave him a threatening air. Hannah pulled out all her gracious hostess tricks, ushering everyone into the sitting room and offering coffee. Chief Powell shook his head.

"As you know, there's been a lot of public interest in this situation."

His eyes sidled over to the newspapers. Matthew sat next to me on the couch, listening with rapt attention. Marjorie stood by the window, holding an unlit cigarette; it was the first time I'd seen her look uncertain. Hannah sat opposite us, her back as stiff as the wing chair that framed her body.

"My purpose today is to get statements from the family, and I'm counting on your full cooperation, Mrs. Lemont."

Chief Powell talked to Hannah as if she was any other suspect, seemingly unimpressed by her wealth or position. Which meant he might actually uncover the truth.

Chief Powell asked to meet with Matthew first, in private. Matthew suggested they talk in the office, and they walked out together, accompanied by one of the policemen and the secretary. The third policeman propped himself in the doorway of the sitting room, keeping a discreet watch on the rest of us. Marjorie asked if we could listen to the radio, and the man shrugged. I was grateful for the gentle hum of Mozart filling the room, suggesting a calm none of us felt. Marjorie laid out a game of solitaire at the card table while I tried to avoid looking at Hannah.

Matthew came back a short while later, looking pale but resolute. Chief Powell nodded at Marjorie, who pulled herself up from her chair with a melodramatic roll of her eyes.

"What happened?" I asked Matthew after they'd left.

He shook his head. "Not much."

"Matthew, . ." Hannah began.

Matthew turned away from her. "No," he said sharply. "Not now."

We sat through a Mendelssohn waltz and a Chopin sonata before Marjorie returned.

"You're next," she said, nodding at me.

My heart pounded during the short walk to the office. Chief Powell would be asking the questions, but there was so much I wanted to know. If I was careful—and clever—I might be able to guide the conversation toward some answers.

Chief Powell was sitting behind the desk. I was nervous facing him head-on; anyone would be, with those eyes staring right into you. After glancing briefly at a small notebook, he asked me to describe the events leading up to the discovery of the body. He nodded as I told the story, confirming that my version matched what he'd been told by the others.

"When's the last time you were inside the maze?" he asked.

"The afternoon of the party. Two days before the body was found."

"It was your husband's idea to tear it down? Because you'd gotten hurt?"

I nodded and gave him a shortened, unemotional account of the time I'd spent lost inside. Chief Powell asked if Matthew had seemed surprised when the workman told him about the skull.

"Yes, he was very upset," I said. "As was I."

"Have you ever discussed Cecily Lemont's disappearance with other members of the family?" he asked.

"Now and then," I said. "It's not something they like to talk about, though."

"Did any of them ever refer to Cecily as dead?"

Marjorie, Matthew, and Hannah all had, at various times. Had one of them known for sure?

"I can't remember," I said, but I could tell by the way Chief Powell looked at me that he'd caught my hesitation. I remembered a piece of advice Ma had given me years ago: the best way to cover up a lie is to confess something else.

"There is one thing I should tell you," I said. "I hired a private detective, not long after I was married, to see if he could find out what happened to Cecily. I thought knowing might bring some comfort to my husband." I looked down at my lap, then slowly, shyly, up at the policeman's face. "The detective wasn't able to give me an answer. Now I know why."

Chief Powell asked me for Mr. Haveleck's name and address and jotted them down in his notebook. I wondered if telling him had been a mistake. What would Hannah do if she found out?

After asking a few other questions—my age, my maiden name, where everyone had been when the body was discovered—Chief Powell nodded.

"That's all for now," he said. "Thank you for your time and candor, Mrs. Lemont. You've been very helpful."

I had? How?

As I stood to go, he added, "You can send in your mother-in-law next."

When I told her, Hannah walked out of the sitting room as regal as ever, showing no trace of fear. The mood seemed to lighten somewhat, and Marjorie convinced Matthew to join her at cards. I shook my head;

I couldn't concentrate on anything, even gin rummy. Instead, I picked up one of the newspapers and began to read.

"Death at Lakecrest!" the headline blared. "Police Baffled!"

> A grisly discovery has added a new chapter to one of the North Shore's most enduring mysteries. A body discovered on the grounds of Lakecrest, the Lemont family estate in East Ridge, has been identified as Miss Cecily Lemont, whose disappearance in 1912 has become the stuff of local legend. The remains were unearthed Tuesday, setting off a flurry of speculation about the cause of Miss Lemont's death. Mr. and Mrs. Matthew Lemont were at home when the fateful discovery was made, along with his mother, Mrs. Jasper Lemont, and sister, Miss Marjorie Lemont.

> Cecily Lemont was last seen on September 14, 1912, entering a maze she had designed on the Lemont estate. At the time of her disappearance, she was thirty-eight years old, the second child and only daughter of noted businessman and art collector Mr. Obadiah Lemont, and a respected writer and artist in her own right. Those who knew her profess to be shocked and saddened by the discovery of her sorry fate.

> One such tribute comes from Miss Lucille Yates, founder of *Fanciful* magazine, which published Miss Lemont's work. "She was a

woman of great talent," said Miss Yates. "Had she wished to pursue a literary career, she could have been among the nation's foremost female authors. I never imagined that one who lived such a quiet life could come to such a sad end."

There was a photograph, one I'd never seen, of Cecily as a young woman. Her hair was tied back loosely with ribbon and swept over one shoulder; her hands held a single rose. It was the kind of sentimental studio portrait that hangs in parlors all over the country, but this one had a charm that set it apart. You could tell Cecily was in on the silliness of it all: the way her mouth tugged just a little wider than a polite smile, eyes that looked amused rather than dreamy. This was Cecily before the breakdowns, before her mysterious decline, before she began muttering to herself behind locked doors. It seemed wrong—cruel—that she should look so fetching in a story about her death.

There was a paragraph about the family's history, with the usual lurid rumors ("Some spoke of strange doings by moonlight . . ."). But no quotes from people who'd seen anything firsthand. There never were in stories about the Lemonts.

The Lake County coroner has confirmed that Miss Lemont's body will undergo an autopsy, but the results will not be revealed until the conclusion of the police investigation. Dr. Thomas Melville, chief surgeon of Cook County Hospital, said it is doubtful a cause of death can be determined after such a considerable passage of time.

"A body buried for nearly twenty years suffers extensive decomposition," he said. "Skeletal remains may be enough to determine foul play if the victim came to a violent end, as the bones may show evidence of a stabbing or crushing blow. A poisoning or suffocation, however, leaves no lasting trace."

I threw down the paper, feeling queasy. I used to laugh at overwrought stories like this, written to revel in each gruesome detail. This time, it was harder to brush off. I thought about how much Matthew would be hurt by reading it and was furious at Marjorie for bringing the papers into the house. We didn't need to make ourselves any more miserable.

Edna brought in sandwiches on trays, and we ate in silence. As the minutes dragged on, the day got hotter, and roasting in that room felt like a punishment for sins I didn't know I'd committed. At some point, Marjorie closed the curtains to block out the glaring sunlight, which only made it worse. Now the sitting room was not only stifling but also gloomy as a tomb. The policeman guarding us pulled off his jacket, and I saw his shirtsleeves were damp with sweat.

Marjorie walked up to him. "I need to make a telephone call, if that's all right with you?"

The policeman nodded, wilting, as if he could barely muster the energy to stand. Matthew offered him a chair, which he took with a nod of thanks. Marjorie went off to the telephone in the front hall, and Matthew picked up a stack of papers he'd brought back with him from the office.

"Might as well do something to pass the time," he said to me. "I'll climb the walls otherwise."

I couldn't imagine he'd get much done; it was impossible to concentrate in that still, sticky air. I lay down on the couch, exhausted even though I'd done nothing all day. I thought longingly of the icy lake.

I didn't care how cold it was; as soon as this interrogation was over, I would walk into the water up to my knees—up to my shoulders!—because I didn't know how much more I could take.

I must have drifted off, because I flinched with surprise when I heard my name. Disoriented, I sat up and looked around. I saw Matthew leaning over me as he shook my shoulder.

"Kate."

I glanced around and was mortified to see a wet mark where I'd drooled on the collar of my dress. But no one was looking at me. All eyes were on Hannah, who was standing in the center of the room with her usual cool expression. Chief Powell, by contrast, looked as if he had just run a race: his face was flushed pink, and his collar and jacket were rumpled and damp.

"We're done for today," he said. "Mrs. Lemont, you said you had the phone number for Dr. McNally?"

Dr. McNally? I flashed a look at Matthew, and he shrugged, looking as mystified as I felt.

"Yes. Give me a minute, would you?"

Matthew and I led Chief Powell to the front hall. Marjorie whispered a few words into the phone and quickly hung up.

"Leaving so soon?" she asked brightly. Nobody smiled.

Matthew leaned in toward the police chief, speaking in a hushed voice. "Have you found out anything on the cause of death?"

Chief Powell shook his head curtly. "Sorry. No word on that yet."

Hannah's heels clattered across the marble floor. She handed the policeman a slip of paper and said, "I'm sure you'll find the doctor's observations useful. Please let us know if there's anything else we can do."

The police chief and his troop left with a quick round of good-byes, leaving the rest of us to stare at each other in uneasy, suspicious silence.

"It's time we talked," Hannah said. "About Cecily."

I sat on the sofa, wedged in the corner, as if I could tuck myself out of sight. Matthew sank down at the other end, one arm outstretched along the back. A pose intended to look casual, but I could tell his body was taut with nerves. Marjorie lit a cigarette and paced. The joking flirtatiousness she'd put on for the policemen was gone, and she glared at her mother with icy distrust.

Hannah lowered herself into an armchair. Slowly, wearily, she took in Marjorie's restlessness and Matthew's apprehension. My purposefully blank expression.

"My dears, I am so sorry you were subjected to that awful interrogation. My only consolation is that we were able to endure it in private."

"Mother!" Marjorie spat the word out like a curse. "What did you tell them?"

Hannah fixed her eyes on me, as if her daughter hadn't spoken. "Kate, I don't think I ever told you how I met my husband, Jasper. It was through my father. Cecily was one of his patients."

I nodded in encouragement.

"She had a breakdown when she was eighteen. Tried to kill herself. Obadiah consulted all sorts of experts, but my father was the only one she confided in. He recognized her at once as a kindred spirit, someone who cared about the larger questions of life and the human mind. He was the one who encouraged the study of ancient languages, as part of her recovery. Once she was feeling better, he supported her wish to travel, to go to Oxford and expand her horizons. Sadly, it was all a bit much for poor Cecily. She failed her exam and came back to Lakecrest in disgrace. Perhaps the humiliation was what drove her to walk into the lake during a summer storm. Who knows what would have happened if one of the men tying down the yacht hadn't seen her? My father began treating her here, at Lakecrest, and I came along as his assistant. Jasper was quite distraught over his sister's condition, and I did what I could to ease his mind."

"How noble," Marjorie said dryly.

"What you must understand," Hannah said, ignoring her daughter, "is that my father and I did our best, but there was no cure for Cecily's melancholy. Her mind was too fragile for the demands of normal life. I suggested Chief Powell consult my father's papers, which are kept in the archives of his clinic in Chicago. Those records make a very strong case that Cecily was unstable and a likely suicide."

"Why?" Matthew demanded. "She had no reason!"

"She didn't need a reason!" Hannah exclaimed. "I protected you and Marjorie from the full extent of her delusions. Don't you think fancying yourself a Greek goddess is evidence of an unsound mind?"

An unsound mind. I couldn't help thinking of Matthew. I kept my face turned away from him, afraid he'd sense my disloyal thoughts.

Hannah took a deep breath. "The night Cecily disappeared, she'd had a terrible fight with Jasper. He was concerned about Cecily's influence on the children. Cecily made a scene, as usual, and Jasper said if she kept it up, he'd destroy everything she'd built. The Temple, the Labyrinth . . . all of it. And he would have, just to spite her.

"I don't know what happened next." Hannah's voice shook. How strange to see her struggle for words. "I blame myself, still. Cecily ran out in tears, and I let her go. I did nothing to help. The next day, she was gone."

"It doesn't make sense," Marjorie said. "If Aunt Cecily killed herself, how could she be buried under the Labyrinth?"

"She wasn't buried," Hannah said simply. "The bones were found inside a wall."

For once, Marjorie was speechless.

"Cecily once told me there were hidden compartments in the Labyrinth, but she was the only one who knew where they were," Hannah said. "I believe she ended her life inside one of them so there'd be no witnesses to her final act."

"I don't believe it." Matthew's voice barely rose above a whisper. "Why wouldn't she leave a note? Why would she leave us to wonder, all these years? Do you have any idea how I've agonized over Cecily's death? My God, Mum—Kate even hired a private investigator to find out what happened because she was so worried about me!"

Hannah didn't look the least surprised, and it came to me in a sudden blow: she already knew. But how? The only person who could have told her was Mr. Haveleck himself. Had he phoned her the minute I left his office, angling for a bigger payout? Or maybe they'd met before. For all I knew, he was on the payroll of Lemont Industries. My head began to throb, and a glaze of sweat coated my skin. I'd barely eaten all day. Marjorie was talking in a swift, brittle voice.

"I don't believe it for a minute. You know how dramatic Aunt Cecily was. She wouldn't hole up like a rat in a trap. She'd want her poor lifeless body on full display!"

Matthew looked shaken by his sister's words. He turned to Hannah, eerily calm. "I saw Aunt Cecily's body, didn't I? You were there."

Hannah shook her head, lips pursed in a frown.

"What?" Marjorie urged her brother. "What did you see?"

"I got up, in the night." Matthew sounded dazed. "I heard a noise outside my door, and I saw Mum in the hall. I followed her to the Labyrinth. I heard shouting—horrible noises. I saw her standing by Cecily, and there was blood down her neck . . ."

"You saw nothing of the sort," Hannah snapped. "You had a nightmare, and it's gotten all mixed up in your mind."

If Hannah was lying, she did so effortlessly. I could see Matthew wavering. What must it feel like to never fully trust your own memory?

"You told me it was a dream," he said to Hannah. "But it wasn't, was it? It really happened."

"Matts!" Marjorie's voice was shrill with panic. "You saw Mum kill Aunt Cecily?"

Matthew shook his head over and over, a flurry of denial. "I saw Aunt Cecily on the ground. Not moving."

"Pull yourself together," Hannah snapped. "I hope to God you didn't share any of this nonsense with the police?"

"Of course not."

"Then it should all sort itself out without causing a scandal."

"Is that what you're worried about?" Marjorie asked. "The scandal is that your own son thinks you're a murderer!"

"Marjorie," Matthew pleaded. He turned to Hannah. "I don't care what you said to the police. Can't you tell the truth to your own family?"

Hannah harrumphed, but her dismissiveness only spurred Matthew on. He sprang up from the couch.

"Tell me!"

Hannah stared back at him. A terrible silence hung over us like a bewitchment. No one moved or spoke for what felt like forever.

"I've always wondered why Marjorie and I are such a mess," Matthew said at last, in a voice drained of all emotion. "It looks like I finally have an answer. I was raised by a monster."

Hannah started shouting and Marjorie screamed back, and their words blended together in a cacophony of hate. I put my hands over my ears to block out the sounds. My chest began to shake with hysterical sobs, the screams coming so fast and hard I could hardly breathe. I gulped, desperate for air, and then it all went black.

CHAPTER FOURTEEN

I woke up in bed, groggy and confused. Specks of dust floated in a ray of sunlight that cut across the room. With some effort, I pulled myself upright and looked out the window at the lawn and the water. The oppressive heat had broken, and my skin prickled as the quilt slipped down from my chest. I glanced at my nightgown, at the glass of water on the bedside table. My bedroom was this bright only in the morning. How long had I been asleep?

"You're awake!"

Matthew stood up from an armchair pulled up beside the bed. His shirt was rumpled, his eyes puffy with exhaustion.

"What happened?" I asked.

Memories came back to me in disjointed images. Marjorie shouting. Matthew accusing Hannah of murder.

"Don't worry," Matthew said. "It's all been worked out."

Worked out? How was that possible? Dull with sleep, I tried to come up with the right words. "You saw your mother. In the Labyrinth, with Cecily."

"So I did. But there was nothing nefarious about it. I misunderstood what I saw."

Matthew smiled, but his calmness didn't reassure me. "How?" I asked.

"Aunt Cecily and her pals liked to pretend they'd traveled back in time to ancient Greece. In the summer, whenever there was a full moon, they'd drink too much wine, scream like banshees, and dance around the Temple. 'Release their inner spirits,' as Mum put it to me. Completely harmless, but not the sort of thing you want the neighbors gossiping about."

"You saw Cecily covered in blood!" I protested.

"I saw her covered in wine," Matthew said. "They poured pitchers of it all over themselves. Once Mum explained, it all made sense."

"You've said yourself you can't trust your own memory! Your mother could have made up this whole story to cover up what really happened."

"Kate," Matthew said, shaking his head slowly. "Can you honestly see Mum as a cold-blooded murderer, lurking around the Labyrinth with a dagger? She's telling the truth, because it all came back. What I saw happened on the night of the fête. That's why I was up so late, why I heard Mum walking down the hall. I remember how hot it was outside and how my pajamas stuck to my skin. Aunt Cecily disappeared in September, months later. What I saw had nothing to do with her death."

I still wasn't sure what to believe, but Matthew seemed so certain. So relieved. "Mum did find me in the Labyrinth that night. I was confused and half-asleep, and she told me it was all a bad dream, thinking I'd forget. She had no idea my mind had twisted what I'd seen and turned it into something else. She feels terrible about it."

I wondered if I'd made a mistake by not confiding in Hannah from the very beginning. If I'd been less suspicious—and less jealous—I'd have told her about Matthew's dreams. She could have saved him months of misery and self-doubt by giving him this perfectly reasonable explanation. The only problem was that I wasn't sure it was true.

"Once I calmed down and thought things through," Matthew went on, "I realized Mum was right. There was so much about Aunt Cecily I never knew. So who's to say what was going through her mind on the night she died?"

He took my hand and looked at me intently. "When we met, you thought I didn't have a care in the world. And yet I'd come close to ending it all myself. Aunt Cecily could have been hiding the same kind of pain."

It was possible, wasn't it? My eyes fell on a newspaper folded on my bedside table.

"Have a look," Matthew said, handing it to me.

The *Chicago Tribune* headline read, "Cecily Lemont: Eternal Mystery."

I read the first few lines.

> The results of a police investigation have found no evidence of foul play in the death of Cecily Lemont some seventeen years ago. Since the discovery of Miss Lemont's body, Chicago has been abuzz with rumors about her mysterious end.

I skipped past the ghoulish theories and innuendo.

> Dr. Anthony Griggs, the coroner of Lake County, stated that the body's decomposition made it impossible to determine the manner of death. "Lacking any evidence of harm, and given the results of the police investigation, Miss Lemont may well have died of natural causes," he said. Miss Lemont was in poor health, according to the records of her per-

sonal physician. The Lake County prosecutor's office has confirmed that no charges will be filed. The remaining members of Miss Lemont's immediate family—Mrs. Jasper Lemont, Mr. and Mrs. Matthew Lemont, and Miss Marjorie Lemont—have remained in seclusion since the body was discovered last week.

Gruesome rumors of a live entombment have shocked Chicago society ever since it was revealed that Miss Lemont's body was found among the walls of her beloved Labyrinth. Dr. Griggs condemned rumors of this supposed imprisonment, noting that no forms of restraint were found at the scene and the body showed no signs of trauma. "It is unlikely she met her end by such foul means," he said.

"Sadly, we shall never know what fate befell Miss Cecily Lemont," said Lake County chief of police Hiram Powell. "We can only pray she rests in peace."

A private funeral is scheduled for Friday.

Friday?

"What day is it?" I asked Matthew.

"Thursday."

I tried to gather my scattered thoughts. "That can't be right. The police . . . they questioned us on Saturday. Or was it Sunday?"

"You've been resting for a while."

"Three . . . four days?"

"Nearly two weeks. As the doctor ordered."

"The doctor?" Alarmed, I ran my hands over my belly.

"Don't worry; the baby's fine. You need to be careful—that's all."

I couldn't remember anything after I collapsed in the sitting room. How could I have slept for two weeks?

"That can't be right," I muttered. "The funeral's tomorrow?"

Matthew nodded.

"Oh God, I don't have any black dresses that'll fit. Maybe I can borrow something from Eva."

"Please don't fret," Matthew said, patting my hands. "It doesn't matter."

"Of course it does. I have to look right."

My head felt fuzzy with confusion and worry and fatigue. I could have easily put my head back on the pillow and gone back to sleep, but that wouldn't do me any good. I had to get moving, to catch up with what was going on.

I asked Matthew to run me a bath, and though my head spun when I raised it from the pillow, it settled somewhat as I slowly scooted off the bed and stood up. Matthew helped me to the bathroom, and the effort was worth it; scrubbing away the sour odor of sweat made me feel halfway human again. Matthew hovered for a while, making me nervous and self-conscious, until I told him I was all right on my own. I lay in the water until my fingertips shriveled, then wrapped myself in a clean robe and shuffled back to the bedroom. Edna was there, holding a tray.

"Mrs. Lemont sent up something to eat."

A bowl of cold leek soup and a glass of milk. If only it had been prime rib or a plate of mashed potatoes! I hadn't realized until then how hungry I was. I sank down on the bed and awkwardly pulled my legs up.

"Here you are," said Edna, handing me the glass.

I looked at the milk doubtfully.

"Is there any lemonade?" I asked.

"Drink up, there's a good girl," Edna urged. As if I were five years old.

I made a point of setting it down without taking a sip. "If you'll get me that lemonade, please."

"It's Mrs. Lemont's orders . . . ," Edna began, then stopped as Hannah herself walked in.

"Of course Kate can have lemonade, if that's what she wants." She waved Edna away and took her place at the side of the bed. "Dr. Westbrook suggested a few glasses of milk a day to build up your strength."

"Did he also suggest a sleeping potion?" In the bathtub, I'd noticed a bruise on my upper arm and the faint remnant of a needle prick at its center.

"He did give you something so you'd rest. Poor thing, you needed it."

How self-satisfied she looked. And no wonder! She'd charmed the police, headed off a criminal investigation, and somehow managed to keep herself clear of any scandal. Grudgingly, I took a few sips of milk and was rewarded with a radiant smile.

"How do you feel, my dear?"

"Better, I think. I don't remember anything since . . . since the police were here."

"Best to put all that out of your mind."

As if I could. "About the funeral . . . ," I began.

Hannah cut me off with a gentle shake of her head. "Oh no. You won't be going."

"I need to be there. For Matthew's sake, at least."

"You're to stay here and rest until the baby's born. Doctor's orders."

I remembered Matthew and Marjorie, imitating their grandfather Dr. Rieger. *Doctor's orders!* they'd laughed. It didn't sound so funny now.

"What do you mean?" I smiled sweetly. "Can I sit outside, at least?"

"You're not to leave this room," Hannah said. "We're not taking any chances with my grandchild."

"That's ridiculous," I said. "I feel fine."

Hannah's voice was icy. "Perhaps I haven't been clear. There will be no more running off to Eva's. No more pitting me against Matthew. From now on, I am the one who decides what's best for the baby. You will stay here, under my care, and do as I say."

"But . . ."

"Do not attempt a battle of wills with me, dear Kate. I always win."

She stalked out without another word. I heard a clink of metal by the door and saw she had pulled out the key. The door closed behind her, and the lock clicked shut. I glanced at the date on the newspaper on the bedside table and worked out the timing. Six weeks until the baby was due.

For six weeks, I'd be Hannah's prisoner.

It took a few days to fully grasp the implications of my sentence. Matthew brought stacks of books up from the library, but most of them smelled like mildew and few held my interest. I'd have happily traded all the collected works of Edgar Allan Poe and Sir Walter Scott for the newest Agatha Christie. When I told him I wanted to go downstairs to use the telephone, he told me he'd already called my mother and Blanche, and they sent their love. Eva and other East Ridge neighbors sent flowers, but I wasn't allowed visitors. The bedroom began to look like a greenhouse thanks to all the bouquets, and it felt like one, too. Even with an electric fan perched on the nightstand, pointed at my face, I could never cool off.

I found myself looking forward to Hannah's visits like a child anticipating Christmas, hoping she might grant permission for a walk in the garden or even a morning on the terrace. I smiled obediently and did whatever she said. All I got in return were vague assurances: "We must ask Dr. Westbrook." Or "We'll see."

With nothing to do all day but brood, it was hard to avoid thoughts of Matthew and Marjorie. Wondering what they might be doing, out of my sight. You can convince yourself of anything if you try hard enough, and I probed my memory of that kiss for evidence that Matthew was innocent. I'd seen her run after him; I'd seen her throw herself into his arms, and he'd clearly been upset afterward. She was the one I blamed; she was the one I longed—and feared—to confront. The scene became so vivid that I could barely look at Marjorie on the few occasions she came to see me, and my sullenness gave her the perfect excuse to cut her visits short. No need to drag out what I'm sure she saw as an unwelcome duty.

A week or so after the funeral, she stopped by in the late afternoon, as I was groggily emerging from my usual nap. She looked as glamorous as ever, with her radiant hair, silky dress, and stack of bracelets that jangled as she walked. But something was different. She greeted me more quietly than usual; her eyes looked concerned rather than restless. She sat in the armchair by the bed and made even that simple gesture a lesson in elegance, sliding her legs down and to the side in perfect alignment. Her fingers tapped against the armrest, fidgeting without their usual cigarette.

"I wanted to stop in and say good-bye," she said. "I'm leaving for Newport in the morning."

Of course; it was August. None of her crowd would be caught dead in Chicago at this time of year.

"Good for you," I managed.

"Do you remember that day in the Labyrinth, when I said I liked you?" she asked. "You looked shocked."

"Because I was."

Marjorie smiled, a gentler version of her usual brash amusement. "The thing is, it's true. I do like you, still. Yet we've never become friends. I don't know if we ever can be."

Because you sicken me, I wanted to say. *Because you'd do anything to keep your brother all to yourself.*

"I saw you kiss Matthew," I said. "By the lake, the day of the fête."

She hadn't been prepared for that. But she was a quick thinker, just like me.

"You must have been confused. I may have hugged him . . ."

"You kissed him. The way a sister should never kiss her brother. How many times has it happened before?"

"What has Matthew told you?"

Nothing, but Marjorie didn't need to know that. "He's told me the truth," I said.

"Then you know it was all childish nonsense. We were best friends, always together. You know how little boys and girls are—of course we were curious about why we looked different under our clothes! It was Mum who made it something it wasn't, that day she found us, and from then on, we were never left alone. There was always a nanny or a governess on watch until we grew out of all that."

All that. A phrase that could mean many different things.

"At the fête, I saw the way Matthew looked at you, and it was the way he used to look at me, and I know it's nasty and unforgivable, but I was so damned jealous. I'd somehow thought your marriage would never come between what he and I once had. I picked a fight, and Matthew tried to walk away—quite rightly—but I wouldn't let him. I kissed him because I was desperate. To see if there was any trace of him I could still claim as mine."

Maybe there was. Maybe that was why he'd given in, if only for a few seconds.

"With all that's happened since then—Aunt Cecily, the investigation—I've barely spoken to him. I think he wants to forget it ever happened. I'm willing to, I promise. If you can, too."

Could I? Marjorie would be in Newport, and then there'd be the baby. Matthew and I would move to a new house, where Marjorie wouldn't constantly be lurking or finding ways to wedge herself between my husband and me. Knowing I'd won allowed my bitterness to soften. I knew I'd miss her gossipy conversation and irreverent jokes and the way she livened up even the stodgiest dinner table.

Besides, if I truly loved Matthew, how could I hate his twin?

"Consider it forgotten," I said.

Marjorie tapped an envelope lying on my nightstand. "I brought this up for you. It came today."

There was no return address. I tore the envelope open and pulled out several sheets of paper. The page on top was signed with a name I didn't recognize, but the letter underneath made my heart pound. It had been written by Cecily.

Marjorie stood up, watching me, unsure whether to leave or stay. I showed her the name, and she sank back in the chair. Stunned.

"There's a note here, at the front," I said. "I'll read it."

July 30, 1929

Dear Mrs. Lemont,

I write to you at the urging of our mutual friend, Mabel Kostrick, who has been contacting friends of Cecily Lemont on your behalf. Please forgive me for not including my name or address; it will soon be apparent why I guard my anonymity so fiercely. While Cecily was alive, I promised to guard her secrets, but the news of her passing has affected me deeply. After great thought, I have decided Matthew deserves to have this. She loved him very much.

I met Cecily in 1896, when I was eighteen years old. We came out the same season, and I was quickly entranced by her confidence and grace. I had undergone some difficulties due to my nervous temperament, but Cecily was very kind, and we soon became the closest of companions. Young women can succumb to powerful feelings of intense friendship, and though some describe it as a form of madness, I would simply say I loved her. When my mother discovered one of Cecily's rather indiscreet notes, she was horrified by references to wine and the passions of the artistic mind. I was sent to live with an aunt in Louisville to avoid further corruption.

It was many years before I dared contact Cecily again. We established an occasional but heartfelt correspondence, sharing our most intimate thoughts. Given my past experience, I burned all our letters after reading them. The only one I saved was this one, the last I ever received from her. I now pass it on to you and Matthew.

I will end with a brief request. I live a quiet life, free of scandal, and wish to continue doing so. Cecily referred to me as Venus in her letters, and I hope that name is enough. Please do not try to find me or pester Mabel. All I know of Cecily's last days is in this letter. Do with it as you wish.

Yours,

"Venus"

I glanced up at Marjorie. She looked like she was trying not to cry. Cecily's letter covered three sheets of paper, with a typewritten story afterward. I handed the story to Marjorie and looked at Cecily's letter. How strange to think of her writing this at Lakecrest almost twenty years ago.

August 13, 1912

My dearest Venus,
Though you protest your life offers little of interest, I greatly enjoyed your stories about Delia and Gregory. I hope I have

said it enough for you to believe me: I do not long for children of my own, for Matthew and Marjorie are as dear to me as any products of my own womb. How astounding it has been to watch them come into their true selves. Matthew is quiet and gracious, with none of the rambunctiousness common in boys of his age. Women flock to him already, fingers patting his cheeks and tousling his hair as if only a touch will convince them such a perfect creature is real. I foresee a trail of broken hearts in his future! Marjorie, for all her charm, has a stubborn streak that reminds me all too much of my brother. The servants shake their heads and call her a handful, which leads me to wonder if Queen Elizabeth and all great women weren't also handfuls in their youth. Marjorie is capable of greatness, I believe, if she modulates her temper to fit society's demands.

Yes, I have become that awful sentimental woman who moans, "How fast they've grown!" and blathers about turning back time as the specter of change looms ahead. The children are of an age when talk has turned to boarding schools, and the fragile peace between Jasper and me is cracking. My summer rite did not bring the usual release (I found myself quite dejected for days afterward), and I am left to wonder if such ceremonies lose their force over time or if it is my own soul that has altered.

This brings us to the man I call Orpheus. You mustn't apologize for your ignorance of the name's meaning in your last letter. It is a story that has intrigued me for years: the devoted lover who rescues his true love from hell. Not a happy ending, I'm afraid, but then you and I know all too well how stories of doomed lovers conclude. This Orpheus beckons me on a path I had not expected to walk at my age, two years shy of forty. I promise to be less mysterious in my next letter, but there is much I have yet to learn about him, and I shy away from confessing too much when it may all come to nothing. I will say he is steady and measured in words and manner, quite the opposite of Jasper and his rages.

I have wondered what my father would have made of this Orpheus; for all the differences in upbringing between them, I believe they would have liked and respected each other. It's been years since Father died, yet I still miss him with a wrenching pain. Together, we created an American Arcadia and proved a prairie home can stand as proud as the palace of Knossos. I only wish Father were still here to rule over Lakecrest. Jasper has been an unworthy heir.

At the time of my last letter, I had turned to writing again, and you were kind to suggest Twelve More Tales *as the title of my next work. Alas, I was able to complete but one tale before my muse deserted me. I consulted stacks of mythologies in search of inspiration, only to encounter one tragic heroine after another. How could I have read these stories so many times yet been blind to their full horror? Poor Leda, seduced by Zeus in the guise of a swan—such a depraved coupling cannot be transformed into art by my poor pen. The princess Andromeda, chained and naked, offered up to a sea monster as punishment for her mother's pride. Mighty, swift Atalanta, besting the men she raced against yet forced into marriage through Aphrodite's trickery.*

The fault, you see, is in the legends themselves, not my talent. The Greek gods were cruel, vengeful creatures, and no retelling is clever enough to change the facts of their terrible deeds. My faith in the wisdom of the ancients rests on such a shaky foundation. Perhaps that is why I reach for the hand that offers escape.

I enclose my latest work and would appreciate your honest thoughts. Do not protest your lack of education—a reader free of prejudice is more valuable to me than the most lauded classical scholar.

Yours with greatest affection,
Cecily

I passed the letter to Marjorie when I was done, then skimmed the story, picturing Cecily as Eurydice, trapped in the underworld. I didn't have the heart to read past the first page, knowing it didn't have a happy ending.

"Do you have any idea who this Orpheus was?" I asked Marjorie when she'd finished.

She shook her head. I'd noticed her brush away tears while she was reading, but now her face looked composed. "Aunt Cecily never had suitors that I was aware of, poor old thing. She allowed herself one night a year to get raging drunk, take off her corset, and howl at the moon, and that got her a reputation! Nowadays, she'd be drinking cocktails and smoking at a nightclub or running off to Paris with this Venus. I've heard women live together there quite openly."

If she'd been born thirty years later, would Cecily's life have turned out differently? Marjorie had choices and opportunities her aunt never did. But I wouldn't describe Marjorie as happy.

"You can keep the letter," I offered, "if you'd like to have something of hers."

Marjorie nodded. "Yes, I would. It's so silly, but I miss her, all of a sudden."

She stood, abruptly, and said she had to get going.

"One bit of sisterly advice before I leave," she said. "I happened to be there when the mailman arrived, but you'd better be careful with your correspondence. Mum's reading all your letters."

The telegram came two weeks later.

THE EARL OF LOTHINGBROOK ASKED FOR MY HAND AND I SAID YES. SAILING FOR LONDON MONDAY. CAPTAIN TO MARRY US AT SEA. MORE SOON ON MY GRAND ADVENTURE. LOVE MARJORIE.

Hannah tossed it on my bed, her clenched jaw hinting at her fury. "What can she be thinking?" Hannah fumed. "Married at sea!"

I could barely believe it myself. Yet I could easily imagine Marjorie's voice, saying those words in her usual mocking tone. Had she decided to marry on a whim, simply to goad her mother?

Or was it because she'd do anything to avoid coming home?

Matthew and Hannah had never met or even heard of the earl. "Clearly, a title of no importance," Hannah snapped. If Marjorie thought she'd make her mother proud by marrying into the British aristocracy, she hadn't set her sights high enough. Perhaps, knowing Marjorie, she'd trade the earl for a duke in a few years.

Marjorie's boldness encouraged me to plan my own escape. I was desperate to get outside, to breathe fresh air and feel the breeze off the lake. How could that possibly hurt the baby? I listened to the car rumbling along the front drive whenever Hannah went out on her rounds, and began scheming. If I timed it right, I could get out of Lakecrest for an hour or so without her knowing. I'd need help; in my weakened, clumsy state, I didn't trust myself not to fall down the stairs. Could I get Alice to take my side? She was young and curious enough to be talked into a grand adventure, unlike boring old Gerta.

I made an effort to be friendlier with Alice than usual over the next few days and was encouraged when she began lingering by my bedside to talk after she'd finished cleaning up and putting away my clothes. Several times, I got the feeling she was steeling herself to ask me something—for a raise, most likely. I'd already decided to go to Hannah on her behalf, if she ever got around to it.

On the afternoon Hannah told me she was off to her monthly garden club meeting, I summoned Alice with the bell on my nightstand. She arrived a few minutes later.

"Yes, ma'am?"

"Come in. Sit down."

"Oh no, I shouldn't."

"Hush," I said. "Mrs. Lemont's not here to see, and I couldn't care less. You make yourself comfortable."

Alice sat gingerly on the edge of the armchair.

"What's going on downstairs?" I asked. "Are you very busy?"

"I was ironing Mr. Lemont's shirts. Gerta's helping Edna with the canning."

Perfect—they'd be busy in the kitchen for hours. If Alice was willing to stand guard, I might get a precious hour to myself on the terrace.

"I wanted to tell you how much I value your loyalty," I began. "To me, you're more than a maid. I've come to think of you as a friend."

To my astonishment, Alice began to cry. I hadn't pegged her as being sentimental.

"Oh, now . . . ," I stammered, trying to lean over far enough to pat her hand. "There's no need for all that."

"There is! Talking about loyalty when I've let someone down!"

I had no idea what she was talking about.

"There's something I've been meaning to tell you for days. You see, I promised to pass on a message, then I got too nervous and afraid of what you'd say."

"A message?" I asked. "Who's it from?"

"Birgitta. She used to see to Miss Cecily."

"You mean she was Cecily's maid?"

Alice nodded. "She was such a help when I started here. Gave me all kinds of good advice. Mama says it's not fair what Mrs. Lemont did to her—oh, but you mustn't tell anyone I said that. I've got three younger brothers counting on the money I bring home."

"I'd never betray a confidence. I hope you know that."

"It was the body, you see. Miss Cecily's. When Birgitta heard about it, she went right to the police and told them what she'd seen, but they wouldn't listen to her."

"What did she see?"

"The night Miss Cecily died, she gave Birgitta a note to deliver, quite late. As Birgitta came out of the room, she saw Mrs. Lemont in the hall. It looked like she'd been snooping around outside. Mrs. Lemont demanded to see the note, and Birgitta handed it over. She had no choice, did she? Birgitta saw Miss Cecily walking to the Labyrinth, from the window, not long afterward. Birgitta was scared something awful when the police came the next day. She didn't know if it was her place to tell them about the note, so she didn't."

A sudden rumble broke the flow of Alice's story. A car engine, approaching up the drive. Had Hannah come home early? It was clear Alice had the same fear; she hurried to the doorway and stuck her head out, listening with tense concern. The noise swelled and then gradually faded as the vehicle passed along the side of the house. A delivery truck, headed for the service entrance.

Alice came back into the room, clutching her hands together. The break in our conversation had allowed doubt to creep in.

I smiled to encourage her. "The note. Did Birgitta tell you what it said?"

"Oh no. It was sealed up in an envelope. Addressed to Karel Pavek."

Karel? My thoughts tried to catch up with her words. Cecily had known Karel. The keeper of the Labyrinth. I remembered the accounts I'd seen in Obadiah's papers, the list of workmen brought in to create Cecily's classical retreat.

Alice continued. "Birgitta was dismissed the next day. Can you imagine Mrs. Lemont being so cold, after all the time Birgitta'd been with the family? Birgitta had a terrible time finding another place. She had to start over by taking in laundry. All these years, she thought Miss Cecily must have written something about leaving Lakecrest, and that's why Mrs. Lemont knew Birgitta wouldn't be needed anymore. Birgitta's always been sure Miss Cecily was alive.

"She was awful upset when she heard about the body. Now she's sure someone in the family did her in and the note had something to do with it. Birgitta marched down to the East Ridge police station and demanded to meet with the chief himself. He asked why she hadn't come forward years ago and got her all confused with their questions, like *she* was the one who'd done something wrong! So she asked if I'd bring up the matter with you."

"Why not Mr. Lemont?" I asked. "Surely you've told her about my . . . condition."

"I've told her about you." Alice looked down, suddenly shy. "How nice you've been. Birgitta thinks you might be more open-minded, not being born into the family and all. You could convince the police to take a second look."

"I can't do a thing from here," I said. "Alice, if you'd help me, I can make it downstairs to the phone. I've met the police chief; I'm sure he'd come talk to me if I ask."

"Oh no, I couldn't. Mrs. Lemont gave me strict orders that you're not to leave the room."

"It's not as if I'm going far. I won't even leave the house."

"But the baby, if something should happen . . . oh, I'd never forgive myself!"

"Please, Alice."

She shook her head and backed away from the bed. Agitated but resolute.

"I promised Birgitta I'd talk to you, and now I have," she said. "But I can't do more than that. Please, Mrs. Lemont."

No doubt Hannah had put the fear of God into all the servants. It probably took all Alice's courage to tell me her friend's story.

"Go find Karel," I told her. "Tell him I want to talk to him, now. If Edna sees you, say I want to thank him for rescuing me from the Labyrinth."

Alice didn't nod or move toward the door. She stared at me, confused.

"Karel's not here," she said.

"Where is he? When will he be back?"

"He's gone. Cleared out his things and left, right after the Labyrinth came down. Didn't you know?"

CHAPTER FIFTEEN

Was Karel the key to everything?

Skulking around the Labyrinth, dropping dark hints about Lakecrest, he knew more than I'd ever suspected, and now he'd vanished. It couldn't be a coincidence, Karel leaving right as Cecily's body was found. Did he know she was buried there? Had he spent all those years tending to the Labyrinth so it wouldn't fall apart and reveal the terrible secret inside?

I struggled to reconcile what I knew and what I thought I knew. I'd gotten a few tantalizing clues, but couldn't make sense of them. Cecily had written a note to Karel on the night she left. He had to be the Orpheus she referred to in her letter. But that letter had been maddeningly vague about the nature of their relationship. Were they lovers? Friends? Conspirators? Whatever Cecily said in her note that last night, Hannah must have read it, and at the very least, Birgitta's story was proof that Hannah was a liar. She'd said nothing to the police about a note, in 1912 or more recently, and she'd said nothing to Matthew or me. That meant her confession about the night of Cecily's death was an act. A performance designed to distract us from what had really happened. There were still things Hannah wanted hidden, and without knowing those secrets, I'd never find out why Cecily died.

My thoughts were slow and jumbled, my brain working at only half speed in the heat. I dragged myself from the bed to look out the window. The same idyllic blue-and-green vista, as if nothing had changed. I wondered what it looked like at the north end of the estate. The bare, scarred earth where the Labyrinth had once stood. The day the workmen arrived, I'd talked to Matthew about building tennis courts or a swimming pool there. Now I knew that land would remain empty. How could we play with our children on the site of Cecily's grave?

I'd asked Alice what the other servants had been saying about Karel, and it wasn't much. He'd lived in a small cottage at the edge of the estate and mostly kept to himself. What I wouldn't give for a private detective now! But I no longer trusted Mr. Haveleck, and even if I did, I couldn't get to the telephone to call him. My theories and suspicions led to no clear answers, and the fatigue that overcame me so often in those days gradually took over. The mystery of Cecily's death, like everything else, would have to wait until after the baby.

If it weren't for the calendar I kept by my bedside, I would have had a hard time distinguishing one day from the next. Every night, I marked an X on the appropriate date, and the forward march of symbols gave me the small satisfaction of progress. Only four weeks to go. Then three.

Dr. Westbrook came to check on me every Monday morning and usually said nothing more than "You're doing fine, little mother."

His condescending tone infuriated me, especially since I was sure he was giving more-detailed reports to Hannah. But there was no point getting angry; any time I acted upset, Hannah suggested another shot to calm me down. Matthew did his best to entertain me in the evenings, but Lemont Medical had him working round the clock. He looked worn out.

Finally, he admitted he'd been having trouble sleeping. "I didn't want you to feel bad, but you've started snoring, and when you turn over . . . well, the entire bed shakes."

He laughed to show it didn't matter, but I insisted he move to one of the guest rooms. Giving up our nights together was a harder sacrifice than I'd imagined, and I felt lonelier than ever. My days were so monotonous that I remember exactly how my heart leapt when I heard a commotion in the front hall one afternoon. Footsteps clattered up the stairs, and a voice called out, "Kate!"

"Blanche!" I shouted back. "Oh, Blanche!"

She careened through the doorway. Hat askew, flushed cheeks.

"Aren't you a sight!" she exclaimed.

It had been so long since anyone other than Matthew, Hannah, or the maids had seen me that I'd stopped putting any effort into my clothes or hair. I must have looked a perfect fright. Despite my embarrassment, I smiled with delight and held out my arms. We hugged and laughed, then laughed even harder when Blanche gaped at the size of my stomach. I heard more footsteps, and Edna appeared in the doorway, frowning with disapproval.

"No visitors," Edna said halfheartedly, as if even she knew that seeing my cousin would do me good. "Mrs. Lemont doesn't want you tired out."

"Be a dear and bring us something to eat, will you?" I asked, eyes pleading for sympathy. "She won't be here long."

Edna gave a curt nod and left.

"Hop in," I urged Blanche.

She kicked off her shoes and cooed with pleasure as she peeled off her stockings. "It's a scorcher," she said. "The walk from the station nearly killed me." She pulled herself onto the bed and propped a pillow behind her back.

"Now, what have they done to you?"

I didn't know what to say. My chest tightened with joy, with hope. Blanche was on my side, and she was the best chance I had at getting out of Lakecrest. But how? She didn't have a car, and Hank had driven Hannah who knows where; she'd stopped in that morning to tell me, but I hadn't been paying attention. As my mind raced with thoughts of freedom, it took an effort to concentrate on what Blanche was saying.

"I've called a bunch of times. Didn't you know? That nasty woman always says you're resting. I figured if something were really wrong, Matthew would have told me, but I couldn't help worrying, and it's not like you to disappear completely, so I just had to come and see for myself."

I reassured her that I wasn't near as bad off as she imagined. As if to make the point, the baby kicked so hard I gasped.

Blanche laughed in delight. "He can't wait to get out!"

I know exactly how he feels, I wanted to say. I wasn't ready to confess how trapped I felt—better to ease her into it.

"I feel terrible about what happened," Blanche said. "The whole business with Cecily. Is it true? Were you here when they found the body?"

"Yes."

I remembered the excavator shutting down. The workman racing across the lawn, waving his arms. It felt like years ago.

"It was all over the papers," Blanche said. "There were pictures of Matthew and Hannah at the funeral, but they said something about you having a nervous collapse."

I remembered screaming. I'd screamed and screamed and couldn't stop.

"Oh, goodness, nothing as bad as that," I said. "I just wasn't up to it."

"Looks like you're doing better now, though." Blanche smiled brightly.

"Tell me what you've been up to," I said. "How's Billy?"

She grinned. "Swell. In fact, he's gotten some very good news. His wife agreed to a divorce. Once everything gets settled with the judge, we're getting married."

A divorced jazz musician wouldn't sound like much of a prize to someone like Hannah, but he was just right for Blanche. I'd known it the first time I saw them together.

"Oh, that's great! What changed her mind?" I asked.

"The money. Didn't Matthew tell you?"

"Um, I don't think so. Then again, I've been awfully forgetful lately."

"Matthew offered to set Billy up with his own band," Blanche explained. "He said it was his mother's idea, that she was completely charmed by Billy when we spent that weekend up here. He *is* charming, isn't he? Matthew told Billy there's always work for a good bandleader, and they set up some kind of partnership. Billy got a nice payment up front, and it was enough to change Elinor's mind—that's his awful wife. I had a feeling all along that she cared more about money than she did about Billy . . ."

She went on as I fit the pieces together. Matthew gave Billy money. Money that allowed Billy to pay off his wife and marry Blanche. And it had all been Hannah's idea. She had no love for jazz or nightclubs, and she'd never shown any particular affection for Blanche. So why did she do it?

I looked at Blanche. Smiling, giggling, happier than I'd ever seen her. I thought of my mother's last letter, in which she'd proudly described her new house. It was the first thing of value Ma had ever owned, and it had been paid for with Hannah's money. I remembered the open invitation to the Lakecrest beach that Hannah had offered to Eva and her family. Just the sort of kindness a mother with three children and a landlocked property would always remember.

One by one, Hannah had sought out the people most loyal to me and given them what they wanted. If Hannah wanted to break up my marriage to Matthew, would Ma risk losing her house to help me? Would Blanche give up her future with Billy for my sake? I could think of no logical reason Hannah would want to get rid of me; I had dedicated myself to her son's well-being, and I was soon to present her with her first grandchild. But I couldn't rid myself of the troubling suspicion that Hannah was biding her time. I pictured the words above Lakecrest's entrance and nearly shivered, despite the heat. If Hannah cast me out, no one would come to my rescue. *Factum est.*

I forced a smile as Blanche described the latest scandal at the Pharaoh's Club.

"It's no wonder we both want to get out of there. Just think, I'll get to be a singer at last. Wouldn't it be great if we toured around the country? What I wouldn't give to see New York!"

Me too, I thought. Self-pity had become an all-too-familiar condition. *The baby,* I told myself. *The baby, the house, then I'll be able to leave.*

"Maybe you'll be off to England yourself sometime," Blanche said. "To visit Marjorie? *Everyone's* been talking about her elopement. I can only imagine what her mother said!"

"She's putting on a brave face for her friends, but she's furious."

"As it so happens, I've got some news from her."

Blanche reached into the pocketbook she'd dropped on the floor and pulled out a thick ivory envelope. I saw Marjorie's swooped handwriting across the front.

"She mailed this to me at the club," Blanche said. "Here, look at the note."

> *Dear Blanche,*
> *Could you see Kate gets this letter? I'd rather no one else reads it, and I can't be sure if I send it to Lakecrest. Prying eyes and all that—I'm sure you understand.*
> *With my very best wishes,*
> *Marjorie Lemont Macfarlane*

Wrapped inside was a sealed envelope, marked simply *Kate.*

"Do the maids really snoop through your mail?" Blanche asked. "I've always thought it would be strange, having people around all the time like that. Now, if Billy's band does well, I'd hire a maid in an instant and send out all the laundry. That would be heaven. You probably haven't had to wash out a pair of knickers in ages."

There was a quick knock at the door, and Edna walked in with a tray of food. I pushed Marjorie's letter under my pillow, saving it for later, though I could tell Blanche was aching to know what it said. My stomach growled, and I told Blanche, "You're in for a treat. Edna's a wonderful cook."

Edna accepted the compliment with a curt nod and placed the tray across my lap. Sandwiches, potato salad, slices of raspberry pie. Lemonade for Blanche and the usual milk for me. Before I could say anything, Blanche reached for the milk and took a sip.

"I love fresh milk! Don't tell me you have cows wandering the grounds?"

Edna stopped fussing with my napkin. She stood perfectly still as Blanche gulped down half the glass. Was it the flicker of concern in her eyes that made me suspicious or the way her lips tightened? My thoughts leapt from one to another, making connections. And then I knew.

It wasn't hard to pretend I'd lost hold of my dessert plate. Chunks of raspberry filling and mangled piecrust smeared across the bed.

"Oh no!" I exclaimed.

I waved Blanche off when she leaned over to help clean up the mess. "It's all right. Edna, would you have Alice bring fresh sheets?"

Edna scowled and stomped away. Now I just had to get rid of Blanche for a few minutes.

"Darling," I told her, "why don't you go into my dressing room and have a look in my jewelry box while we get this sorted out? I've got all sorts of pieces I never wear, and I'd love to give you one as an engagement present. It's on top of a bureau in the corner."

Blanche made the expected protests, but it didn't take much to convince her. When Alice arrived, I hovered at the bedside as she went about her work, whispering so we wouldn't be overheard.

"What has Edna been putting in my milk?"

Sometimes it's best to ask a question as if you already know the answer.

"I'm not sure," Alice said slowly. "Some kind of medicine."

"What kind?"

"I don't know the name. She told me not to touch the bottle."

"What does the bottle look like?"

"Brown? The syrup's pink when she pours it."

I'd seen Edna pour pink syrup from a brown bottle before. She'd given it to Marjorie when she was chained to a bed in the basement.

It all made sense. It wasn't the pregnancy that had me so out of sorts. Twice a day, for weeks, I'd been taking something that left me tired and muddled. Easy to control. What was it Matthew had told me? *We're testing out a formula. A treatment for nervous hysteria. It's made one woman's mania vanish almost entirely.*

"Kate?" Blanche stood in the doorway to the dressing room, holding up a few strands of pearls. "I can't decide."

I dismissed Alice with a jerk of my head.

"Come here and let me have a look," I told Blanche.

She modeled different lengths and took so long deciding that I insisted she take all three. Blanche didn't even bother to politely decline. Sitting with her shoulders hunched over, stifling a yawn, she looked exhausted. All from drinking one glass of my milk.

"Guess the heat is catching up with me," she said.

"Why don't you lie down?" I suggested. "I bet you could do with a nap."

"I could." Too tired to offer more than a halfhearted smile, Blanche curled up in bed next to me. Soon, she was asleep, and I must have followed not long after, because I jolted awake—confused and disoriented—at the sound of tires braking on the front drive. Hannah was home.

Within minutes, I heard the distinctive sound of her shoes click-clacking up the stairs. Though Hannah was surprised to see

Blanche—and Blanche looked mortified—they managed to exchange pleasantries while I tried to hold in my rage. I wanted to scream at Hannah for drugging me. For turning me into her prisoner. Instead, I smiled pleasantly and hugged Blanche good-bye when Hannah offered to have Hank drive her home. I'd wait until Matthew was home. See how she defended herself in front of her son.

"Do you need anything?" Hannah asked before leaving the room.

"It's done me a world of good, seeing Blanche," I said. "I don't feel nearly as tired as usual."

Let her make what she wanted of that, especially after she talked to Edna and found out I hadn't drunk that day's milk. I almost hoped she'd come back and scold me so I could unleash my anger. She didn't. I heard the car drive off and the faint sound of voices downstairs. But Hannah left me alone.

As soon as I felt it was safe, I pulled Marjorie's letter out from under my pillow.

> *My dear Kate—*
> *Funny how it's easier to write you than Matthew. When I imagine telling you what happened, I know just what to say and how to explain myself. With Matthew, I could fill pages and pages and still not find the right words. There's so much history between us.*
>
> *I hope the news of my elopement had the desired effect on Mum (horrified gasps, an attack of the vapors, etc. etc.). You must promise to describe the scene to me one day. I'm sure you're awfully curious about my hus- band (as he will be by the time you receive this). Since I barely know him, I'm afraid there's not much to tell. Sir Edwin Macfarlane, Third Earl of Lothingbrook, is what they call "a decent chap"—blond hair, ruddy complexion, posh accent, a terrible snob. All you'd expect in an earl,*

really. No money, of course—he was quite up front about that—but soon to inherit a huge leaky castle in Scotland very much in need of repairs. His best quality, in my eyes, is his large circle of acquaintances—he's got friends and relatives in Australia, South Africa, India, Egypt. Any of whom, he says, would be happy to have us for an extended stay.

Someday, I'll come up with a lovely romantic story as to how we met, but with you, dear practical Kate, I can be honest. Edwin and I first spoke over dinner, took off for a moonlight drive, and after a night in the backseat of his Cadillac, he declared me his dream girl. I gave him a day to see if it would stick (it did) and then I accepted his proposal: at our ages, you don't waste time. I don't love him, and I don't expect to, not in the way Matthew loves you. Poor Edwin doesn't seem capable of deep emotions, and he's been very honest in his money-grubbing, so it's all aboveboard.

I can see you frowning, Kate—please don't feel sorry for me. Edwin is great fun and always up for an adventure. He'll be good for a few years, at least. (Is it terrible that I already think of him as my first husband? I know you won't approve, but somehow I think you'll understand.)

My only regret is that I don't know when I'll meet Baby Lemont. I promise to send presents from my travels, and you can tell him stories about Daddy's glamorous sister. I don't believe I have it in me to be a mother, but I'll make a good aunt, I think.

This page is half-filled, and I don't want to start another but I still haven't gotten around to the most important part. Typical of me, to leave it to the end.

Please take care of Matthew. I adore him more than anything in this world, as you know. But my love couldn't help him, and I believe it kept him from being truly happy. Leaving Matthew is the most difficult thing I've ever done—my heart's ripped to tatters—but it's the only way to prove my love is pure. Edwin offered me an escape, and I took it.

I hope you'll find a way to explain all this to Matthew in a way that leaves me looking halfway decent and noble. A long time ago, before he met you, Matthew used to call me his ideal woman. I'd like to hold on to a smidgeon of his respect, even if I don't deserve it.

I'll write Mum from the boat—haven't the strength for it now. Will send addresses, travel plans, etc. etc., and I hope you'll write. I truly do.

Your sister,
Marjorie

A collection of Poe stories sat on my nightstand. I'd been amused by the melodramatic gloominess of "The Fall of the House of Usher" when I first read it, but after the discovery of Cecily's body, it had been harder to laugh off. Roderick and Madeline Usher, the brother and sister whose lives were so disturbingly intertwined, no longer seemed like characters from a gothic novel; they could have been Marjorie and Matthew in twenty or thirty years. Caught in a mutual obsession, haunted by their demons, slowing driving each other insane as Lakecrest crumbled around them.

But I'd come along and changed the story. Marriage had saved Matthew, and now Marjorie had saved herself. I pictured her on the deck of an ocean liner, her hair tossed by the wind. I remembered the sensation that had washed over me as I leaned against the railing of the *Franconia*, and hoped Marjorie would one day feel that same sense of boundless possibilities.

As for me, the world was shrinking every day. I could see the years unfold before me in a bleak, unchanging pattern. Carved goose in the dining room at Christmas and lemonade at the summer fête in July. Bridge club on Wednesday afternoons and the Lake County Benefactors Ball each September. I could picture myself, a grandmother confined to this same bed, looking out at the distant glimmer of a lake I'd never touch again.

By the time Matthew came home, I was near tears

"What's gotten into you?" he asked. Kind, as always, but not particularly worried. I could practically hear Dr. Westbrook talking to Matthew man-to-man, confiding that pregnant women could get worked up over nothing: *Do your best to keep her calm. Give her what she wants.*

"Your mother," I whispered. "She's been drugging me."

Irritation flashed across his face, but only for a moment. "Why do you make everything sound so sinister?" he asked. Steady. Reasonable. "Dr. Westbrook and I talked it over with Mum, and we all agreed a mild sedative would do you good."

"Why didn't you tell me?"

"Because we didn't want you to worry."

"It makes me tired. Wobbly."

"You're tired because you're about to have a baby. It's perfectly normal."

"Well, I didn't drink that spiked milk today, and it's the first time in weeks I've felt like myself."

"Really? You don't sound the same to me—you're almost shouting. Don't you see? You're proving my point about getting upset."

The soothing voice. A hand on my cheek. All meant to distract me. I took a deep breath and tried to stay calm.

"I want to stay at your apartment as soon as the baby comes."

"What are you talking about?"

"I can't bring a baby back to Lakecrest. I just can't." There'd be nurses at the hospital, other doctors, people who could call me a taxi. When Hannah showed up, I'd already be gone.

"Oh, goodness . . . ," Matthew murmured. Annoyed.

I was about to lose him. *No tears,* I told myself. *You mustn't crack.*

"You said we'd always come first with each other. You promised. But you've done nothing about finding us our own house. Has your mother gotten to you? Has she convinced you not to leave?"

"No!" Matthew protested. "The thing is—it's not as simple as you think. You have to trust me."

"Then why don't you trust me with the truth?"

Matthew reached for my hand. "There you go again, shouting. Hush. I'll tell you, but you have to promise not to get worked up."

I nodded.

"It's not the ideal time, financially, for us to set up our own household. Lemont Industries has been on shaky ground for some time. We thought we'd make up some of it in the stock market, but with all the speculation it's all a bit unpredictable. We're not penniless, not even close. But we have to tighten our belts for the time being, until Lemont Medical is on a more secure footing."

Tighten our belts. All a bit unpredictable . . . I felt queasy and sank back against my pillow, defeated. Matthew leaned over and kissed my forehead. "You can manage at Lakecrest for a year or two, can't you?"

"Is everything all right?" a voice asked from the doorway.

Hannah. I felt a lurch of panic. Had she heard me, begging to leave?

"We're fine," said Matthew, squeezing my hand.

Hannah walked to the bedside, subtly but firmly pushing Matthew aside. "The waiting's hard, I know," she said. "Don't worry. It will all be over soon."

She reached out to pat my stomach, and it was all I could do not to flinch. I didn't want her touching me. Didn't want her near me.

"I'll feel better once I get some sleep," I said. "Thank you."

"Why don't I send Alice up first, with your milk?"

"No."

"Are you sure?" Hannah asked. Wary.

"Yes. I don't like the way it makes me feel."

The silence lasted no more than a minute, but it felt like a lifetime.

"Whatever you want," she said at last. "Good night, my dear."

Despite my aching back and swollen legs, standing up for myself made me feel better than I had in weeks. I asked Matthew to sleep with me that night rather than down the hall. It wasn't easy to get comfortable in the still, sticky air, with the bulk of my stomach between us. But we laughed and found a way to fit together, and I fell asleep with my husband's arm lying protectively over my chest.

What was it that made me want Matthew beside me on that particular night? Call it mother's intuition, because it was only a few hours later that I woke up to a strange, damp sensation on my upper thighs.

My water had broken. The baby was on its way at last.

CHAPTER SIXTEEN

"Matthew!"

I showed him the wet sheet, and he understood instantly. After bringing me a towel to dry off, he said, "I'll go get Mum."

I lay in bed, jittery with nerves, anticipating the ordeal to come. I took a deep breath, released it slowly, and felt my muscles ease. *You can do this.*

Hannah walked in, not nearly as disheveled as I would have expected at three o'clock in the morning. Her hair was brushed back into its usual neat bun, and her nightdress looked as if it had been freshly ironed. Had she known this would be the night?

"How are you, dear?" she asked.

"All right," I said. "Is Matthew bringing the car round?"

"The car?"

"To go to the hospital."

"Oh no. Dr. Westbrook doesn't want you moved. Matthew's calling him now."

"Calling him?"

"He'll attend to you here, at home."

"No!"

I'd been counting on the hospital, a safe haven where the nurses and doctors would protect me. But the sickening dread that washed over me was more visceral than that. I couldn't let my child come into the world at Lakecrest. He'd be tainted forever.

"Where's Matthew?" I demanded. "I want to talk to Matthew!"

I tried to push myself upright, but only succeeded in slumping sideways. I'd never felt so awkward in my own body. So helpless. Hannah shook her head in condescending pity, thinking she'd won. Infuriated, I pulled myself to the side of the bed and slid my legs toward the floor. They shook with the effort.

"Kate," Hannah murmured in the smooth, persuasive voice I knew so well. "Calm yourself. It's all for the best."

"It's my baby! I'll decide what's best."

"Will you?" The shift from kindly concern to iron-willed threat was so fast it frightened me. "This baby is a Lemont. Ours. Not yours."

Barefoot and sweaty, I willed myself to move. To walk away from the bed. All I had to do was get to the door and call out to Matthew. Then everything would be all right. He'd help me downstairs and Hank would drive us to the hospital, and I'd be rid of Lakecrest forever. Hannah watched my pathetically slow progress, making no attempt to stop me. With each step, I felt my resolve harden. Finally, I leaned my body against the doorjamb and grabbed the knob. It didn't budge. I glanced at the keyhole underneath. Empty. Hannah had locked it from the inside.

"Help!" I shouted, pounding on the door. Before I could cry out again, Hannah was behind me, her hands under my arms, pulling me firmly back to bed.

"Don't be frightened," she murmured. "When the doctor gets here, he'll give you something for the pain."

"I don't want his drugs! Who knows what he'll try on me this time?"

"My dear girl, do you think I'd take any chances with the health of my grandchild?" She pulled the sheet over my legs and ran her thumb across my forehead to smooth the hair out of my eyes. The maternal gesture repulsed me.

The door rattled, and I heard Matthew call out from the other side. Hannah pulled the key from her pocket and unlocked it. Matthew rushed straight to the bedside. His hair was tousled, his robe tied crookedly over his pajamas, yet to me he looked like Prince Charming, coming to save his true love. If only a kiss could rescue me.

Matthew squeezed my hand. "Are you all right?"

I nodded. I couldn't say anything else with Hannah hovering.

Matthew turned to his mother. "Dr. Westbrook says he'll come when Kate's pains are a few minutes apart. What do you think?"

"They haven't started yet. It may be some time."

Eva had labored for two days. How would I stand it? Already, the room felt suffocating.

"I offered to fetch some supplies from the hospital so everything's ready when the doctor arrives," Matthew said. "If you'll excuse us, Mum, I'll get dressed."

"Of course. I'll be downstairs."

As soon as Hannah left—leaving the key in the door, I noted—I began whispering furiously to Matthew.

"I'm not having the baby here. You have to call Dr. Westbrook and tell him we're going to the hospital."

How many times had I seen that caring yet bewildered expression on Matthew's face? Maybe I'd cried wolf so many times he no longer bothered to believe me.

"I know it's upsetting," Matthew said. "But I'm not going against the doctor's advice. We've got to think of the baby."

The baby. Never me. Was that how it would be from now on?

Matthew walked over to his armoire and began pulling out clothes. Already his attention was wandering; whether to wear a plain white shirt or one with stripes appeared to be a more pressing concern than his terrified wife.

"Why can't you send Hank to the hospital?" I asked.

"It's Sunday." Hank's day off. "I'm the only one who can drive the car."

Matthew walked into the bathroom, and I heard water splashing in the sink. I felt calmer, knowing he was close by. Husbands weren't supposed to be hanging around birthing rooms; they were shooed away to play golf or smoke cigars with their friends. But I knew Matthew would stay if I asked him. He'd look out for me. I had a sudden, vivid image of Hannah swooping in and snatching the baby out of my arms. I even knew what she'd say: *You rest and I'll take care of the little one. It's for your own good.*

"You'll come right back, after you're done?" I called out.

Matthew came out of the bathroom in a clean undershirt and drawers. "Whatever you want," he said.

I forced a smile. "I'd feel better, with you here."

Matthew quickly pulled on his trousers and shirt and fastened his tie with a few flips of his wrists. "I'm off, then. Won't be long, I promise."

He leaned in for a kiss, and I grabbed his arms to pull him closer. Pressed my hands against his solid shoulders and back, reassured by his protection. Then he was gone, closing the door softly behind him.

Unlocked.

I slid out of bed and opened the door carefully to avoid any squeaks. No sign of Hannah. No maids scurrying down the hall. The only sounds I could hear were voices in the entryway, directly below.

". . . give her something," Matthew was saying.

Murmurs from Hannah. Then, "You know how she gets."

"You can't blame her for being scared." Matthew, indignant. Taking my side.

Hannah again. "Not good for the baby. Quite dangerous if she becomes too agitated."

A very long pause. Then Matthew. "Do what you have to. I trust your judgment."

They were going to knock me out.

I slipped back into my room and began pacing in a panic. I'd made a point of speaking to Matthew in a calm, rational voice, yet he still trusted his mother over me. Still believed she had my best interests at heart. What easy prey he was, for women like Hannah and Marjorie! So eager to please, so anxious to make everything right.

I knew, deep down, that the baby was fine, that the story about its delicate health had been concocted to keep me under Hannah's control. To her, I was a broodmare, meant only to pop out the next generation of Lemonts. How easily I could become one of those wives pictured on my dressing room wall, women who faded from history, leaving no trace of themselves behind. She wouldn't hurt me as long as I was carrying the family heir, but what would happen afterward? Hannah wanted her grandchild raised at Lakecrest under her supervision. And the Lemonts always got what they wanted.

The only question was how she'd do it. A shot in the arm while I was distracted by labor pangs? I'd wake up and find the baby had already been whisked off to the nursery. Hannah would arrange a stay for me at a rest home, someplace I could recover from an ailment I didn't have. Dr. Westbrook or Dr. McNally would produce a report that painted me as an unfit mother, and just like that, I'd lose my child. And lose Matthew. I'd be cast out of the family forever.

Or would she go even further? There are so many ways childbirth can go wrong, especially an old-fashioned home birth. I might never wake up. *Complications,* Hannah would say sadly. Matthew would be devastated, but his mother would be there to comfort him. To claim him back.

Shaky with nerves, I pulled on a silk robe and glanced at the clock. Nearly four in the morning. Hank would be arriving for work in a few hours. It wouldn't be fair, asking him to risk his job for my sake. But he was the only person at Lakecrest who might be willing to help. I rushed to my dressing table and opened my jewelry box. It had been empty a year ago when Blanche gave it to me as a wedding present. Now it sparkled with gold and silver and glittering gemstones. Each piece was a token of Matthew's love.

I'd put away money, too, after my ill-fated attempt to run home to Ma. A bill here and there taken from Matthew's billfold or slipped out of the drawer where Hannah kept the household accounts. I flipped through the roll. Two hundred dollars, enough to cover at least a few months of Hank's salary. I put the money in one pocket of my robe and a handful of diamond bracelets in the other. Hopefully it would be enough to convince him.

I crept back to my bedroom and stuck my head out the doorway. I heard footsteps and the distinctive creak of the front door opening. Matthew was leaving, which meant Hannah would be back upstairs any minute. I snuck out into the second-floor hallway, assessing each room I passed. Could I fit under one of the beds? Slip behind a thick curtain? I heard Hannah's heels tapping up the marble stairs. She'd discover me instantly if I started rummaging around one of the guest rooms. The only way to gain more time was to keep going, up the service stairs to the third floor. I didn't know which of the wooden steps were loose, and I cringed when one made a squeaky groan. My only advantage was that Hannah would be heading in the opposite direction, toward my bedroom. I had a few minutes before she started searching for me in earnest.

I'd been to the servants' wing before, during those rainy days when I'd wandered around in search of Lakecrest's secrets. It must have been bustling back in Obadiah and Cecily's time. Now, the rooms were silent and deserted, Spartan spaces with two beds, one dresser, and little else. I kept going toward the attic that took up the other half of the top floor. In the daytime, it was relatively bright, with square windows set into the dormers, but now it was pitch black and almost impossible to navigate.

I stumbled against an old rocking chair, sucking in my breath to avoid crying out when my toe twisted against the wood. I sank down on top of a trunk, panting. This momentary ache was nothing compared to the labor pains that would be assaulting me at any minute.

Though it was stifling hot and I was damp with sweat, I began to shiver. There'd be a search on for me by now. Hannah and Edna were the only ones at home—Gerta and Alice, like Hank, didn't start work until eight—and it would take the two of them some time to check all the rooms on the first and second floors. But sooner or later, they'd come up here.

The sky began to lighten with the first hints of dawn, and I crept over to a window. To my great relief, there was a latch, and I was able to pull it open. Fresh air drifted in like a gift from God, and I stuck my face out to drink it in. It was going to be a beautiful sunrise; the sky over the lake was already tinted with pink and gold. Outside, the estate spread around me in all its late-summer beauty: lush trees and flower beds formed patterns of green and yellow and red around the swirling pathways. In the distance, I saw an enormous slab of bare earth where the Labyrinth had once stood. There was no rubble to mark the spot, not a single brick. Nothing to show it had ever existed.

For the first time, I saw a small building the Labyrinth had previously kept hidden. Modest, with only two windows and a sagging roof. Karel's cottage, I guessed. Eerie, to think of him living there all those years, so close to Cecily's body. The woman he'd killed? The woman he'd loved?

Possibly both.

With the attic gradually getting lighter, I was better able to search for a hiding place. I scoured the dusty piles of furniture and lamps and paintings, careful not to disturb anything that might make noise. I saw the trunk I'd gone through months ago, when I'd found the scrapbook of Cecily's newspaper clippings. There hadn't been anything else interesting inside, only stacks of musty bedding. I looked at the trunk and suddenly thought of Ma. It looked like the one she'd brought on her visit, the one with "O'Meara" painted on the front. I examined the trunk more closely and gently pushed aside the large mirror leaning against the back. There I saw what I'd hardly dared to hope for: the name Cecily Lemont.

It was hers. I flipped it open and saw the piles of cloth I'd tossed aside so carelessly before. I let one piece of fabric fall open and realized it was a dress, one of the white gowns Cecily and her acolytes must have worn for their ceremonies at the Temple. I searched through the stack; there were at least ten of them. Some had faint remnants of mud along the hem. There was a quilt, a few blankets—had these come from Cecily's bed? I pawed through them, hoping to feel some lingering trace of her. But there was nothing.

From far away, I heard the thump of footsteps coming up the service stairs. What an idiot I'd been, wasting time on Cecily! I hurled everything back into the trunk and closed the top, then glanced frantically around the attic. I saw a grandfather clock wedged in a corner, one of its hands dangling off. Paintings leaned in a stack around it, and a few were big enough that I might be able to squeeze myself behind them.

Thud. Thud. The steps were pausing at each of the servants' rooms. Getting closer. Trying not to let fear overwhelm my caution, I tiptoed to the clock and carefully leaned one of the paintings to the side. Wincing from the effort, I crouched down and crawled to the base of the clock, then pulled the canvases around me as a shelter. It wasn't long afterward that I heard the floor across the room creaking. Someone had come in.

My heart was pounding so hard I was sure it would give me away. *Poe's tell-tale heart,* I thought giddily, trying to keep my breathing steady. I couldn't see out, but the lumbering pace sounded like Edna. To my horror, the muscles in my legs began to shake; I didn't know how long I'd be able to maintain this awkward, hunched position. I pushed my hand against my mouth to keep in the moans that threatened to escape. Thankfully, the footsteps moved to the other side of the room, then grew fainter as Edna returned to the stairs. I was safe for the moment. But I knew I couldn't stay up there much longer. The only thing worse than giving birth in my room would be doing it in the attic, alone.

And what if Dr. Westbrook was right? If the baby was weak, I'd be responsible if something went wrong.

I couldn't tell exactly what time it was, but from the sunlight coming in the windows, it had to be at least seven. Hank would be in the garage by now. I knew a set of stairs led directly from the servants' quarters to the kitchen, and if I could get down those without being seen, I could escape out the side door.

I pushed aside the paintings and pulled myself up. Matthew must be back by now; was he looking for me, too? He'd be beside himself. Devastated that I'd run off without telling him—again. *I'll explain it to him later,* I told myself, *when I've gotten him away from Hannah.* I still believed we could break away and start fresh.

Wasn't that the American way?

I found a set of stairs leading directly from the attic. Clutching the banister for support, I eased myself down one step, then another. Fear made me clumsy, and when my foot nearly slid out from under me, I froze and curled over, keeping myself as still as possible until my breathing eased. The staircase came to an end after one flight on a landing somewhere above the second floor. Doorways opened to a series of cramped spaces: a storage closet filled with blankets and pillows, a room with ironing boards and hangers, another with a sink and buckets and mops. Places the servants could work out of sight that looked like they hadn't been used in decades.

The workrooms led from one into another, always ending back at the same landing. I had no idea where I was, and there was no clear way out; it felt like the Labyrinth all over again. I felt a throbbing in my stomach, like a clock ticking, urging me out. Finally, I looked out one of the narrow windows to get my bearings. I saw the lake and the beach, which meant I was directly over the kitchen. So close! I went back to the stairs, certain there must be another way down. I examined the landing more carefully and at last I saw it: a door concealed in the paneling, all but invisible unless you were standing directly in front of it. I pushed against the door—it swung open easily and silently—and found myself in the second-floor hallway. Opposite Hannah's bedroom.

I stood still and listened. Nothing. Could everyone be outside searching the grounds? Carefully, I moved along the hall. I'd seen Alice and Gerta bring sheets up to the linen closet from the laundry room below, which meant there was another set of service stairs at the center of the house. I found it easily and began walking down, taking each step as lightly as possible, alert to any sound. The kitchen was the only room at Lakecrest that never felt deserted; there was almost always someone there, cooking or cleaning or brewing tea. I passed through the laundry room, then the butler's pantry. I peeked around the corner, ducking down to make myself less visible.

The kitchen was empty.

I hurried to the door. Pulled it open and did a quick check of the kitchen garden. No one. Ahead of me was the gravel path that curved around the side of the house. If I could get to the front drive, I'd be only a few hundred feet from the garage. Hank. The car. I tried to run, but my body fought against the effort, my stomach weighing me down. *Don't stop,* I told myself. *Not when you're so close.*

I turned the corner, and the garage appeared before me like a beacon guiding me to safety. Only a few more steps. Another. My feet stumbled on the uneven ground, and I nearly fell. I saw Hank, emerging from behind the car, staring at me. He rushed toward me, arms outstretched, and I collapsed into him, sagging with relief. He sat me down gently on the grass and took a step back.

"Mrs. Lemont? Are you all right?"

"Hank, you have to take me to the hospital. The baby's coming."

"Mr. Lemont's worried sick. I was about to drive down to the Monroes' to look for you."

"We have to go, right now." I reached into the sagging pockets of my robe. "Here's a payment for your trouble. Jewelry, too; I'm sure it's quite valuable. You can give it to your wife or pawn it if you'd like."

The bracelets slithered from my hand to the ground. Hank looked at them as if they were poison.

"Please, Hank, you're the only one I trust."

He glanced toward the house, uncertain. I grabbed his hands, squeezing his fingers as I begged, and that's what doomed me. Hank twisted out of my grip and stepped back, his face a mix of anguished sympathy and fear. *Lemonts are never overly familiar with staff.* Especially not their Negro drivers. I'd put his job and his family in danger, and I can't blame him for putting his future over my own.

Hank looked behind me and shouted, "She's here! I've found her!"

I heard thudding footsteps, and then hands were reaching under my arms, pulling me up. Matthew on one side, Gerta on the other, but all I could see was Hank, stepping back as ten- and twenty-dollar bills cascaded around my feet. As if in punishment for my disloyalty, a dull ache radiated across my lower back. It wouldn't be long before my pains started. I began to sob, dreading the ordeal to come.

No one else made a sound.

Matthew and Gerta half carried and half dragged me into the house and up the front stairs. When we reached my bedroom—my cell!—I clutched at Matthew and pleaded with him to take me away, but my words were slurred and jumbled, and he simply looked ahead, his face pale. Gerta pulled off my robe and laid me back in bed. I saw Hannah at the bedside, watching. As always.

"No!" I shouted. "Matthew, please! Get her out!"

Matthew looked from me to his mother. Bewildered. "What should I do?" he asked. I couldn't tell whom he was speaking to.

"You shouldn't see her like this," Hannah said. "Go call the doctor. Tell him it's almost time."

"Don't leave me alone with her," I cried. "She wants to kill me!"

I couldn't have chosen worse words to evoke sympathy. Matthew looked furious.

"Don't worry," Hannah told him, infuriatingly calm. "Women say all sorts of nonsense during childbirth."

Matthew stomped off, and any hope for escape left along with him. My arms and legs were quivering, and my nightgown was damp with sweat. Hannah's face sagged, her usual self-satisfied smirk replaced by a wistful sadness.

"Do you really think I'd hurt you?" she asked.

I didn't answer. Are executioners ever moved by last minute pleas?

"Of course you don't trust me," Hannah said. "I haven't earned it." With a weary sigh, she sat down in Matthew's armchair. "We have a little while before the doctor arrives. I'll tell you everything. An offering, if you will. You wonder if I killed Cecily, don't you? I suppose the answer is yes. I did."

CHAPTER SEVENTEEN

"I can't blame you for being suspicious," Hannah began. "All I ask is that you hear me out. Give me a chance, just as I gave you."

She leaned over to fluff up my pillow. "That's better, isn't it? Honestly, you needn't look so scared. You've heard too many stories—that's the problem. Told a few yourself, haven't you, Kate?"

"What do you mean?"

"You're such a smart girl—I can't believe you never guessed I've known all about you from the start. As soon as Matthew told me about the charming young governess he'd met on the boat, I called Mr. Haveleck. Yes, the very same; he's worked for Lemont Industries for years. He went to Ohio to investigate you, and even I was surprised by the depravity he found. Your drunk of a father wasn't much of a surprise, given your heritage. A taste for alcohol is a common weakness among the Irish, isn't it? I could even forgive your mother her murderous outburst, given her treatment at his hands. However, the line of work she chose afterward? That was a shock."

All this time, Hannah knew.

"I was quite prepared to put a stop to your romance with Matthew after reading Mr. Haveleck's first report," Hannah said with a condescending smile. "Then he wrote a second letter, and that one gave me pause. He started with a glowing account of your aunt, Nellie—very respectable, in excellent health, the mother of four thriving children. He'd spoken to another woman as well, the housemother at your college dormitory. What was her name?"

"Mrs. Llewellyn," I whispered.

"Ah, yes. She was particularly helpful and quite effusive in her praise of you. She told Mr. Haveleck a very interesting story about a certain young man."

I couldn't stop the mortified flush that rose up every time I thought of Randall. How could Mrs. Llewellyn have betrayed my trust? Was anyone immune to the Lemonts' money? The muscles of my stomach tightened, and I took quick, shallow breaths, trying to present Hannah with a blank, unconcerned expression.

"Kate, Kate," Hannah murmured. "I don't care what happened; I truly don't. What struck me was how you handled yourself. What might have been a disastrous incident was hushed up with no damage to anyone's reputation, thanks to your quick thinking. Not many girls your age would have known what to do. I was quite impressed.

"The boy's name was Bigelow, wasn't it? It's a curious thing—I found out not long after that his father had mortgaged their hotels to the hilt. Made a terrible mess of the family's finances. It's shocking, the mistakes people make when they get greedy. I had a word with the Palmers about it—they didn't make the Palmer House into one of the world's finest hotels without knowing the business inside and out—and wouldn't you know? They decided to branch out to Ohio. They say Mr. Bigelow was so desperate he sold at a loss. Shipped his son off to South America. He'd become a bit of an embarrassment, it seems."

For years, I'd wondered what I'd do if I ran into Randall, whether I'd be able to look into his arrogant eyes and pretend I didn't care what happened. Now, thanks to Hannah, I wouldn't have to.

"I can make things happen, you see," Hannah said. "I could have stopped your marriage to Matthew by telling him any one of your lies. But I didn't, because I came to believe you were exactly the sort of wife Matthew needed. Oh, I knew you were after his money, but you weren't coldhearted. You had some affection for him. That was clear. You were simply determined to better yourself, and who could blame you, after the way you'd been raised? Would it surprise you to know that I rather admired your spirit? That I hoped some of it might rub off on Matthew?

"You'll soon know what it's like to fret over your child's future. I've always known Matthew was more fragile than other boys. Not physically, of course. With his looks, no one guessed a thing. I was the only one who knew how much he questioned himself. Hated himself, at times. Cecily saw it, too. Encouraged him to wallow in it, just as she did."

"Cecily . . . ," I said.

"Yes, yes, we'll get to her. But I must make you understand about Matthew first. I did everything I could for him—encouraged him to make friends with the right sort of people at Choate and join the best fraternity at Yale. I was surprised when he decided to study medicine, but to be honest, I didn't think he'd last through the training. I didn't understand how desperate he was to prove himself."

Hannah sighed, steeling herself. "The war didn't make Matthew a man," she said. "It wrecked him, as surely as if he'd been shelled in a trench. Kate, whatever he's told you about his time afterward . . . it was worse than you can imagine. He acted like a madman, mumbling about ghosts and blood and all sorts of horrible things. He nearly threw himself out the bedroom window because it was the only way to make the visions stop! I cried when I first saw him in that cellar, tied down to the bed. I was forced to do it, out of love. It was the only way to protect Matthew from himself.

"In time, his terrors eased. I was the only one who knew he'd never truly be well. That's why I couldn't let him marry anyone in our social set. It's one thing for people to gossip about an eccentric aunt, but quite another for Matthew's mental instability to be common knowledge throughout Chicago. I hoped a new setting and new people might lure Matthew out of his gloom, so we spent a few years abroad. It worked for a time, but never for long. I nearly gave up on the idea of him marrying.

"And then Matthew met you. The very unexpected answer to my prayers. Someone who wouldn't run back to her family when her new husband started raving about his visions. No protective father to challenge Matthew about his odd behavior. Whatever your motives were for marrying my son, I knew you wouldn't be cruel to him. You'd stick it out, keep your mouth shut, and do everything you could to prove yourself a good wife."

And so I had. More or less.

"I'm sorry I wasn't able to tell you any of this at the time. I had to be an absolute terror to test your resolve. Would you abandon Matthew for the right price? But you didn't. You made your grand stand, and I admired you for it.

"You were just the wife I hoped you'd be. So wonderful at calming Matthew's moods. He'd never have been able to run Lemont Medical otherwise. Oh, I make the hard decisions to spare him the worry, and someday you'll do the same. What's important is that he *believes* he's in charge. It's such a boost to his confidence."

Hannah's voice was so hypnotic that it soothed my fear of the impending childbirth. What a relief it was to no longer run. To surrender to Hannah's story.

"I've never been your enemy, Kate. It wasn't until tonight that I realized how deeply you misunderstood me. How much Cecily has stood between us, even all these years after her death. The problem is that women like Cecily craft fantasies out of their own lives. How could you possibly understand her from the bits and pieces you've heard? She actually saw herself as a character from one of her stories. A tragic heroine! The Lemonts excel at many things, Kate, but I believe their greatest talent is for self-invention.

"You remember that book, with its nonsense about Henri de Le Mont fleeing the French Revolution? A pampered nobleman wouldn't have the first idea how to survive in the wilderness! Oh no, if he was tracking and skinning animals better than any other white man of his day, his origins must have been far . . . let us say, *earthier*. He's the one they credit with the motto *Factum est*. So bold, isn't it? Like the Lemonts themselves! I don't believe there was any romance with an Indian princess. Henri simply took the woman he wanted, as he would any other animal caught in one of his traps."

I remembered the note Matthew had written on board the *Franconia*, the one I'd found so charming: *The thought of giving up our lively conversations is enough to send me jumping off the deck at the earliest opportunity, so your answer must be yes.* No *please* or *if you like*. I wasn't given a choice.

"The men in this family were raised to believe they should get whatever they wanted," Hannah said. "Henri's son George was utterly ruthless, from what I've heard, and Obadiah . . . there was a man you wouldn't dare cross. He could ruin a man's business with one word to his bankers. Berthe Palmer and her society friends might have turned up their noses at Lakecrest's garishness, but they never refused an invitation from Obadiah. The Lemonts' wealth has always protected them.

"It's strange, when you come to think of it, that the only two people who defied Obadiah's orders were women. His daughter and his wife."

"Leticia," I said. "I always wondered why no one talked about her."

"She killed herself."

I knew Leticia only as a face in a portrait, but I felt a twinge of grief all the same. Another poor, lost Lemont.

"Jasper was the one who told me. Said his mother had taken the coward's way out. You'd think a loss like that would have left a mark, but he said it with absolutely no expression. She was Obadiah's first cousin, you know. A Lemont by birth. I couldn't stop thinking about Leticia and Obadiah, blood relations, and how both their children had turned out so strange. That's part of the reason I was so anxious that Matthew marry wisely. The Lemonts needed fresh stock. People like you and me."

I already felt somewhat less than human, sprawled on the bed, at the mercy of my body. Now Hannah was comparing me to livestock?

"Obadiah understood," she went on. "It's the only reason he favored my marriage to Jasper. Believe me, I wasn't at all what he'd planned for his son. I was only a few steps above the household help! But he recognized my father's ambition. And mine. How it might be useful to his family.

"I've never told you how I first met Cecily, have I? It was at Father's clinic, when I was fifteen years old. She had bandages on her wrists to cover the slashes she'd made in her skin. There was dried blood all over her arms before Mother washed it off. Cecily was only three years older than me, but it might as well have been twenty. She had such a style and elegance to her, even with matted hair and dark circles under her eyes. Her nightgown looked more expensive than my best Sunday dress, and her voice . . . well, she had a manner of speaking you simply couldn't ignore. It took me years and years to talk like a Lemont, but for Cecily it was a birthright. I didn't even mind her ordering me around and complaining about Mother's food. It made me feel special to have her attention.

"You'd never believe how nervous I was when Obadiah and Jasper made their first visit. Beauty can be quite blinding, can't it? Jasper took hold of my hands and thanked me for my kindness to his sister, and I fell in love with him right then and there. You'd never have thought it of me, would you? Mooning over a man like a sentimental fool?"

Hannah's lips twisted into a rueful smile, mocking her former self.

"Cecily stayed in Father's care nearly a month," she continued. "He tried all his modern treatments, but do you know what cured her? Poetry. I can see you don't believe me, but it's true. She asked Father about a book he was carrying, and before you know it, he was offering to teach her ancient Greek. Father understood that her mind needed to be challenged so it wouldn't wander down self-destructive paths. Cecily became his star student and his proudest achievement."

I could hear the subtext from the brightly bitter way Hannah said the words: *He loved her more than he loved me.*

"The triumphant tour to England was a mistake. Cecily simply wasn't strong enough. She failed the exam at Oxford and came back despondent. Tried to drown herself at Lakecrest. Obadiah realized she needed round-the-clock care, so Father sent me to stay with her. And Jasper was always there, checking on his sister and talking to me. When he proposed, I felt like the luckiest girl in the world, even though I suspected—correctly—that Obadiah had pushed his son into doing it. He'd been at Jasper for years to get married, and he thought I'd be a good influence, just as my Father had helped poor Cecily. Still, I didn't think Jasper would have agreed if he wasn't fond of me to some degree. It wasn't until our wedding night that Jasper made the terms of our marriage clear. Very matter-of-fact, as if it were perfectly natural, he told me he wouldn't be held to the same rules as other men. I'd have a comfortable life as long as I ignored his infidelity. Would you have accepted such a bargain, Kate?"

I shook my head. A tightening sensation snaked around my stomach and back. Uncomfortable, but not severe. Not yet.

"I hesitate to discuss what should remain behind closed doors," Hannah continued. "I only speak of this because it has bearing on what happened later. Jasper drank to excess and stayed out all hours. I turned my mind to dinner parties and the latest fashion in hats to keep from brooding. And I avoided the north end of the estate. That was Cecily's domain.

"The first time I entered the Labyrinth was on the night of the summer fête, some years after I was married. Those affairs put today's parties to shame—five hundred guests, a six-course dinner laid out in the Arabian Room, a full orchestra in the ballroom. We had the staff to do that sort of thing back then. As the last guests were leaving, I saw Cecily and her latest cohort of girls sneak off across the lawn. There'd been something odd about her manner all night, a certain devilish anticipation. I decided to follow them."

Just as I'd followed Matthew and Marjorie. Only to discover something I wish I'd never seen.

"They were chanting some nonsense in the Temple. Drinking wine out of silver goblets, though most were already showing the effects of too much punch. There was a certain beauty to the scene, I will admit. The white gowns and columns gleaming in the moonlight. Then they began shouting—shrieking, really—and ran off into the Labyrinth. I went after them. Sometimes we're too curious for our own good, aren't we? I heard their footsteps, leading the way. When I reached the center, I kept my body hidden behind a wall and peeked around the edge.

"It was bedlam. The girls were flinging themselves about, tearing at their clothes, working themselves into an absolute frenzy. Cecily was at the center. She'd ripped her dress right down the center, and she was pouring wine from a jug over her face and chest. She drenched the rest of them in wine as well, and they pawed at each other like animals. Practically howling! And then, to my horror, the Minotaur stepped forward."

I must have looked upset, because Hannah insisted I take a sip of water before she continued.

"I was mistaken, of course. It was a man dressed in black stepping out from behind the statue. His face was covered. The girls swarmed around him, grabbing at his arms and chest. Cecily pushed her way forward . . ." Hannah looked down modestly. "You can guess what happened next."

Marjorie had joked about orgies, and I felt strangely let down to find out she was right. It all sounded so tawdry, such a betrayal of Cecily's noble ideals.

"The others watched, with no shame at all! Then Cecily motioned one of the girls over, and the man called out. It was only one word—'Come'—but it was enough. I recognized my father's voice."

Hannah's voice had dropped to a murmur, as if she barely had the strength to accept what she'd witnessed.

"You've read his book," she said. "I saw it, here in your room. He was a brilliant scholar. He'd studied such perversions, but to act on them? I'd never have believed it if I hadn't seen for myself."

I remembered the inscription Dr. Rieger had written to Cecily: *My muse and inspiration for a most divine madness.* He'd spent his whole life studying and treating madness. And Cecily had inspired him to experience it himself.

"What happened next?" I asked.

"I ran out of there in tears! Never said a word to either of them about what I'd seen. I learned I was expecting not long after, which was a mercy. Children give women a purpose. It's why I know this baby will be good for you."

If Hannah was set on telling the truth, it was time she answered for everything. "Did you do something to make sure I'd get pregnant?" I asked.

"Oh, my dear, what kind of powers do you think I have?" She shook her head dismissively. "I was so happy in those early years, after the twins were born. I thought they'd put everything right, and for a time, they did. Jasper was such a proud father, and Cecily softened toward me, too. I worried about her influence on Matthew and Marjorie—who wouldn't?—but I couldn't deny how good she was with them. And they adored her.

"As the children grew older, Jasper spent more time away from Lakecrest. Times were changing, with shipping lines giving way to railroads, and the Lemont fortune suffered accordingly. Every investment Jasper made to cover the shortfall went bad. It's quite an awful realization, Kate, to find out your husband is a fool and your family is close to ruin. Jasper's personal failures were even worse. I know you are familiar with the chamber beneath Obadiah's office. After Obadiah's death, Jasper cleared out the things that had been stored there and claimed the room for his own purposes. I don't feel comfortable describing his preferences to someone in your delicate condition. Suffice to say, Jasper took pleasure in punishment, and he brought in women who satisfied his unsavory tastes. I saw him once, escorting one of his fancy girls out the service entrance. She had the same tumbling curls and wide eyes as Cecily. He'd even dressed her up in one of his sister's white gowns, though whatever he'd done had left the fabric in shreds. There were welts all over her cheeks and arms.

"I'm sorry if this disturbs you. It's the only way you'll understand. Jasper was infatuated with Cecily. His rages were nothing but bluster to hide his shameful feelings. He loved her and he hated her, because he knew she'd never be his.

"Cecily wasn't innocent, of course. She enjoyed provoking Jasper, as I'm sure she enjoyed toying with my father. But the children had a calming effect. She spent hours with Matthew and Marjorie, playing and telling stories. Whatever else I thought of her, I never doubted her love for them. She began painting more, spending time outside in the gardens, having fewer girls to stay. When my father died—a heart attack at a medical conference in Vienna—I assumed her debaucheries at the Labyrinth were over. For years, we lived together in peace. And then, when the twins were ten or eleven, Cecily fell in love."

"Karel?" I guessed.

Hannah nodded. If she was surprised that I knew, she didn't show it. "You'd never guess it now, but he used to be quite handsome. Not that I paid much mind to the groundskeepers, but Cecily was just the kind of person to find a laborer romantic! She managed to keep their liaison secret from almost everyone, but I saw them holding hands and whispering. I thought it was nothing more than a flirtation. I had no idea how deep Cecily's feelings went. I truly didn't; otherwise, I might have understood the repercussions of my actions."

Hannah paused, collecting herself. I'd never seen her look so genuinely upset.

"When the summer fête came round," Hannah went on, "I kept my eye on Cecily. I didn't trust her not to make trouble, not on that night. She was acting very odd: laughing too loud, slurring her words, always checking the watch she wore on a chain around her neck. I was quite sure she was planning to meet Karel under that full moon, but she was still at Lakecrest when the party ended. I said good night to her and Jasper at the top of the stairs and retired to my room. I changed into my nightdress and brushed out my hair, and then I heard a door creak and footsteps pattering down the hall. Not long after, I heard another door open—Jasper's, next to mine—and more footsteps. I peeked out and saw Jasper going downstairs.

"I looked out my window and saw Cecily on the lakefront path. Jasper was lurking in the trees behind her. Well, I thought, if Jasper wants to spy on Cecily, then I'll spy on him. I was flustered, in a rush, and I suppose I wasn't as quiet as I should have been. I had no idea Matthew heard all the commotion and followed me. I went straight to the Labyrinth, and I was about to enter when I saw Karel approaching. He was clearly startled to see me, and before I could think what to say, he'd mumbled some excuse and left. I was sure he'd come to meet Cecily and didn't want me to see them together. I was about to leave myself, when I heard sounds from inside the Labyrinth.

"The walls blocked most of the moonlight, and I could barely see where I was going. I kept having the odd sensation that I was being watched—which I was, by Matthew—but whenever I turned around, there was no one there. When I arrived at the opening that led into the clearing, I saw Cecily lying on her side, looking like some kind of pagan goddess. She'd pulled down the shoulders of her gown, and wine dripped from her chin and down her neck. Slowly and deliberately, she poured wine over her chest. As if her body were some kind of offering! Her eyes looked heavy, as if she were half-asleep. Then I heard Jasper say, 'You will be my destruction,' and Cecily laughed.

"My heart nearly stopped. I scurried back and tumbled into Matthew. Behind me, I could hear sounds—my God, like animals!— and I was terrified Matthew would see. I dragged him away, back to the house. I told him over and over it was only a dream. It was all I could think to say. And worse was to come. By the end of the summer, I'd worked out that Cecily was expecting."

I grimaced as a ripple of pain made my stomach clench. Hannah wiped my face with a damp towel. The contraction eased, and I sucked in a breath, trying to calm my racing heart.

"I waited for Cecily to confide in me, but she didn't," Hannah said. "I assumed she'd do what any woman with money does in her position: arrange a trip abroad and have the child adopted. But she had other plans. I only found out about it when I saw her maid with a note to be delivered to Karel. I read it, of course, and why wouldn't I? Who knows what kind of scheme she was plotting? The note instructed Karel to meet her in the Labyrinth at midnight—they'd made plans to elope.

"It was ludicrous. Cecily running away with a gardener? Matthew and Marjorie would be laughingstocks! As for the child . . . it could be the product of relations with her own brother! No, no. Cecily couldn't possibly keep that baby, and I was the only one who could ensure she gave it up.

"I went to Karel's cottage that night, and he admitted everything. He swore he and Cecily had only given in to temptation once, during a rainstorm when she'd taken refuge at his cottage. It was clear he didn't know anything about pregnancy—I remembered the date of the storm and could tell Cecily was farther along than that. That's when I knew she was carrying Jasper's child.

"I didn't tell Karel, of course. I gave him two choices: go with Cecily, who was a good ten years older and would soon be cut off from her money by her furious brother, or leave Lakecrest alone, with a generous payment and excellent references. Karel quickly came to the right decision. He agreed to leave in the next few days, after I'd been able to gather the money. I even felt a bit sorry for Cecily when I saw how willingly he deserted her.

"Cecily's note to Karel had said to meet in a hidden compartment of the Labyrinth. I decided to let her wait in vain. You may think me petty, but I thought it would do her good to be brought down a peg. I was as surprised as anyone when I heard her bed hadn't been slept in. She must have heard the policemen tramping across the estate the next day, calling her name, but she never came out. Even then I wasn't worried. I thought she was out there, sulking. After everyone left that night, Jasper poured a glass of whiskey—Lord knows how many he'd had that day—and I could see he was holding back tears. It gave me such satisfaction to have the upper hand at last! I didn't tell him I knew where Cecily was; I chose to let him suffer. And that's not the worst of it. Not by a half.

"When Jasper was so drunk he could hardly stand, I called his valet to see him to bed, then I left Lakecrest. It was beautiful out: stars sprinkled across the sky, the moonlight reflected on the water. Even so, it took all the strength I had to enter the Labyrinth that night. I shouted out Cecily's name, knowing no one would hear, and this time she came out. Looking such a wreck I almost felt sorry for her. I told her Karel wasn't coming and that we should discuss her situation back at the house. The look she gave me . . . well, it was the kind a queen gives the lowliest servant. 'How dare you give me orders,' she said, as if I were of no account. A nobody, utterly beneath her.

"Had she shown a moment of weakness, I might have been kinder. Instead, I lashed out. I told her she was vile and depraved, that I'd never allow the child of such evil at Lakecrest. 'Evil?' she asked. 'The baby was

258

created in an act of great beauty.' Honestly, Kate, it was all such gibber-ish, but she believed it! She honestly believed what she got up to in the Labyrinth had some sort of sacred meaning! Then she prattled on about me being a snob simply because the child was Karel's, and it took me some time to understand because I was so confused.

"Kate—she didn't know. The wine she drank was mixed with leaves that brought on visions. The same kind used in ancient Greece, natu-rally. Cecily thought Karel had come to her in the form of the Minotaur. I was the one who told her it was Jasper.

"Dear God, her face. Her entire body collapsed. There wasn't much to say after that. I left her on the ground, sobbing, and went to bed. The next day, Cecily's room was still empty. I assumed she'd skulk in eventually when she needed food. Jasper was frantic, but I still believed Cecily would turn up at the house any minute. After supper, when Jasper turned back to his whiskey, I returned to the Labyrinth. Cecily was lying right where I'd left her, and I thought she was asleep. Until I saw the knife by her side. It was the kind the gardeners used to trim branches; I suppose it might have been Karel's—Kate, you can't under-stand what I did unless you know how awful it was. She was coated in blood. She'd cut her wrists—there were gouges all over her arms—but the worst was her stomach. She'd butchered herself! Herself and the baby . . ."

I wanted to press my hands against my ears and block out the horrifying images Hannah was describing. But I couldn't. My fingers clenched into fists.

"In any other circumstances, I would have called the police, but I couldn't let news of the baby come out. The whole family would be shunned. If only I'd let her run away, I thought in a panic, and then the idea lingered. What if her body simply disappeared? The police would continue searching, and people might talk, but no one would know the truth. In time, Cecily would be forgotten. So I grabbed her arms and dragged her inside the wall."

In a haze, I heard Hannah describe how she'd pulled off her stockings to wipe the blood off the grass. How she'd punished Jasper by never telling him the truth about Cecily. How Karel had begged to stay at Lakecrest, hoping Cecily would one day come back.

"I did what needed to be done, for the family's sake. Still, there are moments I wonder if Cecily's death is on my hands."

I looked at Hannah's wan face, her sagging shoulders. Then I felt a pressure in my body, and I gasped. Hannah turned away to talk to someone in the doorway; I couldn't see who it was.

"Matthew," I whispered.

"He's at the Monroes'. I didn't want him to hear this."

The pain relented, and I gulped for air.

"I may be a monster," Hannah said, the words spilling out in a rush, "but everything I did was to protect the Lemont name. *Your* name. I know you don't like me. Perhaps you never will. But I wasn't born to this life any more than you were! The past you tried so hard to hide is gone—you are Kate Lemont of Lakecrest. One day, you'll be hosting teas and planning your daughter's debut at the Drake and shaking your head at your grandchildren's fashions. You'll be the person who holds this family together after I'm gone."

I was dimly aware of voices outside. A commotion in the hall. I caught a glimpse of Alice's face, tight with concern. I saw Dr. Westbrook enter the room, pushing a wheeled canister.

Hannah wiped my face. "Now, now. You'll be all right. You'll have a nice rest, and when you wake up, you'll meet your new baby."

Hannah was talking to the doctor, but I couldn't hear what they were saying. Two hands pressed a breathing mask over my nose and mouth. I tried to push it away, but my palms were slippery, and I couldn't grab on. The rubber edges dug into my cheeks. Flailing, panicking, I sucked in a breath. And another.

Then I didn't feel anything at all.

CHAPTER EIGHTEEN

Slowly, I opened my eyes. I saw the sheet pulled smooth against my chest and tucked under my arms. Matthew was perched on the side of the bed, looking at me expectantly.

It took me a minute to remember he was my husband.

"Darling." He patted my cheek. Cautious. "How do you feel?"

I tried to identify the sensations scattered throughout my body. Throbbing head, tingling breasts. A dull ache further down. The vague sense that I was hovering above the bed, observing myself from a distance.

I looked around. I was in my bedroom at Lakecrest. The curtains were closed, the lamps lit. Nighttime. I heard the distinctive squeak of the door hinges, and Dr. Westbrook's head appeared over Matthew's shoulder.

"Ah! You're awake."

For one disorienting minute, I couldn't put a name to his face, and I tried to hide my agitation. Then I remembered. I glanced down and saw how the covers were flat against my stomach.

"The baby," I whispered.

"Hearty and healthy," Dr. Westbrook assured me.

I reached out for Matthew, felt his hand in mine.

"It's all right," he murmured. "Everything's all right."

I tried to sort through the jumble of memories clouding my brain. Hannah, talking about Cecily's dead body. Had I dreamed it? Why couldn't I remember my own baby being born?

As if reading my thoughts, Dr. Westbrook said, "We had to put you under full sedation, Mrs. Lemont. You were quite agitated when I arrived."

Agitated? Fragments of conversation flickered at the edge of my understanding.

She butchered herself.

I did what needed to be done.

You'll be the person who holds this family together.

"No cause for worry," Dr. Westbrook went on cheerfully. "Look who's come to meet you."

A high-pitched whimper made me turn. Hannah was walking into the room, holding a white bundle. She placed the baby in my arms, beaming, and I looked down at a tiny, red-faced creature.

"A girl," Hannah said. "A beautiful baby girl."

That's when the tears welled up. All along, I'd expected a boy, a son for Matthew and an heir for the Lemonts. But this little girl would be mine. She wouldn't be pushed into the family business or carry the burden of passing on the Lemont name. I could protect her.

All Matthew's doubts about being a father seemed to have vanished. We smiled and laughed and cried, and I saw Alice, Edna, and Gerta in the doorway, basking in our joy. I felt weak with relief. With happiness.

"Stella, is it?" Matthew asked. "Or Holly?" We'd put so much thought into boys' names that we'd never settled on a definite choice for a girl.

I stared into the baby's face. She was so small, so new. How could I be sure what name would fit once she developed into her own person?

"Stella," I cooed, and the baby twisted her face into what I took as agreement. Already, I was charmed by every movement of her lips and arms, and I pulled away the blanket to tickle her toes.

"I've brought my colleague, Nurse Gage, to take you through the feeding when you're ready," Dr. Westbrook said. "I find most patients prefer to do a few weeks themselves before the baby nurse takes over."

"Time we left the new parents alone to get acquainted," Hannah announced. "Kate, would you like something to eat? You must be famished."

Surprisingly, I was. I nodded, and Hannah smiled with brisk satisfaction. Her entire confession felt like a distant memory, a story I'd heard years before. The woman who'd driven her sister-in-law to suicide, who'd kept the secret of Cecily's death a secret for nearly twenty years, was still in control of everyone and everything around her.

Once we were alone, Matthew climbed up on the bed next to me, oohing and aahing over Stella's scrunched-up face. With the ether wearing off, I was starting to feel sore, and I winced when he put a hand around my shoulder and pulled me tight for a hug.

"It's all right," I said when he tried to apologize. "I'm so glad you're here."

"I always will be." A gentle peck on my forehead.

I thought of us pushing a carriage along the lakefront path and watching Stella build sand castles on the beach. Perhaps she would be tied to this land as much as Obadiah was when he surveyed the edge of the prairie and built the estate that would be his legacy. I passed Stella into Matthew's arms, and as I watched them, father and daughter, I felt almost crushed by my love for both of them.

I finally understood what Hannah had been trying to tell me. History depicts families as generations of men passing down talents and weaknesses along with their last names. But every birth is a blend of old and new, a mingling of the father's blood with that of another line whose name is lost as soon as the wedding vows are said. Every great dynasty is an intricate stew of mothers and fathers, recreating itself with each generation.

The Lemonts' reputation was formed by Henri's ambition and Obadiah's quest for wealth. But every Lemont had also been shaped by the family's forgotten women. Matthew and Marjorie inherited their father's arrogance and their aunt's eccentricities, but they were also Hannah's children, gifted with her perseverance and strength. Marjorie, for all her brittleness, had a fundamental decency she tried to hide, and Matthew fought to stay loyal and kind despite his troubled mind. Hannah hadn't been a perfect wife or mother, but she'd done her best. In the end, her children had turned out better than Cecily and Jasper. My daughter with Matthew would do even better.

Stella let out a mewling sort of cry, and Matthew looked to me for reassurance.

"You're doing fine," I said.

From the corner of my eye, I could see a face peering through a crack in the doorway. Hannah, hovering. I felt the familiar irritation swell up, then almost instantly subside. For the first time, I saw Hannah for who she was: a woman on the brink of old age, trying desperately to maintain her grip on power. She ruled Lakecrest; she ruled Lemont Industries; she ruled her own son. But she would not reign forever. Step by step, day by day, I'd make myself indispensable. I'd learn about the business and demand a seat on the board of directors. Convince Matthew to tear the gargoyles and turrets off Lakecrest and transform it into a modern showplace. Raise Stella to look to the future, not the past.

Hannah had never denied meddling with my family-planning supplies; I still believed she'd done it. If it weren't for Stella, Matthew and I might be in Africa right now, or Paris, or New York. We might have escaped Lakecrest. I looked over Matthew's shoulder, directly at Hannah, holding her gaze.

This baby is mine, my eyes told her. *I win.*

EPILOGUE

The Depression didn't wipe us out, but life at Lakecrest changed. There were no more parties, and my redecorating plans had to be put aside. I listened to the dismal economic news with only halfhearted interest. Childbirth had changed me more than just physically; it was as if the struggle to bring Stella into the world had destroyed my ambition. It was enough to sit with Stella in my lap, watching her grab at my hair or skirt. When I was bored of mothering, I handed her to the baby nurse and napped or read a book. When I bothered to reflect on what my life had become, I was mystified by my lassitude. It took a long time to realize that what I was feeling was contentment. Never before had I experienced it so completely.

Years passed as if they were days, with little to distinguish one from another. Blanche sent letters from New York and Miami, and I answered with note cards, unable to find enough news to fill a whole page. I made appearances at appropriate events: meetings of the Ladies' Club and a Young Mothers card group with Eva. By the time Stella was walking, Matthew and I had agreed to have another child, and Robbie was born in the spring of 1932. An easy birth for an easy baby. From the beginning, he wanted nothing more than cuddles and affection, and my most vivid memories of that summer are of sitting under a beach umbrella with Robbie kicking on a blanket and Stella splashing at the water's edge. I was sunstruck and lazy, free of the inner turmoil that had propelled me into this privileged life. When Matthew came home from work to join us, the children looked at him with the same stunned awe I used to feel early in my married life: what a wonder that such a gorgeous man should be ours!

My battles with Hannah faded into insignificance. I was relieved to be spared the running of the household and allowed her to supervise the nurse and the children's schedules. There were signs here and there that she hadn't given up her interfering ways. An offhand comment she made about boarding schools that I chose to ignore. Her insistence we spend August in Maine, despite the expense, because the "right people" would be there. I went along without complaint, biding my time. As my children became more independent, flickers of my old self sparked to life. With every step Robbie took, a piece shifted back into place.

Turning points are often best viewed in hindsight, but I knew right away the phone call from Terrence Fry could change everything. He was a well-known architect working with rich clients who wanted a lakeside home. Might some of our property be for sale? Despite the times, there were apparently still people with enough money to pay handsomely for a water view. It sounded like an offer heaven-sent to solve two problems at once. We'd be rid of the bleak, deserted north estate, and we'd finally be able to afford a renovation of Lakecrest.

Matthew and I were immediately in favor of selling, but not Hannah. We first discussed it over dinner, resolved nothing by dessert, then dragged the arguments along with us into the next day. I turned on the charm, and Matthew pulled out the family accounts to make his case, but Hannah wouldn't budge. It was then that I realized my life and my children's future were still firmly in her hands.

I began tallying up the slights I'd previously brushed off, the constant instructions to do things this way or that. Early motherhood had been a cocoon, nestling me as I transformed into a sharper, clearer version of myself. Before I had children, I prided myself on being strong and independent; now, I saw how weak I'd really been. Cowed by Hannah's anger and scared of Matthew's mood swings, I'd allowed a leaky house and bossy old lady to drive me nearly crazy. Matthew's dreams were long gone, thanks to Lemont Medical's magical syrup, but if they ever started up again, I knew I'd no longer cringe at the edge of the bed if he attacked me in the night. I'd fight back.

Pent-up anger builds in secret, like a volcano beneath the surface. You never know when the tremor will hit that sets it off.

It was an ordinary summer day, the heat building but not yet oppressive. Hannah and I were following Stella and Robbie and the nanny on our usual midmorning walk. There'd be luncheon in an hour, then a nap for Robbie and an afternoon at the beach with Eva and her children. The routine was ingrained, and nothing in those fateful minutes warned of approaching danger. But isn't that often the way of it, right before your life inexorably changes?

The nanny held Robbie's hand while Stella skipped ahead. She became a speck in the distance, a whirl of blonde and white in the waist-high prairie grass. Around her hovered the ghosts of buildings past. I would never be able to look at this landscape without seeing the Temple and the Labyrinth, without picturing Cecily stabbing herself to death.

I stopped and turned to Hannah. We had understood each other once on the day Stella was born. I appealed to the Hannah buried beneath the stern self-righteousness, the woman who had acknowledged my importance to her family.

"Don't you want to be free of all this?" I pleaded. "There'd be a new family, a new house. A fence. We wouldn't have to face this constant reminder of what happened."

"There's no need to be dramatic," she said. "And to think you accuse me of dwelling in the past!"

Irked by her dismissive tone, I struck back. "If that were true, you'd welcome the changes I planned for Lakecrest."

"You know very well that we can't afford to redecorate."

I could have stopped right there and accepted that Hannah was being Hannah and stomped off after the children. But the pride I'd kept caged was pushing to break free. I wanted to provoke Hannah and show her I wasn't beaten.

"We'd have the money if we sold the land!" I exclaimed. "Matthew's all for it."

"Matthew will say whatever he must to keep you happy."

Knowing that was true didn't make me any less angry. "If we're nearly in the poorhouse, why is there money for boarding school?"

"That is entirely different," Hannah said. "School is an investment in Stella and Robert's future. If they don't go to the right schools, they won't move in the right circles."

"Well, I'm not sending my children away. No snobby French governesses, either. I'm going to enroll Stella in the East Ridge school."

Hannah looked as if I'd suggested sending her to the moon. "You can't!"

My laugh sounded more like a snort. "Can't I? I am her mother. Why not close up Lakecrest while we're at it? You're always telling me it costs a fortune to run. Matthew and I could rent a house in town. That would be the financially wise choice, wouldn't it? I'm sure we could find a cozy little apartment for you nearby."

Stella shrieked with a wild kind of joy. I saw Robbie toddling after her, the nanny almost obscured by weeds. Even as I threatened to move, I knew I'd never do it. My children loved this land.

"That's ridiculous," Hannah said. "Lemonts belong at Lakecrest."

Her eyes went soft, a trick she used to make it seem as if she cared. After all this time, I still couldn't tell when her motherly concern was genuine or put on.

"You've seemed so happy, ever since the children," she said soothingly. "Why would you want that to change? I'll talk to Matthew and see if we can't find some money to freshen up your bedroom. That would help, wouldn't it?"

A classic Lemont tactic: buying me off.

"There's no need to worry about school yet," Hannah went on. "We should consider all possibilities carefully rather than make rash decisions. You can't understand what's appropriate for our sort of family"—she made a show of looking conflicted—"given the way you were raised."

Allusions to my upbringing used to make me wilt with shame. Now, I held my ground, giving Hannah my iciest glare. Aching to shock the smug expression off her face.

"I should trust you to raise my children?" I asked sarcastically. "Look how well you did with Matthew and Marjorie! How old were they before you noticed they were taking each other's clothes off?"

My words hit their mark. Hannah's lower lip dropped, and her cheeks sagged. She stared at me with horrified eyes, her self-possession so quickly shattered that I knew I'd gone too far.

Hannah turned away and stumbled toward the lake, as if the open panorama held the promise of escape. I tried to savor my victory, but the taste made me sick. Tentatively, I approached the edge of the bluff. The water rippled in gentle circles around the rocks below. My hair was sticky with sweat underneath my hat, and I thought longingly of that coolness lapping around my feet on the beach. I would apologize, we would rejoin the children, and the day would continue as usual.

"I'm sorry . . . ," I began, but Hannah turned so quickly that I went silent. Her eyes were blazing.

"Don't you *ever* speak of Matthew that way. Your own husband!"

"I was angry. It was wrong of me."

"You think you're a fit mother for Matthew's children? A liar and gold digger? I promise you, Kate, if you continue to defy me, I will tell Matthew everything. The truth about his sweet, innocent wife. I have the documents to prove it—safely locked up where you'll never find them."

The reports from Mr. Haveleck. Interviews with Aunt Nellie and Mrs. Llewellyn. If Matthew read them, would he ever forgive me?

"I could easily talk him into a divorce once he found out about your lies," Hannah said. "He'd get custody of Stella and Robert, of course. A man like Matthew wouldn't want to be a bachelor father for long. When he married again, I'd make sure it was someone with money, someone who made a useful contribution to this family."

The words came at me like blows, each one landing with a crush of pain. Everything I had was at Hannah's mercy. Whenever she wanted, she could show those papers to Matthew and get rid of me; maybe she was already working up to it. She would take Matthew and Stella and Robbie and Lakecrest, a place I'd once hated but now felt bound to because it was my children's home. She had the ultimate power over everything I loved.

Rage swelled up in my belly and surged through my chest and arms and face. It expanded into a heat that burned so strong I was propelled forward under its force. My hands flew out and pushed. Hannah's feet caught on the edge of the cliff. Her knees buckled, and she seemed to hover for a moment, her face looking up in disoriented panic. Then she fell onto the rocks below.

She died instantly, the doctor told us later, after I'd tearfully described her tripping and losing her balance. Thank God the end was swift. If I'd seen her move or heard her moan in pain, would I have had the courage to finish the job?

I heard Stella's cascading laughter and Robbie's high-pitched shrieks. Soon, I'd have to go back to the house and tell Edna and the maids, call Matthew at the office. There'd be a funeral to plan and guests to put up. It would all be hard on the children—why not allow them a few more minutes of blissful, ignorant play?

I looked down at Hannah's lifeless body and thought of my mother lashing out at my father with a swipe of her knife. Of Hannah telling Cecily what she'd done with her own brother. Women who'd done terrible things for the sake of their children. Hannah's last outburst—the insults that had driven me to murder—had been her last futile attempt to claim Matthew for herself.

"Mrs. Lemont?" I heard the nanny call out.

I turned away from the lake and prepared to do my duty. From now on, there was only one Mrs. Lemont. And I would get what I wanted.

ACKNOWLEDGMENTS

This book is dedicated to my sister-in-law, Elizabeth Blackwell, who welcomed me into the Blackwell clan with kindness and love. There's no one else I'd rather share a name with. I'm also grateful to my brother-in-law, Alec Breckenridge; my father-in-law, Robert Blackwell Sr.; and my mother-in-law, the late Sandy Blackwell. Unlike the Lemonts, they were nothing but nice from the very beginning.

My parents, Mike and Judy Canning, and my sister, Rachel, were a huge source of support during the writing of this book. As my unofficial (unpaid) therapists, I'm pretty sure they were as excited as I was when it was finally finished. I'd also like to give a special shout-out to Simon Motamed, brother-in-law extraordinaire and my West Coast PR director.

My husband, Bob, was on the front lines during the long, tortured process that resulted in this book, and he deserves some kind of "Writer Spouse" medal. Clara, James, and Alan: I'm sorry for all the times I snapped, "I can't talk—I have to finish this scene!"

If *In the Shadow of Lakecrest* had a coauthor, it would be my agent, Danielle Egan-Miller. This story never would have come together without her input and her urging to "Go big!" Hugs of gratitude also to Joanna MacKenzie and Abby Saul. I love talking books and drinking pink champagne with all of you. Thanks also to editors Jodi Warshaw and Jenna Free for their spot-on suggestions.

In the Shadow of Lakecrest, much like Lakecrest itself, felt at times like a sprawling monstrosity with many dead ends. As I wrote and rewrote, a few brave souls kept asking how my work was going, even if it meant subjecting themselves to my whining and self-doubt. I have to end by acknowledging those friends and fellow writers who lifted my spirits along the way, whether it was one inspirational conversation or a years-long dialogue: Michael Austin, Nicole Baart, Mary Jean Babic, Mike Bailey, Adam Beechen, Loretta Nyhan, Tom Samorian, and Jenny Szostak. And to every single person who not only made it through the book but also all the way to these final pages: thank you for reading!

ABOUT THE AUTHOR

Photo © 2013 Heidi Jo Brady/HJB Photo

Elizabeth Blackwell is the author of *While Beauty Slept*. A graduate of Northwestern University and the Columbia University Graduate School of Journalism, she lives outside Chicago with her family and piles of books she is absolutely, positively going to read someday. Find out what else she's up to at elizabethblackwellbooks.com.